# Hey, Nicky!

## LEIA SKYY

Copyright © 2022 by Leia Skyy
www.LeiaSkyy.com



First Edition: November 2022

ISBN 978-1-959039-56-3 (ebook)
ISBN 978-1-959039-58-7 (paperback)

Published by Books to Hook Publishing, LLC.
www.BooksToHook.com

# Contents

# Chapter One

A whole lot of stories have been written about the senior year of high school. The whole world's expecting you to figure out your life, but you're just trying to figure out what to wear to prom. Everyone says that high school romances never last, but you're expected to have some. I've read a dozen books about the teenage angst that is senior year. But this story is different. Well, maybe it won't seem like it to everyone, but it is to me. Because this is my story. The story of one Remi Lucas trying to survive the drama of the century or, at least, of senior year.

I suppose we should start where these kinds of stories usually begin. The high school cafeteria. As far as high school cafeterias went, mine was pretty average. The lunch ladies in the kitchen at the left, who cooked their disdain for their work into each depressing hamburger. The usual school cliches and groups of friends occupied the tables. I always sat with my best friend, Mikayla Dunkin, at our table. Today she's talking about our upcoming gymnastics competition.

"I'm just saying that if they don't let us compete this year, I'm going to do a front-flip into Coach Amy's face," Mikayla declared, her arms crossed.

"They were going to let us last year; you were the one who decided not to miss cheerleading," I reminded her.

"Still!" she insisted, sucking furiously on a Capri Sun.

"Even if we are going to compete this year, we still need a new routine, you know," I said. Our old routine was practically rusting with age. "The Mayflay High team is going to be determined to beat us this year."

"They're determined every year, the ugly balls of sun-dried tomatoes," Mikayla hissed, her drink's straw trapped between her teeth.

I giggled. Mikayla's insults were the best in the school, and I was here for it.

"Ooh, check it!" Mikayla exclaimed, the drink falling on the table, forgotten. "Group of tens, on your six!"

"Do you even know what any of that means?" I asked. I didn't always know which part of Mikayla's dialogue was our code for hot guys and which were colloquialisms she found on Urban Dictionary.

"Just look behind you!" Mikayla insisted.

I turned slightly to see the guys she had pointed out. My eyes locked onto one of them. His name was Nicholas. He looked up just as I did, and our eyes met. I started to smile at him, but he dropped his eyes and sped up to get by me. I watched him and his group of friends as they sat at a table toward the back of the cafeteria.

"Wait, who was that?" Mikayla asked. "The lead one with the blonde hair. He looked familiar. Have I seen him before? What's his name?"

"I mean, he's been here forever," I mumbled. "His name is Nicholas. He and I used to be friends for a while."

"Really? Woah. Think you could set me up?" Mikayla asked jokingly.

I gave a half-hearted giggle. "Nah, we're not friends anymore."

'We're not friends anymore' was one of the saddest sentences in the English language. Right above 'my dog died' and 'we ran out of ice cream'. I smiled to myself, internally laughing at my own jokes.

"What're you thinking?" Mikayla asked. She knew me so well.

"Nothing. Just how much we've changed since freshman year. I used to be really good friends with that guy, you know... now I'm invisible."

"Things have changed," Mikayla said. "I remember freshman year I was dating Denny Davinsqe. Can you believe it? My standards were so low a stingray couldn't slip underneath them."

"Yeah." I laughed. We'd all had dumb crushes freshman year. I was actually starting to get feelings for Nicholas before... I felt the smile fall off my face.

"Enough serious talk," Mikayla declared, snapping a carrot stick in half. "I have tea about the Mayflay team."

"What? Did you find out something?" I asked, immediately distracted. Mayflay High had been our rivals in gymnastics since before forever. We were always looking for new ways to get an edge on them.

"They have a foreign exchange student. I don't know where they're from, but the word in the locker room is that they have mastered like seven aerial tricks. Seven!" Mikayla whispered as if she was transferring national secrets.

"No way!" I said, "But no one on our team knows any aerials!"

"Yeah, that's the point! We need to get on that, as soon as possible!"

"Right," I mumbled, but hesitantly. "Are you sure we need aerials? I mean if their new team member already has them mastered... is it even worth learning them?"

"Come on, Remi, you were totally close to mastering them yourself but—"

"Yeah, yeah, you're right," I said hastily, cutting her off. "We do need to learn them, but all I'm saying is..."

"Remi?"

We both looked up to where Philip Mollins, a linebacker on the school's football team, was standing behind us. We'd talked to him before, of course. As cheerleaders, we were friendly with all of the football guys. But he had never come up to us in the cafeteria before.

"Mikayla, can I steal Remi for a second?" he asked, flashing the smile that made all the freshmen fall instantly in love with him.

As a senior, Mikayla was immune to his magic, so she shrugged and said, "Sure."

She shot me a curious glance but slid down the table's long bench and tapped our other friend and gymnastics team member, Jackie, on the shoulder.

"Hey, Jackie! Did you hear about..."

I turned to Philip.

"What's up?" I asked.

"I was wondering if you'd like to go to the movies with me this weekend?" Philip asked kindly.

I thought about it for a moment, trying to come up with an answer before the silence between us grew too awkward. For some reason, my eyes were drawn to where Nicolas was sitting with his friends.

"Thanks, but I can't," I replied, trying to be as kind as possible.

Then, a flash of brilliance!

"You know cheerleaders aren't allowed to go out with the football players," I said, citing an old rule that literally no one followed.

Philip's eyebrows went up.

"No one follows that rule," he said, "And since when did you follow rules, anyway?"

It was a fair point. I was constantly getting into trouble. But I had my answer ready.

"Hey, it's senior year, we're supposed to be mature and role models... or something like that. And I'm trying not to get suspended from cheer... again. I don't know how much longer Coach will tolerate me."

Philip laughed.

"All right," he said with a smile, "Maybe another time then. See you at the next game!"

"See you!"

I turned back around to my lunch, confident in that rejection. It was always nice to let the guy leave with a smile. Then I began to think about all the times I'd rejected guys over the years... it was a lot.

"So...?" Mikayla came sliding back over to me with an air of expectancy in her voice.

"So?" I teased her.

"Did he ask you out or not?!" she demanded urgently.

I laughed, "Yeah."

"And what did you say...?"

"I said no..."

"What?!"

I shrugged and bit off a piece of my pizza.

"Remi. My friend. What on earth were you thinking? He's totally hot!" Mikayla said, exasperated.

"I just didn't want to."

"You didn't want to." She sighed. "Well, you didn't want to when Charles asked you out, and he's totally rich. And you didn't want to when Franklin asked you out, and he's the cutest guy on the drama team! Rejecting Harden, I understand. He was a bit of a creep. But Philip?! Are you planning on being single forever?"

I didn't answer for a moment. My eyes wandered again over to Nicholas.

"Him?" Mikayla squeaked. "Oh, man. I should have seen this coming. Am I totally blind? You literally keep staring at him! Nicholas, was he? Come on, Remi, spill the tea. You weren't just friends, were you? You were together? He's an ex and you want him back!"

"No, we were never together," I said whimsically, "But we could have been..."

"Unrequited love, huh?" Mikayla sighed. "Girl, you need to move on."

A small flash of color caught my eye just then.

"There! Mikayla, see?" I said.

"See what?" She asked.

I pointed toward Nicolas as inconspicuously as possible.

"You're going to have to tell me; I don't see anything but a bunch of moody teenagers," Mikayla said at last.

"He had the friendship bracelet I made him! Years ago, when we were friends! He just put it in his backpack."

"Are you sure?"

"Positive!" I declared, "I'd know it anywhere! I have to get him back, Mikayla. I'll do anything to get him back!"

"Sounds like you never had him in the first place," Mikayla said, munching on another carrot stick.

"Are you going to help me or not?" I asked.

"Of course! I'm not going to let my bestie do anything dumb without me by her side to help! And to laugh and film her... but mostly help!"

I glared at her, and she smiled sweetly at me. We burst into laughter.

Oh, yeah. I was going to get Nicholas back. Whatever it took. And this time, we would be more than friends.

# Chapter Two

All right, now that the scene has been set, let's go back a couple of years. Nicholas and I are eleven. Right now it's summer break we're in my backyard doing what was my favorite thing in the world at that age: catching lightning bugs.

"Did you know that fireflies eat other fireflies?" Nicholas declared as his firefly crawled up his fingers.

"Eww... gross," I said, putting another lightning bug into the home I had made for them out of a box with holes in the top. I had made little beds for them out of cotton and even added a playground made of cotton swabs and toothpicks. I was convinced Nicholas was jealous. He only had a jar.

"And they're not called fireflies," I insisted, "They're lightning bugs."

"Nah, they're fireflies," he argued then. To back up his argument, he hit me with another fun fact. "Did you know that fireflies only live for one to two years?"

"No, I didn't," I said honestly. I hadn't considered the lifespan of any kind of bug until that point. I just assumed that they died when I smushed them.

"Did you know that they're actually in the beetle family?" Nicholas said.

Now he had gone too far.

"So, first they're flies with fire, now they're beetles?" I demanded, hands on my hips.

"They are beetles, they are just called fireflies! And 'lightning bug' is no better. They don't have lightning!"

"Well, what do they have in them?"

"It's called bioluminescence," Nicholas said proudly. Looking back, he butchered the pronunciation, and it sounded more like 'bio-lion-sense', but it was a big word for an eleven-year-old.

"That's the glow?" I asked, not scared to admit when I didn't know something. I loved to learn, and asking questions was the start of learning.

"Yeah. So, they should be called bioluminescence beetles."

I burst into laughter, repeating the funny phrase.

"Bioluminescence beetles!"

We both laughed until our sides hurt and we collapsed into the grass. We let our bugs go one by one, watching them crawl up our fingers to the very tip, then spread their tiny wings and take off.

"Oh, I made you something!" I said, pulling a bracelet out of my pocket. It was made of knotted, fraying yarn, but I handed it to him as if it had been made of gold.

"You finished one!" he exclaimed, taking it carefully, "And it didn't fall apart like all the others!"

"Yeah, that's why I wanted you to have it! The first one that didn't fall apart," I said, with the biggest smile on my face. Nicholas returned my grin.

"Thank you!" he whispers.

"Nicholas!"

We both look up sharply. His mother was calling him from across the street.

"I got to go," he says, grabbing his now-empty jar and running across the property lines.

"Thank you!" he called over his shoulder.

I waved back at him. I stayed in the backyard until I saw the light go on in Nicholas's window. His window faced mine, and we never went to sleep without flashing our lights at each other three times. On, off, on, off, on, off, every night since we were tall enough to flip the switch. It was our own secret goodnight signal.

I let the rest of my lightning bugs go and hurried up to my room to get ready for bed... and Nicholas's goodnight signal.

# Chapter Three

And we're back from that trip to the past. I'm pacing around my bedroom at the moment, the dark blue furry carpet under my feet distracting me from my planning. I didn't like typing out ideas, so I recorded myself on my phone.

"I need to do something to get Nicholas's attention," I said. My phone obediently converted my speech into text.

"How am I supposed to get his attention? He's been ignoring me for years." I sighed and flopped down on my bed. I stuck one of my hands up in the air, not sure why, but it felt right.

"What gets a guy's attention? Makeup? Cute outfits? I wear those every day though, and Nicholas still doesn't pay me any attention."

My words appeared in my notes app as I said them. I leaned over to my nightstand and grabbed my phone, reading over my ideas.

"None of these will work," I said, scrolling back up over my thoughts.

"Nothing will work! He'll never notice me."

I rolled back over and buried my face in my pillow, groaning.

"I should just do something dumb like tell him how I feel to his face," I mumbled, my voice muffled by the pillow.

I lifted my head.

"That's not a bad idea. Maybe not to his face... but what if I wrote him a note? It can't be cheesy or sappy... but if it's honest and sincere, maybe he won't hate me for it?"

I jumped up and hurried over to my desk. I grabbed a piece of lined notebook paper and my favorite blue pen for moral support.

"But what should I say?" I asked the paper. It had no answers. I sighed again.

"Just be honest, Remi. Be honest. Just like you're honestly talking to yourself."

I was losing my mind for this boy.

"Don't think, just write!"

I put the pen on the paper and just wrote.

*Dear Nicholas.*

I started, then immediately doubted myself. I scratched out the 'Dear' part, but that looked awful, so I threw away the paper and got out a new one from a stack on my desk.

*Nicholas, My Love.*

Was I insane? That paper went into the trash as well.

*Nicholas,*

I wrote, happy with that beginning.

*I know that we're not really friends anymore, but I wanted to write you a note to ask you why.*

Nope, that didn't make sense.

*I'm really sorry that we're not friends anymore. I miss you.*

Was that too needy? I wasn't sure, so I just kept writing.

*Would you want to hang out sometime? If not that's okay.*

I wasn't sure that last part sounded right, so I scratched it out. But that looked bad, so I copied everything I had so far on a new piece of paper.

*Would you want to hang out sometime? If we did hang out, could we hang out as more than friends? I really like you.*

I was overthinking so much I was practically shaking. I took a breath to calm myself and finished as fast as I could.

*Anyway, I miss you.*

*-Remi*

I took another breath and immediately felt better.

"Now, for the fun part!"

I grabbed my markers and set about doodling lightning bugs all over the note. It might have been a childish thing to do, but I wanted to remind him of all the good times we had together. And drawing helped to relax me, so it was a win-win.

"Now I just have to deliver it," I mumbled to myself. That would be the hard part. I slipped the note into an envelope and wrote Nicholas's name on the front, butterflies dancing in my stomach.

I crawled into bed that night, excited and nervous beyond belief. How was I ever going to get to sleep?

Turns out, I slept just fine because the next thing I knew my alarm clock was going off. While I would usually pound the snooze and roll back over with a groan, today I jumped out of bed, ready to start the day. I got breakfast quickly and drove myself to school thirty minutes early.

The doors were unlocked, all the teachers were there, and a few kids roamed the halls. It was a new experience for me. I was usually late.

I took advantage of the emptier halls to run through them, stopping first to drop off my bag in my locker. I grabbed the note for Nicholas out of a pocket in my bag, took a breath, then turned to run through the halls again.

"Slow down!" a teacher yelled at me.

I slowed my pace to a walk, calling over my shoulder, "Sorry!"

I knew exactly where Nicholas's locker was. Mikayla would have called it stalking. It wasn't stalking in my opinion; it was just general knowledge. Right?

I stopped by his locker. With a deep breath, I stared at the note in my hand. I rocked back and forth on my heels for a minute. It was now or never.

"Never," the reasonable voice in my mind said, begging me to run back to my backpack.

"Now!" said the voice in my head that had seen way too many romantic comedies.

"Shut up!" I said aloud. A teacher who was standing in a nearby doorway gave me a strange look.

"Sorry, Mrs. Jackson, not you."

The teacher retreated into their classroom, mumbling something about young people these days.

With a deep breath, I took a last look at the note in my hands and closed my eyes tight.

"Here goes nothing," I mumbled.

And, with my heart beating out of my chest, I took a deep breath and slipped the note into his locker.

# Chapter Four

Hey, I'm Nicholas Savage. This is my part of the story, the part that Remi can't write about because... well, she didn't know most of it.

Remi and I used to be close friends. Things changed in high school, as they usually do. I got busy, she got busy, and we drifted apart. It's one of my biggest regrets of freshman year. But I found something after that. Something that would help massively change my relationship with Remi. But I can't get ahead of myself.

My part of the story starts the morning Remi left the note in my locker.

I was late to school the morning Remi left me the note. My dad dropped me off on his way to work. I was in a rush to get all the books and stuff I needed for my first period because we had a test that morning. I'd hadn't studied for it, so I was already stressed. It took me two tries to get the lock on my locker open. It usually stuck, but today it just made me mad. I smacked the bottom of my locker door in frustration and heard something fall inside. Curious, I fiddled with the lock with new energy.

As soon as I opened the door, the envelope fell out of my locker onto the floor. I thought it was from a teacher at first because I had one teacher that would return homework in our lockers. I was disappointed for a moment. With a sigh, I leaned over to pick it up and got an adrenaline rush as I saw the name. I recognized Remi's handwriting as I picked it up.

I looked around to see if she was there, but I didn't see her in the hallway. So, I opened the note.

*Nicholas*

I sucked in a breath. I couldn't believe this was happening.

*I'm really sorry that we're not friends anymore. I miss you.*

She missed me!

*Would you want to hang out sometime? If we did hang out, could we hang out as more than friends? I really like you.*

I was overwhelmed. My heart was going a mile a minute.

"Finally!" I whispered to myself, unable to contain my excitement. "Finally! It's working!"

It had been so long since Remi paid me any attention. It had been so long since we had even had a decent conversation. All those nights we spent together as kids seemed far away and long ago, but here was the reminder of them in my hand! All the nights of catching fireflies in her backyard...

It had been so long; I was beginning to wonder if she would ever be interested in me. But now I was holding a note from her, from Remi! And it was practically a love note!

I read it over again. She was interested in me!

"Finally!" I said again and shut my locker.

I put the note in my backpack and began walking to my class. Every instinct inside of me was telling me to run to Remi's homeroom and declare that I feel the same way for her. I'd been waiting so long for this, why would I wait another moment?

But of course, I had to wait. I had to. The book said to.

I sat down at my desk. I should have been studying for the upcoming test, but this was much more important. I pulled a different kind of textbook out of my backpack. A very important book called, *True Love Needs Persuasion: Making Any Woman Fall in Love with You.*

I had been studying it for years. I had read every page and memorized large sections. I had been living by its words every day at school for so long, maybe too long. This was the first time it seemed to be working. And if it worked, all my study, trial, and error would be worth it. If Remi was mine, anything would be worth it.

I scanned over the familiar sections for my next course of action.

"I can't admit anything to her yet," I whispered to myself. "Not a word. I need to..." I scanned the book. "Capture her affection first. And the only way to do that is to ignore her."

I sighed. Ignoring Remi was the hardest thing I had to do. One would think I would be used to it by now. I'd been doing it for literally years. But it never got easier. Every time I saw her beautiful face from across the room, I wanted to run up and ask her about her day. If she ever looked sad, it took all my strength not to let her cry on my shoulder like she used to. The worst of it was when another guy talked to her. I wanted to be sitting next to her, watching her back. I just wanted to be close to her.

But no. I had to look away, walk away, and keep my distance.

"Just for a little while longer," I whispered, "I won't respond to this note at all. She'll be desperate for me. She'll fall for me hard and fast. I just have to wait a little while longer..."

The book said the longer I kept her waiting, the more she would want me. But every moment that passed without Remi, the more I wanted *her*. I had to be strong and wait. I knew I did.

But it was still hard.

# Chapter Five

"Remi!" Mikayla shook my arm.

"Huh?" I looked up at her, trying to shake away my thoughts. I couldn't, and they clung with me as she continued speaking.

"Remi, what's with you?" Mikayla asked.

"What?" I replied, not listening to her at all.

I was too busy to hear her. I was busy wondering what had happened with my note. Had Nicholas found it? Had he read it? What if it had gotten lost? What if he hated me for it?

"Remi!" Mikayla tried again. "Are you okay?"

"Yeah," I shook myself out of it, "Yeah I'm okay. Why?"

"We're on page twenty-one. You're still on page fourteen."

I looked down at the book on my desk.

"Oh. Thanks," I said, flipping to the right page.

"What's on your mind?" Mikayla said, leaning in to whisper to me.

"Nothing," I replied, trying to avoid eye contact with her.

"Remi, I know you," she insisted, "What's wrong?"

I couldn't keep it in anymore.

"I wrote Nicholas a note!"

Mikayla was silent a moment because the teacher glared at us, and we had to pretend that we were innocently reading. The minute the teacher looked away, Mikayla turned back to me.

"Why on earth would you do that?" she demanded.

"Because I like him! I have for a long time! He had to know how I felt."

"No, he did not! We all get stupid crushes sometimes; that doesn't mean we tell them! What were you thinking?" Mikayla hissed.

"I don't see what the big issue here is!" I replied.

"He's a nerd, Remi. You could have any other guy you want, any guy on the football team, and you're chasing a nerd?! He spends all his time in computer club!"

"What's wrong with computer club?"

"Spending hours glued to a video game is not healthy, Remi! Have you ever seen him exercise? At least you know the football players get outside sometimes!"

"Nicholas gets outside sometimes," I replied sourly.

"And not to mention that he's ghosted you for, um, let me think, years?! Remind me why you care about this dweeb again?" Mikayla asked, entirely baffled.

"I just do, Mikayla." I sighed. "And he's not a dweeb."

"Says you," Mikayla mumbled.

We were both quiet for the rest of class, turning the pages of our textbooks silently as our teacher's voice droned on and on from the front of the classroom.

Mikayla met me at the classroom door the minute the bell rang.

"What did the note say?" she asked.

"What note?" I asked innocently, trying to avoid the question.

Mikayla glared at me.

"Fine," I admitted, "I told him that I missed him and asked if we could hang out... as more than friends."

Mikayla groaned, "No, girl, you didn't."

"It seemed like a good idea last night when I wrote it!" I insisted, starting to doubt myself.

"You should have texted me! I would have kept you from this whole mess. Oh, tell me you didn't give it to him in person, right? Please, tell me that you didn't give it to him in person!"

"No, I put it in his locker."

"Good!" Mikayla sighed in relief. "Thank goodness."

Then, brightening up, Mikayla asked, "Did you sign it? Did you sign your name?"

"Yeah..."

"Oh." Mikayla's face fell. "Well, why did you do that?!"

"I wanted him to know it was from me!"

"Remi, Remi, what am I going to do with you!" Mikayla said, exasperated.

"I still don't see what all the fuss is about," I said as we stopped at our lockers. Mikayla's was right next to mine.

Mikayla slammed her locker door more forcefully than usual.

"He's a dweeb, he ignored you for years, he threw away your friendship, you could have any guy in school, need I go on? I'm not going to let my best friend throw her heart away to some indifferent computer mouse!"

"It's not that big of a deal, Mikayla," I said, though I was starting to bitterly regret my note.

"Not that big of a deal," Mikayla sighed, shaking her head.

The two of us turned and started walking down the hallway to our next class.

"And, besides," I said, turning to Mikayla as I thought of a new argument, "I like who I like, okay? I can't change how I feel about him."

"I still don't have to like it!" Mikayla retorted.

Frustrated, I turned back around to keep walking to class... and ran straight into Nicholas.

I froze. It was like my whole body shut down. I could feel my face flush. I knew it was getting redder and redder, but I couldn't do anything about it. I could only stand there, in front of the boy I liked so much, with a face as red as a cherry.

He locked eyes with me. Oh, those blue eyes... I could stare into them forever. Nicholas took a breath. He was going to say something! Did he read my note? Did he like me back!?

Then his eyes dropped. And he put his head down... and he walked away.

I could breathe again. The rosy flush wilted and ran off my cheeks. My eyes glazed over, seeing nothing. But I could breathe again.

"Hey." Mikayla took my arm, speaking quietly. "We need to get to class."

"Yeah," I said as if in a daze, "Class."

She led me to my next class, being the saint that she is. I barely remembered that class period. She took notes for me. I don't deserve her. All I could think about was the look in his eyes right before they dropped to the floor.

It was a goodbye. I knew it was.

Part of me wanted to give up. Part of me thought it was hopeless. I didn't give up. But that moment was the closest I came.

I had told him the truth. And he hadn't even spoken to me.

And part of me just wanted to cry.

# Chapter Six

I wanted to kiss her in that hallway. I wanted to wrap my arms around her waist and pull her close to me. I would hold her so tightly. She would be mine at last! I would hear her heartbeat and feel her breath on my cheek. I would hold her hand for the rest of the day.

I wanted to kiss Remi so badly it physically hurt. My hands were shaking as I walked away, and my breath was coming in gasps.

But no. It was working. The book was working. And it said to ignore her. I couldn't stop now... not yet... I had to wait.

I sat down at a desk in the library to think. The note was a promising sign. The book had explained them. It meant she was starting to get interested. But I had to wait! It was imperative that I wait! I was patient enough. I knew I was.

But the look on her face...

Why did it hurt? The memory, it was still so fresh! Like a picture that was taken moments ago, but why did it make my eyes sting and my chest tight?

She had looked so hopeful. Those beautiful blue-green eyes stared so deeply into mine with such hope and joy, like she was watching a sunrise or... a firefly.

I smiled, but my smile was short-lived.

I had taken one peek over my shoulder as I walked away. I knew that I shouldn't have. It was against the book, after all. But I didn't have that much strength.

I had wanted to know how much she wanted me. I wanted to see her staring after me with adoration, longing, or love. I hadn't wanted what I saw.

I hadn't wanted heartbreak.

I opened one of my textbooks and stared blankly at the page, not seeing it.

Remi always had that spark of light in her eyes. It shone brighter when she was doing something she loved or was with someone she cared about. I watched it, longed for it, did everything I could to make it shine brighter and stay longer... at least, I did.

Now I had seen it go out like a candle in the wind. In the blink of an eye, it was gone. And I had done that. It was my fault.

"I'm hurting her," I whispered aloud. I looked around quickly, but no one was nearby, and no one heard.

I sighed. It was a bad habit, talking to myself. But I preferred it to talking to other people... except Remi. Why couldn't I get her off my mind?

"I'm hurting her," I said, even more quietly. "I don't want to hurt her."

Of course, I didn't want to hurt her. She was the love of my life! I didn't want anyone or anything to hurt her. And yet, there I was.

"But the book is working!" I insisted, arguing with myself.

"But if it's hurting Remi is it really working?"

"It's making her want me."

"But she looked so heartbroken..."

"Nicholas?"

I nearly jumped out of my skin.

"Timothy!" I sighed in relief. Timothy was in my computer

class. We weren't really friends, but we had worked together on a few projects.

"You're talking to yourself again," Timothy said, shoving his large-rimmed glasses further up his nose.

"Yeah, I know," I replied.

"You're late to math class."

"Am I?! Oh," I checked my watch and hurried to gather my stuff, "I forgot they moved my math period. Thanks for warning me!"

I started toward the door, then stopped.

"Wait, aren't you in my math class?" I asked.

"Yes," Timothy said simply.

"Then aren't you late, too?"

Timothy nodded.

"Come on, then!"

Timothy followed me into class, and we slipped in just as the bell rang.

"Thanks for coming to get me. I already have three tardy marks in this class, another would mean detention."

"I know."

"You know?" Now I was curious. Until this point, Timothy and I hadn't spoken very much, except for a team project.

"I volunteer as the teacher's assistant."

"Oh," I said, "Well, thanks... it was really nice of you."

"I wanted a favor from you, actually."

"Oh!" For the third time in five minutes, Timothy had surprised me.

"What favor?" I asked.

"I need tutoring in computers."

"Okay." I said, "I can do that."

"Study hall?"

"Sounds good."

Timothy opened a notebook and started taking notes. I stared at him in utter confusion for a moment. Then I smiled. I guess I'd made a friend.

That brought the situation with Remi up in my mind again, and I grimaced.

"What?" Timothy asked, his voice a whisper.

"Nothing," I replied. Then, after considering, I said, "Troublesome math problem."

Timothy nodded, satisfied, and turned back to his work.

I sighed as I tried to focus on the equations in front of me. But my mind was in Remi's class with her. Was she truly hurt? Did she despise me for not speaking with her? Was the book wrong? Could I have done something differently?

I hated myself at that moment. I pulled the book out of my backpack out of habit. The cover was reassuring.

*True Love Needs Persuasion: Making Any Woman Fall in Love with You.*

The familiar title made me sigh in relief. I flipped through the dog-eared pages, looking for some reassurance. I reread the sections I knew so well, the parts I had memorized, and the chapters I was still learning.

*Women only fall in love with the men they can't have.*

I had memorized that line. I repeated it to myself whenever Remi glanced over at me in the cafeteria.

*If you're in love with a woman, be the man she can't have, and she will fall helplessly in love with you.*

I had that line memorized, too. Especially the last bit. *Helplessly in love...* I repeated that when the friendship bracelet in my backpack brought back memories that made me long for her all the more.

And not just memories of Remi.

I couldn't be the guy who threw himself at a woman, begging for her love. I couldn't be the guy who begged a woman to stay.

I couldn't be my father, chasing my mother's car down the road, screaming for her to stay with him.

I slammed the book closed and shoved it in my backpack.

*There is no happily after, not if you show your hand too early. Patience is the most important thing. You must wait.*

I had to wait. It was the hardest thing I'd done, and it grew harder every day. But I couldn't show my cards yet. I had to wait.

That line was getting old quickly.

I allowed myself the luxury of daydreaming about Remi and me for the rest of the day. All the dates I would take her on, all the things I would buy her. I'd treat her like a queen, of course, my precious princess. It was perfect and beautiful in my imagination.

But in real life, I took a back door into the cafeteria so I wouldn't have to walk past her. I couldn't handle seeing the hurt in her eyes. Not again.

I didn't know how much longer I could wait.

# Chapter Seven

Remi was adorable at six years old. I assume I was, too, but I didn't see myself in the way I saw Remi. I saw her every afternoon. We'd spend the morning together in first grade. Then we'd play together in my backyard after school. We'd run around the yard, play on Remi's swings, and, most of all, we would play in my glorious sandbox. It was one of my most prized possessions as a six-year-old. It was my kingdom. And I ruled it side by side with my wonderful queen.

"This is my town," I declared, finishing a few houses in the sand that looked much more like lumps of sand.

"This is my tower!" Remi said, determined to one-up me by making a taller sand lump. She held up the sand and let it run through her fingers.

"Look, it's raining on my tower!" she said.

"Well, this is my skyscraper! And it's snowing on my tower." I topped my house with a pointed top. It was only a few inches taller than Remi's tower, but it was enough to make her angry at me.

"No fair!" She pouted.

"I'll make a castle then," she decided.

"Not if I make one first!"

The race was on!

I made my castle by neatly packing sand into brick-shaped molds and stacking them on top of one another. Every tower was topped with a red flag. The red flags were mine; the purple ones were Remi's. She built her castle by scooping large piles of sand together and sculpting them from there, sticking a flag on the ones she liked the best.

After a while, my castle fell apart and I was forced to make repairs. Remi's castle firmly refused to stay together, and she grew more and more frustrated. Finally, she dug her fingers into the center, causing the whole thing to collapse.

"No!" she exclaimed. "Let's do something else."

"What?" I asked. My castle was coming along nicely, but Remi always had the best ideas for new games, so I was open to the idea.

"Let's make a real castle! One we can really live in!" Remi said, getting excited about her idea.

"With doors and windows and a moat and everything?" I asked, my eyes wide.

"Yeah!" Remi squealed, gathering the buckets we had laying around.

"What are we going to build it out of?" I asked, not entirely convinced.

"Sand!" Remi said, then she sat back on her heels and considered the matter further. "Unless you can think of something else?"

I couldn't think of anything, so we set about building our life-sized sandcastle.

I lay the foundation of bricks, while Remi dug a ditch around the edge of the sandbox for our moat. We worked on the sandcastle for an hour, but the walls kept falling. The sand couldn't support the weight we put upon it. Our walls stayed stubbornly at only ten inches tall.

Remi threw her pail at them, making a dent. I turned to her, angry, only to see her bottom lip quivering.

"I want a castle!" she insisted, on the verge of tears.

"Don't cry, Remi," I said, scared that she would cry. I hugged her tightly. She sniffed and didn't cry, but still looked very upset.

"I wanted a castle."

"I'll get you one," I promised.

"How?" she asked, rubbing her grubby hands in her eyes.

"I'll figure it out."

"Remi!" Remi's mother called from their yard, "Daddy got McDonald's!"

"McDonald's!" Remi exclaimed, brightening instantly. "See you tomorrow, Nicholas!"

She ran off with barely a wave in my direction. I couldn't compete with the lure of McDonald's. I waved until she disappeared inside her house. Then I got to work.

I spent the rest of the afternoon building with all the Legos that I owned. I ate dinner in a rush and ran back to my room. At night after my mom had tucked me in, I got up with a flashlight and worked some more. The next day, I moved it all into the sandpit, and I waited for Remi.

The look on her face as she ran into my yard was worth everything in the world.

"Nicholas!" She squealed, "You build us a castle!"

"Yeah," I giggled, "Do you want to see the inside?"

"Yes!"

We hurried inside our Lego Castle. It was simple, four walls with a hole in one for a door, and a couple of towers, but it was the greatest thing on earth to Remi. She redecorated with my Legos a little, but I didn't mind. She was the queen in her castle.

We played until her mom made her come in for dinner. As she left, she gave me a huge hug.

"Thanks, Nicholas," she whispered. "You really can do anything!"

I flushed with pride and the smile stayed on my face for the rest of the week.

I could do anything.

# Chapter Eight

The atmosphere at the gym always put me in a good mood. The floor was cold and slightly sticky under my bare feet. The air conditioning was turned down so low that I could practically taste the cold. The air smelled like hand chalk and every now and then I would hear the squeaky springs of some trampoline.

"Remi, focus!"

I took a breath and did the flip. I landed smoothly and turned to my coach.

"Good! Next."

I walked to the side to stand with my teammates. I'd been on this team, the Dragons, for years. I started when I was seven on the Junior Dragons and grew up with my teammates. We've formed a sisterhood over the years. We'd go out and do fun stuff as a team. We shared all our secrets and when one of the girls was riled up about something, we were all riled up.

And nothing riled us up more than competing against the Mayflay Firecrackers.

"Did you hear about the new Firecracker?" Maisy asked me.

"Yeah. She can do aerials."

"He, I heard it's a guy."

"Really? No way."

"I wonder if he's cute." Jackie giggled.

"No, Jackie! No fraternizing with the enemy!" I insisted.

"Aw," she said, pretending to be disappointed.

"Yeah, we don't want a Romeo and Juliet situation, Jackie, we need you alive for our competition season," Mikayla said, walking up to us.

We all laughed together.

"All right, nice work, girls!" our coach said.

"Everyone take a break, get some water. Remi, can I talk with you?"

"Ooh someone's in trouble," chorused the girls.

"Shut up," I hissed at them. They just giggled as they walked away.

"What's up, Coach?" I asked.

"I wanted to talk to you about aerial tricks. You heard about the Firecrackers new teammate?"

I gulped. "Yeah?"

"Look, I know you're the star on the floor and the beam. But I really need you to work on adding aerials into your routine. Mikayla and Alice can do the typical floor routines, and Jackie and Maisy can do balance beam, but I don't have anyone who is ready for a routine with ariels. Anyone but you."

"Coach, I-" I started, but Coach cut me off.

"I know this is new for you, but you have more experience than everyone else. You tried before. We'll just work on a simple one to start, but I need to throw in a couple in your floor routine. If you're up for it, we'll add in some on the beam."

"I can't, Coach," I tried again, but again was interrupted.

"You know I don't like that word! We don't say 'can't' here. We say 'not yet'."

"Not yet then," I pleaded. "Coach, aerials just aren't for me. They're not my thing!"

"You're going to need to make them your thing, Remi. If you want to take your gymnastics skills to the next level, this is the next step. I've paired you up with Florence, she can spot you.

Practice a front aerial for a while. You remember how to do that one, right? I'll be over in a minute to check on your progress."

I wanted to protest, but Coach walked away before I could.

"Come on, Remi. You can totally do this! At least try?" Florence tried to encourage me.

"Fine," I said.

Sullenly I followed Florence to the mat.

"Spot me?" I asked. She nodded.

I sighed. The mat in front of me had never looked so daunting. A million thoughts ran through my head. What if I landed wrong? What if I got hurt? What if I was out for the rest of the season?

"Deep breaths, Remi," Florence reminded me.

I nodded. Deep breaths.

I pulled my arms up to my ears, lifting my leading leg in a ready position.

Deep breaths.

I stepped into my first lunge, raising my back leg and preparing to flip. I couldn't help but close my eyes as I pushed off and jumped with my base leg.

I was in the air for all of half a second, but it felt like an eternity of falling through the air. I landed on my leading leg just fine, but the panic from the falling feeling made me stumble backward. I fell on my back on the mat, staring up at the ceiling high above me in defeat.

Florence's face appeared above me.

"At least you landed it," she said, offering me her hand.

I took it, and she pulled me to my feet.

"Yeah," I said.

"Try not to close your eyes; it'll throw you off balance. And get a little more push on your base leg?" Florence instructed with a helpful tone.

"I'll try that, thanks."

"Do you want to try again now?"

I looked over at the clock.

"Practice is over in five minutes and I need to shower..." I trailed off. My excuse sounded pathetic even to my own ears.

"Okay. Better luck next time?"

"Yeah. Thanks, Flo."

"Anytime."

"Girls!" Coach called us back over for our end of practice talk.

I couldn't hear any of it. I walked on autopilot to the locker rooms and barely remembered taking a shower. It was only when Mikayla spoke to me that I broke out of my daze.

"Hey, are you okay?"

"Yeah," I replied. "It was just the aerial."

"What aerial?" Mikayla asked.

"Coach wants me to put some aerials in my routine, so I can go against that new kid on the Firecrackers."

"Ooh, so that's what Coach was talking to you about! Well, that's great, isn't it? You get some more complicated tricks."

"Yeah, I guess," I said quietly.

"That isn't what's really bothering you, is it?" Mikayla asked. She stopped what she was doing and walked over to me.

"It's that Nicholas kid, isn't it? Girl, you saw him in the halls, he isn't into you! You've got to get over him. You know you can do so much better! Give me the word. I'll set you up with any guy you want! Anyone, in the whole school!"

"Nicholas?" I requested sweetly.

"Not funny!" Mikayla scowled.

"What's all this about Nicholas?" Maisy asked, leaning in to eavesdrop.

"Nothing!" I insisted, but Mikayla told them everything.

"Remi's in love with a guy at school, Nicholas. They were friends as kids, then he totally ghosted her freshman year, and she's been in love with him ever since. But they haven't even talked since ninth grade! And he's a nerd, guys, and not in a cute, shy way. In a 'spend seven hours in front of the tv playing Legend of Zelda and only occasionally taking a break to cosplay a Star Trek character' way."

"He wouldn't do that..." I tried to argue, but no one was listening to me.

"Ooh," Florence said, scooting closer to hear the drama. "Does he know?"

"Oh, yes. She told him. This morning, wasn't it?" Mikayla turned momentarily to me.

I opened my mouth to answer, but she didn't wait for a reply.

"She wrote him a note and slipped it in his locker. A note! A cheesy one, too."

"It wasn't that cheesy," I said, feeling smaller by the second.

"It was, trust me. She slipped it in his locker and was a wreck for all of first period. She was all like 'did he get it? What will he think about it?'" Mikayla mocked me as the team listened. Even Jackie and Alice, who didn't usually get involved in drama, came over to listen.

"And then she bumped into him. Like literally, turned around and ran smack into his chest. And he didn't say a thing to her! Just avoided eye contact and walked away."

"Oof, rejection," Jackie said and there was a murmur of agreement.

"He didn't say that he didn't feel the same way," I said. All the girls looked at me with pity.

"Of course, he didn't, with a note like that. You've got to do something more than that!" Florence said.

"I want to, I do! I'd do anything to get him back!" I exclaimed.

"Anything?" Alice asked with a mysterious smile.

"Yes! He means everything to me. And I don't mind that he's a nerd, I love him anyway." I pouted.

"He's really that important to you?" Mikayla asked, turning back to me.

"Of course, he is! She's been hung up on him since freshman year? And you're a senior now, right? That's four years! We've got to get this Nicholas to fall for Remi, and fast," Jackie said, pounding her fist into her leg.

"We?" I questioned.

"Yes! Girls, are we a team or not?"
"Yes!" the team chorused.
"All right, then let's do this!"
And before I knew it, my whole gymnastics team was helping me hatch a plan to get Nicholas back.

# Chapter Nine

Timothy was a typically quiet person. Unless he got to know you very well, in that case, he would talk your ear off. Today, he was talking my ear off about some crazy Star Trek theory.

"I'm telling you, Nicholas," he said, "Transporters destroy the original version of you and create a copy of you where you're trying to go. And the copy is so good, that you can't tell it's a copy! How else can you convert matter into energy?"

"That makes no sense, Tim," I said, but I didn't have the mental energy to argue with him about it. Usually, I would, but today my mind was consumed with thoughts of Remi.

"It does, but I can tell you're not listening to me," Tim said quietly. "Am I talking too much?"

"No, I just don't feel like a debate today," I replied honestly. "Can we talk about something else?"

"Sure." Timothy considered a moment, then said, "Did you hear about the robotics club?"

"What robotics club?" I asked, immediately intrigued. I had tried to start a robotics club for years, but no one else was interested in joining.

"Some junior kid is starting one. They just need the Assistant Principal to approve the funds for supplies," Tim replied.

"That's epic! Who? Which junior kid? I want to help!"

"I think his name was Matthew? Come on, we can find him at lunch. There aren't that many juniors this year; we can ask around. I'd like to join a robotics club, too."

I was going to answer Timothy, but just then, an angel walked into my view. Not an actual angel, of course, but close to one. Remi, my beautiful Remi! She was so close to me I stopped breathing for a second.

Then she caught my eye! The magical moment made my heart stop. She grinned at me with that adorable smile and flipped her long silky hair over one shoulder. I smiled without meaning to. She was being friendly to me! Was she flirting with me? She was! The book was working! Patience was working!

"Hey there, Nicky! I'll see you at lunch today. I think there might be a surprise coming your way!" Remi called, then giggled and was whisked away by her friends.

I watched her go, my eyes glazed over and my heart pounding. I had barely heard what she had said, my thoughts were so consumed by her sweet voice.

"Nicky, huh?" Timothy asked, staring at me with an amused smirk.

I shook myself.

"No, I hate that nickname," I said.

It was true, I hated that nickname. But Remi could call me any name she liked, and I would always love it.

Tim raised his eyebrows.

"Why do you always ignore her, anyway? I always see you staring at her in class. But when she stares at you, you look away. It's so obvious she's in love with you and, let's be honest, she's like the hottest girl in school," Timothy said quizzically.

Rather than launch into a whole lecture about my reasoning, I brushed Tim off with a line from my book.

"Women only want you if you ignore them," I said simply.

Timothy looked at me like I had just said 'pigs only like you if you launch them into outer space'. But then he shrugged.

"Whatever. All I know is that if a gorgeous girl like that wanted me, I wouldn't keep her waiting. There's a ton of guys in this school, Nicholas. And we are in our senior year. You're running out of time."

"Yeah," I admitted.

We kept walking to Spanish class. Timothy talked about robotics club some more, but my mind was miles away.

What if I was running out of time? The book had worked so far, but would it continue to work?

And what was the surprise waiting for me at lunch?

<h1 style="text-align:center">Chapter Ten</h1>

It turned out that I didn't have to wait long to see what Remi's surprise was. That was a good thing, too, because I was driving myself nearly crazy wondering what it could be. I'd been nervous all morning and could barely pay attention in class. What did she have planned?

I entered the cafeteria at lunch, nervous but excited. The first thing I noticed was that Remi and her friends weren't at their usual lunch table. I thought that was odd. Were her friends in on the surprise? Were they helping her with it?

I sat down at my usual table with my friends. I nibbled on my lunch, constantly looking around the cafeteria for any signs of Remi, her friends, or the surprise.

Ten minutes into lunch, I had just about given up on the surprise and focused on eating my lunch. At that moment, Remi and her friends burst into the cafeteria.

What happened next could only be described as a High School Musical number. It was Remi, all of her cheerleading friends, and a few girls from Remi's gymnastics team. I recognized most of them. I liked to know who Remi's friends were, even if I never met them in person. From what I had guessed, they were nice, sensible, logical girls.

I guessed wrong. Because whatever Junior Broadway drama-kid supernova that happened in front of me was the opposite of nice, sensible, and logical. Not that the routine wasn't good, it was.

Mikayla, Remi's best friend, stood at the back with a speaker to play the music. I didn't recognize the song, but that didn't seem to matter. They changed the lyrics to suit them anyway. I think the name in the song was supposed to be Mickey, but every time it was said, the girls sang Nicky too loud to hear the real lyric. That was when it really struck me that this dance was for me!

Until this point I had been staring blankly, watching this unfold before my eyes like a bad 90's musical where you skip all the songs anyway. But this was real, and it was for me.

Remi was in the very middle, dancing her heart out. She looked breathtaking in her cheerleading uniform. I felt my face flush just seeing her. I hadn't seen any of her cheerleading performances in a long time. But she had only gotten better at the routines over time.

She was beaming, the smile on her face lighting up the room. She nailed the routine. I watched as she did a cartwheel in front of me. Then she did an aerial flip off an empty table!

My heart flipped for her. Her head was so close to the ground, I could only wonder what would happen if she couldn't land it. I couldn't live without her!

But those thoughts only lasted for a split second, because she did land it. She stumbled a bit as she hit the floor, but one of her friends steadied her without a second thought. Remi smiled at her friend and continued as if nothing happened.

The routine ended with Remi doing a full split in front of me.

She looked up at me so expectantly, with that adorable smile on her face. There was something behind it this time, though. Something I had seen before.

She was trying to be confident, but I could see the worry behind her eyes. She had the same look our first day of kinder-garten, and then the first day of every grade since then. Every gymnastics competition, every cheerleading routine, every test, I had watched her. It was the same look. She tried so hard to be brave. And she was! She would walk into every school year like she owned it, and she did own it. Every gymnastics competition or routine, win or lose, she would walk in and out like a queen.

And only I knew that the act was to protect herself. She couldn't admit how afraid she was. Of rejection, of falling, of failure... the thoughts were too frightening, so she pretended that she didn't have them.

I always hated that fake smile, that mask. And now she was wearing it for me. Did she think I couldn't see? Or did she want me to?

The cafeteria was dead silent. Everyone was waiting to see how I would react. Timothy nudged me, but I didn't turn my eyes away from Remi's.

Her eyes were begging me to say something. Anything. They were growing more desperate by the second.

I had to say something. I physically had to. But the book... the plan.

I took a breath and saw the light come back into Remi's eyes for a split second.

"That was some routine," I said, my voice echoing throughout the silent cafeteria.

Then I grabbed my backpack and ran out of the room.

# Chapter Eleven

I thought we nailed the routine. We ran into the lunchroom united, as a team, in a v-formation in front of Nicholas's table. I was at the center, of course. Mikayla stood off to one side, playing "Hey Mickey" from her Bluetooth speaker. We did the routine singing the song but switching out the word Mickey for Nicky.

It was one of our old competition routines. We had practiced it a million times and did it to warm up every now and again. But I wanted to throw in something special. So, I did a cartwheel to build my confidence; it was my favorite trick. Then I did the aerial off of an empty table.

I was terrified while I was in the air. The adrenaline was already pumping from performing, especially in these circumstances. I was practically in shock. But it was for Nicholas, and I landed it for him. Florence helped me when I stumbled, giving me an encouraging smile. I smiled back and went on with the dance.

I did the splits in front of him at the very end. He had told me once a long time ago that it was his favorite trick of mine. He never understood how I could do it. So, I learned it for him. I perfected it for him. And I did it for him.

Then I waited. I looked up into his eyes, silently pleading with him. He always could understand me when we were kids; why couldn't he understand me now?

I kept my performance smile plastered on my face for confidence. But as the seconds went by, it became harder and harder to keep the act up.

That's when he spoke.

"That was some routine."

I didn't see him leave the cafeteria. The words echoed in my ears over and over, in sync with the pounding of my heart, which had shattered.

The cafeteria was silent with pity. All my friends were staring at me, not knowing what to do or say.

I spoke up. It felt like I was yelling, but I didn't care. I poured all my pain into a face smile and cheery voice.

"Oh well," I said. I could barely hear myself over the rushing in my ears. "That's the life of a cheerleader! You win some, you lose some."

My friends all nodded, their smiles returning.

Mikayla met my eyes, then cracked a loud joke, making nearly everyone laugh. In another second, the cafeteria had come back to life. My friends were finding seats at their usual tables, giggling awkwardly amongst themselves.

Mikayla motioned for me to follow her to our usual table, but I shook my head. She nodded. She understood.

I walked quietly out of the cafeteria.

I was planning on going to the bathroom to cry, but I found that I didn't have the energy. It was strange. I didn't want to cry, I wanted to sleep. All of this worrying, all of this angst and preparation... and he rejected me. I should have seen it sooner. Maybe then I wouldn't have completely humiliated myself. But it was worth a shot, right?

He was worth a shot.

I stopped at my locker. I was looking for something, anything, that would comfort me. What would give me enough strength to finish the day? Music? No. Some lip balm, maybe. It was worth a try.

I grabbed it, closed my locker, and headed toward the bathrooms.

That's when I saw Nicholas at the end of the hallway, coming out of the boy's bathroom. I tried to swerve to avoid him, but there was nowhere to go. I didn't have enough strength to put on a fake smile and walk past him. I just wanted to disappear.

I watched him walk up to his locker. Nicholas reached his hand in for something, but it came out empty. Had he been looking for comfort, too?

Nicholas caught my eye then.

I stared at him, not knowing what to do, or what to say. He watched me too. He seemed to be struggling the same way I was.

I raised my hand in an awkward, pathetic wave.

That caught him off guard. He stumbled for a second, then called out to me.

"That was an impressive flip."

"Thank you," I said. My voice was dry and empty, but the flush rose on my face. I know it was impressive. I was proud of myself.

"I guess you've been practicing since I saw you do a routine..."

I closed my eyes for a second to control my emotions. It had been long. So, so long. He used to come to all of my competitions and a lot of my practices. I used to teach him some of the moves and I would see him doing them on the sidelines. He always brought me a present when I won something, even if it was only a sticker or a penny.

"I've gotten a little better, yeah." Now even I could notice the change in my voice. There wasn't that distinctive whine when someone is about to cry, but it was low and weighted anyway.

"I'm still not great at anything aerial. Yet, anyway," I said, just wanting to break the silence. "I'm still afraid-"

"Of falling and hitting your head? Yeah. I remember. Because you fell and hit your head on the basement floor when you were seven and tried to do a flip off of the chest freezer."

I hated myself and I wanted to die. The embarrassment filled my head and pounded around on the inside.

"You remember that, huh?"

"I remember I told you that it wasn't a good idea."

That was it. I was done. All my mental energy was gone, and I was ready to release some pent-up fury.

"And what I'm doing now? What I just did in the cafeteria? Is that a good idea? Or am I only going to get myself hurt again?"

Nicholas was shocked. I watched him try to process my outburst. He seemed almost hurt at first, but the glimmer of pain was replaced by something I thought looked too much like arrogance.

"I have to go. See you later, Remi."

He walked by me, stomping on the pieces of my heart I had once again offered him.

And I watched him go.

I put on the lip balm in the bathroom. Fresh mascara, too, and my very favorite purple glittery eye shadow. I looked amazing. But I couldn't see myself through the tears in my eyes.

I marched back into the cafeteria, completely numb. I flipped my hair over my shoulder and smiled at everyone who caught my eye.

I slammed my lunch tray down at the usual table with my friends. They all stared at me with pity.

Mikayla said, "I'm sorry it turned out that way, Remi. Try not to take it personally, though. We did some digging. Nicholas turns down every girl who makes a move on him. Maybe he's ace, or too busy for a girlfriend, or just a jerk..."

I didn't respond.

"I guess you're done trying to romance him now, at least?" Florence asked.

Yes. The right answer was yes. My mind was done. I had tried and the logical side of me knew when to quit. I knew deep down that had lost him.

But I couldn't believe that. My heart wouldn't accept it. I would keep offering pieces until he broke every last one. I had only fragments left, but they would still be his. They would always be his.

"Nope," I said.

The fake smile was back.

"I'm just getting started."

# Chapter Twelve

I didn't think I could do it anymore. Walking away from Remi, again and again, was ripping pieces out of my heart. Every time hurt more than the last.

But what was I supposed to do? It was working! I guessed that it was like ripping off a band-aid. I had to do it and get it over with. Then I would have Remi! And all the pain in the world would be worth it. She was worth any suffering.

I couldn't stop now.

I let myself daydream of her. She looked so cute bouncing around during her cheer routine. And not just cute but graceful, athletic, and just downright hot. It was a complicated routine, too!

I blushed and tried to hide it in my textbook. Now that I had a chance to stop and think about it, I was thrilled. Remi had done a routine in front of the entire school just for me!

She had done all of that for me. Me! She had gotten her whole gymnastics team and her cheerleading squad to choreograph a routine just for me. She was totally starting to fall in love with me!

I was incredibly flattered that she liked me enough to go through so much trouble for me. I hadn't imagined in my wildest dreams that the book would work so well!

"How about you and me?"

The flurry of thoughts buzzing around in my head was popped in an instant. I stared blankly down at the hand that was softly touching my arm. Upon further inspection, I found that the hand belonged to a girl. A girl named Erica.

"What?" I asked. I assumed that this girl had been trying to get my attention for a while now, perhaps had even been speaking to me.

"You're pretty distracted, aren't you?" she said with one of those giggles that's so fake and cheesy you can practically feel the stickiness of it.

"I guess a smart guy like you doesn't have to pay any attention in class," she went on, much to my dismay. "Mr. Denton just told everyone to pair up to swap critiques on our rough drafts. I was asking if you wanted to partner with me?"

That was when reality fully returned to my mind. I remembered this girl, this Erica. She had tried to flirt with me a few times in the past. At the time, I brushed her off, and it had done the trick. And by 'brushed her off', I meant low-key insulted her. I wasn't proud of it, though!

No, that's a lie. I was very proud of it.

She flirted with me all day and I asked her if she knew what subtlety was. I was very proud of that line. But I felt bad when her face fell, so I tried to make up for it by explaining that being subtle is better when you're trying to win someone over romantically. At least then, if the other person has to reject you, you can save face and not have to take an overt rejection.

That didn't help at all.

She had looked at the ground and asked quietly, bottom lip quivering if I was talking about her.

I believe I asked her, "What do you think?" Which I admit, wasn't the nicest response I could have said. But it worked, anyway. That had been nearly a month ago, and Erica hadn't bothered me since. It has been a reprieve I've been very grateful for.

Not to brag, but I do find myself in situations like this rather frequently. I can be a nerd at times, but I am apparently a very good-looking nerd. But I don't have time for flings or meaningless make-out sessions. I'm holding out for something real. I'm holding out for Remi. I'm not about to let random girls who don't mean anything to me get between us.

But where was I? Oh, yes. Erica. She seemed to be back to bother me again. It was just my luck, I suppose.

"Come on, Nicholas, don't stare at me like that." She spoke up again, her voice like nails on a chalkboard, "I just need a partner for this project!"

She did not just need a partner for this project. There was a large section of the book, *True Love Needs Persuasion: Making Any Woman Fall in Love with You,* dedicated to body language. I could see the flirtatious glimmer in Erica's eyes. Her smile was a little too wide, and a little too coy.

She had repealed her hand at this point, of which I was grateful. But just as I gathered my scattered thoughts, her hand reached out again and brushed against my hand.

I stiffened and pulled away. I looked around desperately for a savior, someone else to partner with. I would have taken anyone at this point! Even Jackson, who stuck a pencil in the ear of every guy he was partnered with! I was that hopeless!

But alas, no one came to my rescue. I had been far too lost in thoughts of Remi. They had moved on without me, choosing partners and leaving me to the proverbial wolves.

"Looks like you have no choice!" Erica said and again burst into a fit of ear-grating giggles.

Then, seeing my crestfallen face, put on a fake, pouty frown and mumbled, "Aww, so tragic for you. Is it really so awful to have to talk to me for ten minutes?"

Yes. Yes, it was. But all the nights of bitterly regretting being rude at our last conversation prevented me from saying this out loud. I bit my tongue and thought before I spoke.

"No, of course not," I lied. "Let me see your paper."

I pulled my rough draft out of my binder and passed it over. I had spent three hours on it, and I was very proud. I had done my essay on who I thought the hero was in the classic novel, *The Great Gatsby*. It was one of my favorite books and, in my opinion, a tragic romance seconded only by Shakespeare's *Romeo and Juliet*.

Erica passed me her paper, which was printed on green paper.

"I did mine on Tuck Everlasting," she said with a smile.

"The kid's book?" I asked. I regretted the words as they left my mouth. I had to learn to think before speaking! But this girl's face annoyed me so much...

"It's not a kid's book!" She argued, "It's a great classic!"

I just nodded. We turned and looked over each other's papers silently for a few minutes, but I could almost hear the cogs whirling in her head.

"I guess Remi could use your little lecture on subtlety," Erica leaned over and whispered in my ear.

I flinched. This girl was on my last nerve.

I tried to calm myself with a few deep breaths before saying, "Or maybe she's the sort of girl who can come on as strong as she wants and is still adorable and charming. Not all girls have that gift, you know."

Erica scoffed, but I wasn't done.

"For other girls, that routine might have been tacky and embarrassing, but she pulled it off. Wouldn't you agree?"

Erica looked shaken. She opened her mouth to reply, but the words seemed to be stuck between her head and her mouth. Her lips opened and closed a few times, comically reminding me of a pufferfish.

I finished reading over her paper while she stuttered. Although, it was barely readable. The main point was unclear, the spelling and grammar were wrong and, the most grievous mistake of all, she had left in several details that showed that she had not read the book at all. She had left in points that came only from the movie adaptation. This was a crime against all book-readers and essay-writers in the world. I passed it back with all the disdain and disgust it deserved, which was the equivalent of carbonated milk.

"The entire essay needs rewriting."

"What's wrong with it?" Erica asked shakily.

I had written most of my notes across the top. It wasn't my fault that the girl couldn't read. But, nice guy that I was, I summarized the issues for her.

"It's all fluff. There's no substance."

She didn't speak a word to me the whole rest of the class period. And, I might add, the only problem she found in my essay was a misspelling of the word 'apparently'.

# Chapter Thirteen

Seven-year-old me loved gymnastics more than anything. This was before I joined the Dragons and met all my friends there. My mom was just starting to think about letting me join a competitive team. I was begging her for that chance every day, and every day I went to lessons, I practiced my little heart out.

Leaps and beams I would do every day. I worked hard to perfect whatever routine I was given and, for the most part, I succeeded. I could even perform rings if I was asked.

My only problems were my flips and aerial tricks.

I tried them in the gym with my coach. She had told me very specifically not to practice them at home, because I wasn't ready to do them without her there. I very specifically didn't listen, because I wanted to get good at the tricks and get good at them as quickly as I possibly could.

That was why I did the aerial flip in the basement with Nicholas. We had been talking about my gymnastics dreams and what I was learning. In reality, I had just wanted to show off to him, to impress him.

I will never forget that feeling of my head hitting the concrete. I wanted to cry or scream. But most of all I wanted to lay there. I didn't want to get up or move or do anything ever again. I wanted to live and die right there, on the concrete.

Nicholas had screamed for my mom. It hurt my ears. She took me to the emergency room, which sent me to a doctor. He said I just had a big bump and a minor concussion and that I would be fine in a few weeks. I remember Nicholas's dad coming over as our car pulled back in the driveway. Nicholas was worried, she said. He visited me with our homework and video games every day after school until I was better.

It hurt, but it was more than that. It was as if fear had been implanted in my mind, transferring directly from the concrete into my skull.

Every time I try to do anything airborne with my head facing the ground, I'm seized with fear. For a while, I thought it was just nerves. I thought it would go away when I landed my first flip. The aerial came and went. Mom even got me ice cream to celebrate. But the fear didn't leave.

So, I thought it would go away when I got better at it. I worked on it harder, pushing myself to practice more. But the fear didn't leave.

I had one routine with an aerial. It was the one routine I completely failed. The aerial through me off mentally, so much so that I blanked in the middle of a flip and had to improvise. It was awful, and I knew it. But the rush of panic the aerial gave me sucked all of the training from my mind.

After a while, I stopped trying. I didn't have the mental energy to push past the explosion of adrenaline and terror whenever I did the trick. And I got by on the skills I knew by heart, beams, leaps, bars, and rings. For a while, I was the most skilled gymnast in my age category. I had a shelf of trophies, medals, and banners to prove it.

But now the other girls in my age category were catching up and surpassing me. They were already starting to become very skilled at aerial tricks. For the first time in my competitive life, I was in danger of being left behind if I couldn't get beyond my fear.

All this was why I was out on the trampoline that night. I had to get over the fear so I could have a routine with an aerial in it!

Dad bought me the trampoline for Christmas one year. He had explained that if I fell on the trampoline, I wouldn't get hurt as I did in the basement.

I appreciated the gesture. I knew Mom and Dad were both terrified when I fell in the basement. But they understood how much gymnastics meant to me, and they weren't afraid to push me to pick myself up and try again.

That was the problem, though. I did try. I tried and tried, but nothing changed. I was still afraid, and the fear still ruined my routines.

I bounced up and down slowly. I loved the feeling of rising and falling on the trampoline. At the gym, on special occasions, we'd be allowed to play on the trampoline it had embedded in the ground. It would bounce you so much higher than the one Dad had got me. But I loved this one more, nonetheless.

This one was all mine. I could try dumb jumps and look stupid on it all I wanted. My hair could frizz up from the static without my friends teasing me about it. I could enjoy the rising feeling without someone else waiting for a turn.

I bounced higher. I watched the afternoon light fade as it got closer to twilight. I'd been outside on that trampoline for hours and hadn't yet mustered up the courage to do a flip.

I wanted to keep up with my friends. I wanted to keep winning competitions. I wanted to keep competing in college and get scholarships because of it. I wanted that thrill I got when I mastered something new back.

I hated feeling like I was at the end of my gymnastics career. It hadn't even started! I had to get past this.

The sky went from blue to orange and then to gold as I watched. I knew that my dad was going to call me in for dinner at any moment.

I gathered all of my courage, took a deep breath, and bounced three times to gain some height.

I threw my legs up and tucked in my arms, propelling myself into a flip. I felt the twisting feeling that made my stomach drop. I saw the sky overhead, then underneath me. What was up? What was down? Where was the ground? In just a moment, my head will be facing the ground.

I panicked. I forgot about the bouncy, squishy trampoline underneath me.

I was back in the basement, with hard concrete underneath me, filled with fear, and bracing myself for the impact.

I freaked out, twisting my legs wildly, trying to turn myself right-side-up again. It half worked. I landed face-first, pulling a muscle in my side.

I rolled myself over to stare at the sky, wanting to cry. I knew I could do it. I had done it! But today I was just in my own head. I had psyched myself out. I knew that! I would do better tomorrow.

Still, today, I felt like a failure.

"That was really good, Remi."

The voice yanked my stomach back from where it had fallen to my feet.

I stood on the trampoline and looked over to see Nicholas in his backyard.

"How long have you been watching me?" I demanded, my arms instinctually crossing over my chest.

"Not long," he said in a perfectly calm voice.

I hated that. How dare he talk calmly to me? Any embarrassment I had felt at lunch was gone, replaced with frustration and fury.

"It wasn't good at all, dimwit," I snapped, "It was awful. I was trying to do a flip and I fell."

Nicholas looked confused.

"You jumped, though," he said.

"Yeah, and I failed. Big hurray to me," I replied, in no mood for games.

"But Remi... you were afraid to jump. But you made yourself do it. You jumped," Nicholas insisted.

A million things flooded my mind. What did he care? Why was he trying to encourage me? He out-right rejected me, only now to come and make me feel better? What was his problem?

"Remi, dinner!" my dad's voice came from inside.

"Coming, Dad!" I replied.

Then, turning to Nicholas, I said, "I guess I did jump."

"Yeah," he said as I climbed off the trampoline, "And you can jump again. Who knows? Maybe next time you'll land that flip."

I didn't reply.

# Chapter Fourteen

I walked home from cheerleading practice. I had cheerleading on Mondays and Thursdays, and I had gymnastics Tuesdays, Wednesdays, and Fridays. Saturdays were competition days for both my sports, usually not at the same time.

Most days I loved cheerleading. It was a fun and relatively easy workout for my off-gymnastics days. I got to use a lot of my gymnastics skills and show off to my friends. It was also a great group of girls and we'd all hang out together after school.

Today's practice, however, was miserable. I spent the whole practice dodging sympathetic looks and pitying glances from my teammates. To make things worse, a lot of them came up and apologized for my routine's failure.

"I'm sorry it didn't work, Remi," said Emily, one of my friends.

"It's all right. I didn't expect it to. Besides, you win some and you lose some, right?" I answered cheerfully.

I made it through most of the practice all right. But then the football players came out to practice.

"Hey, Remi!" one of them yelled at me.

I didn't know who he was, but apparently, he knew me. I

wondered if everyone knew me after today. I tried to ignore him, but he yelled again.

"What was up with that whole display yesterday? Do you think you're in a movie or something? Are you going to chase him through an airport next?"

The team laughed and jostled the guy who had spoken.

My team, to their credit, gave the football players dirty looks and came closer to comfort me. I played it cool and laughed it off like I was in on the joke.

It felt awful, having everyone feel sorry for me. I hadn't expected this kind of consequence when we were planning the idea. It had seemed like such a wonderful plan at the time. But now...

Here I was, the popular cheerleader who could have any guy I wanted. And I threw all my credibility and my reputation away for a quiet, nerdy guy... just to have him run away from me as fast as he could.

I could finally admit to myself that I was embarrassed. Not just that, no, I was utterly and completely humiliated. I wanted a large hole to appear in the earth and swallow me up, never to be seen again. I wanted to crawl in a very small hole and remain there until everyone forgot I existed. Everyone except Nicholas.

Maybe it was time for me to move on... but no. No, I couldn't. I didn't think I ever could. Nicholas was worth my embarrassment. He was worth anything.

But that didn't change the embarrassment I was feeling the rest of practice and as I walked home.

I dropped my bags on the floor as I walked in, too tired to deal with them. I stumbled to the kitchen, hoping for a post-practice snack. What I found was my mom, sitting at the kitchen table, consumed by her work.

Mom was an accountant who ran her own tax preparation business. It sounded painfully boring to me, but Mom insisted that she enjoyed it. She said she loved math and numbers, something I couldn't understand.

She often worked long hours, so seeing her there wasn't a surprise. But still, it startled me. I guess my nerves were on edge after the long day I had.

"Hey, honey. Cookies are on the table," my mom said.

"Cookies?" I asked, perking up considerably.

"Sugar cookies. They had extra at work, and I know they're your favorite."

"Yes! Thanks, Mom. I could use a pick-me-up after the day I had."

I shoved my face full of sugar cookies with a pitiful sigh.

"What happened?" my mom asked.

I stopped eating. I knew that tone in her voice. That was the tone she had when she knew exactly what had happened but wanted me to tell her in my own words.

"How did you find out?" I groaned.

"One of my friends, Barbra Burncoat, you remember her? She was subbing for Mrs. Lindsey today. She was out sick. She saw your little routine in the lunchroom and gave me a call. Were you planning on telling me, or?"

"Yes, I was," Remi said. "Just... after I started dating Nicholas."

"Remi," my mom sighed.

"Okay, Mom, just give me the lecture and get it over with? I'm tired."

"I wasn't going to lecture you, sweetie, I'm just worried that you're coming on too strong. I haven't seen you and Nicholas hang out in years. Maybe there is a reason for that? Friends drift apart and that's all right!"

"No, I can't drift apart with him, Mom! I love him!"

"You don't mean that. You're still young. I know it feels like the end of the world to you at your age, but it's not. You'll find someone else, someone who actually wants you too..."

"But Mom, what if he does like me back and he's just too shy to say so? I have to take the chance. I have to see if he feels the same way. After we graduate, he won't be in my life anymore. I might not ever see him again. He could move away and be out of my life forever. I don't even know where he's thinking about going to college!"

"What does that matter? Remi, you won't follow him to college anyway."

"Who said I wouldn't?" Remi replied.

"I do. I wouldn't let you throw away your gymnastic career to follow that boy to some college. You'll go where gymnastics takes you or if you want a major at a different college, that's fine too. But you won't be wasting thousands of dollars a year to go to a college just to be with him," my mom said firmly.

"But Mom!"

My mom sighed.

"I don't understand it, Remi. But I do remember being your age too."

"Oh, no," Remi said quietly.

"Oh, no? What?" my mom asked.

"You've got that look," I said.

"What look?"

"The look that says you're about to meddle in my business."

My mom laughed.

"If it's my baby's business, it's my business. I'm just trying to think of a better way to get to the root of how Nicholas feels about you. Maybe a way that doesn't involve you putting your whole heart out there in front of your entire school?"

"Well, I did put a note in his locker first," I said with a sigh, sinking my head into my hands from embarrassment.

"Did he respond to the note?" my mom asked, putting her hand on my shoulder comfortingly.

"No..."

"Not at all?"

I thought hard, trying to come up with some kind of response from Nicholas. But in the end, even I had to admit the truth.

"No, not at all. He ignored me completely."

"Maybe he didn't want to hurt your feelings? Maybe he didn't want to outright reject you?" my mom asked softly.

"But Mom, you don't understand! He does like me! He has to!" I protested, hearing none of my mom's reason and logic, as emotional as I was.

"Honey, if he didn't respond to the note and he shut you down at school today, I really don't think..."

"But he remembers things about me, Mom! He remembered that I'm afraid of flips and other complicated aerial gymnastic tricks. And I'm almost positive that I saw a friendship bracelet I made for him when we were little in his backpack!" I argued.

"That doesn't mean he likes you romantically, Remi, that could just mean he has fond memories with you," my mom replied, still trying to be reasonable.

"But Mom, he still has the *bracelet*! Why would he keep that if it was just a fond memory? Why would he have it with him at school? That has to mean something! Right...?"

My mom chewed on her lip and stared sadly at me. That made more of an impact than any of her arguments. I could see the pity in her eyes.

"I know, Mom..." I said quietly. "But I can't give up yet. I'll move on after graduation if I can't manage to get him by then. But just... let me have these last few months?"

My mom hugged me close.

"Of course, honey. But remember, he won't be the last guy you fall for."

"No," I whispered, "But he was the first."

# Chapter Fifteen

Timothy and I had started talking more frequently. I hadn't known it at the time, but he would become one of my closest friends. He was one of the only guys I knew that understood me. So, we talked nearly every night. Usually, I enjoyed talking to him.

But not tonight.

Tonight, Tim was ranting about Remi's performance in the cafeteria, and I honestly wanted to just hang up.

"She got her whole cheerleading team for you, Nicholas!"

"Yeah, I know..."

"And that whole routine? That took time to choreograph!"

"Yeah, I'm sure it did."

"And did you see their outfits? They looked amazing!"

"I know, I saw."

"And that song, personalized just for you, dude, epic!"

"I know, I was there."

"Man, Nicholas, you're so lucky. Remi is beautiful and she's obviously crazy for you. Your hard-to-get routine worked like an enchanted charm," Tim said with a longing sigh.

"Not yet, it hasn't," I replied, my voice low with the internal impatience I was feeling.

Tim was frustrated, too.

"Nicholas, you cannot be serious. She literally threw herself at your feet, and you're going to keep ignoring her? You're keeping this whole routine up? For how long? How long do you expect her to wait? It's only a few months until graduation!" Tim exclaimed.

"I know, I know! Believe me," I sighed, "I know. But I have to wait just a little while longer. Just until I'm' certain that I have her!"

"You *do* have her, you idiot! You could not possibly have her any more than you do right now! The entire cafeteria saw how much you have her, and you *walked out the door*! I mean, everyone thought you were nervous or embarrassed, so it wasn't too humiliating on your part. But did you see her? She played it off well, of course, but dude, you totally destroyed her confidence. Wiped it out like a dry-erase marker on a sheet protector. How do you even sleep at night?"

"Are you done already?" I snapped, "You don't think this is hard for me, too? It's torture! I love this girl and having to hold myself back every day is killing me! I'd give anything on earth just to hold her in my arms for one minute!"

"Then freaking do it, Nicholas!"

"I CAN'T!"

"Nicholas?" my dad called from downstairs, "Who are you yelling at?"

"No one, Dad! Sorry," I replied, covering the phone with my hand.

I returned to the conversation with Timothy, slightly calmer.

"I'm sorry. I just... I just have to wait."

"All right, it's your girl, your funeral... I just didn't think you were actually going to keep making her chase you."

"It sure is fun being chased, though," I admitted.

"Ouch, heartless of you. You should have seen her face when you ran out, you wouldn't think so. Actually, go online and see if you can find a video. Everyone was filming. Anyway, don't keep up your fun too long. Eventually, it won't be any fun for Remi and a lot of other guys won't make her work so hard. Honestly, I have no idea why she hasn't moved on already. She should. I would."

"Shut up," I sighed, "Can we talk about something else?"

"Like what. Oh, the robotics club? I do have some updates to tell you. We got a room and some school funding!"

"Really?"

"Yeah! If we make it stretch and get some more kids and maybe some teachers on broad, we could have a nice battle robot team this year! I know of a competition in Jurysville that's happening at the end of the year. Maybe we could put together a bot for that?"

"Yeah, I know Mr. Jasnson, the 11th-grade math teacher, likes robotics and programming. We could get him on board!"

"Yeah!"

We talked for another fifteen minutes about the club. It was nice to get my mind off Remi for a while. But the moment I hung up the phone and I got ready for bed, she was all I could think about.

Maybe what Timothy said was right. Maybe I was cruel and heartless, making Remi jump through hoops like a trained puppy and chasing her tail after my affections. She must have put in a lot of effort to make that routine happen. I daydreamed Remi and her friends putting together the moves and practicing hard, all to impress me.

My face flushed as I felt a rush of joy and warmth.

"She wanted to impress me," I whispered, thoroughly pleased.

Timothy was right. I'd given Remi no sign at all that I was interested. I had to give her something, just a little something, to keep her coming after me.

I did remember a section in the book about giving a woman just enough attention to keep her hopes up. The book said that I should be subtle and ambiguous. I shouldn't do anything that can be seen as outright confirmation that I reciprocate her feelings. It has to be something that only makes her think that *maybe* I like her as well. I'd never done this part of the book until now because I would have quickly gone too far. The temptation to declare my undying love for Remi would have been too great for me to handle.

I paced around my bedroom, thinking of what to do.

"Nicholas, I can hear you walking around up there! It's past your bedtime, young man!" my dad called.

"I'm a senior in high school, Mom, I don't have a bedtime anymore!" I replied.

"You still need your sleep! At least stop pacing around, you'll bring the ceiling down with your clomping!"

I sighed and sat down on my bed.

"Goodnight, Nicholas!" my dad yelled from downstairs.

"Goodnight, Mom!" I yelled in reply, laying back on my bed.

I leaned over and flicked off my lights, staring at the dark void where my ceiling should be until my eyes adjusted enough to see the cracks above me.

Through the slats in my blinds, I could see the light in Remi's room. I tried not to watch Remi very often. It was creepy to just stare at her bedroom through my window. And usually, she kept the blinds closed anyway.

Then the flash of brilliance hit me. I knew exactly what gesture would be enough to encourage Remi and give her something that, after the grand gesture of hers, would be an appropriate thank-you. At least, it was ambiguous and would keep her wanting me, but at the same leave her unsure of where she stands with me.

I leaned over again and flipped the lights on and off three times in a row.

*On, off.*

This was our good-night signal as kids. I remember the nights I would stay up long past my bedtime waiting for that signal because Remi had late gymnastics practices and I couldn't go to sleep without my goodnight.

*On, off.*

I would stare out at the stars and the fireflies and think about Remi. She was my best friend then. We did everything together. Now, during these awful years without her, I thought often of those days. I had taken the time we had spent together for granted. Now I would give anything to sit on the swings with her again.

*On, off.*

It was just for a little while more, I kept telling myself. But that line was old. It had lost all persuasion in my mind and my love was held at bay by my willpower alone. I wanted Remi so much it hurt.

I stared between the flaps in my blinds at her window. The blinds were closed, as they usually were, but her light was still on.

I took a deep breath. On nights like this, it felt so impossible. I wondered if we'd ever be together, or if all these years would be in vain.

I wondered if she noticed my lights. Maybe she wasn't even in her room and didn't see it. Maybe she did and didn't remember or, so much worse, didn't care.

Anxiety gripped my chest as I stared out at the closed blinds.

"Please, Remi..."

Then her lights flicked on and off three times.

I let out the breath I didn't realize I had been holding.

"She says goodnight," I whispered, a smile on my face.

"Goodnight, Remi."

# Chapter Sixteen

Needless to say, Nicholas's good-night message sent me into a frenzied spiral. I called all of my friends to let them know, stopping only when my mom stormed upstairs and took away my phone, reminding me that the walls were paper-thin and she was trying to sleep.

I apologized but couldn't sleep. I knew my mom didn't want me to put myself out there for someone who might not want anything to do with me, but I wasn't listening. He remembered my flipping fear, he had the friendship bracelet, and he remembered the good-night signal. That was enough for me.

*He hasn't done that in so long, not since we stopped being friends. Does he want me back in his life? It's working! I have to keep going because it's working!*

I thought.

I spent the next morning at school trying to figure out how to make my next move. And doing schoolwork, but that took a backseat. Nicholas remembered something about me from years ago, so I had to throw away the day's education and focus on whatever grand gesture of affection I was going to subject him to next. He remembered something about me; maybe I should base my next move on something I remembered about him? To show him that I remember, too?

I wracked my brain, trying to think of something and, at the same time, trying to pass a Spanish quiz. I failed the quiz and failed to come up with a new idea.

*What could I do next? Something with science? With legos? I can't think of anything! All these ideas are too cheesy.*

I slammed my locker closed between classes, then realized I had forgotten the books I would need next period, so I opened it again. It was all a part of the struggles of being in love, I supposed.

That was when I saw her. Evil took human form in a girl named Erica.

Needless to say, we had never gotten along well. Erica joined the cheerleading team very briefly two years ago when her family first moved to town. They moved from a nearby city, and Erica wanted to get plugged in and make some friends. But aside from being outrageously pretty, she was awful at even the simplest routine. Not only that, but she could not get along with any of the other cheerleaders. None of them! I remembered meeting with the team to discuss asking her to leave. But she must have got the memo without us having to say it to her face because she quit the team two weeks later. She'd been salty toward us cheerleaders ever since. I couldn't blame her for that, at least. But she could have tried to be nicer if she'd wanted to be on the team that much.

I never had a personal problem with Erica. I was against her because she bullied some of the other cheerleaders, and we stood together. But I try not to get into petty squabbles or drama with cheerleaders or ex-cheerleaders. I hate the stereotype of cheerleaders being backstabbers and catty. I always try to be supportive of my teammates and deal with conflicts in a mature way.

I was reminded of all this as I walked by Erica in the hallway. The look on Erica's face had me thinking that she was trying to stir up trouble.

"Hey, Erica!" I called, giving her a friendly smile and even throwing in a wave to be extra polite.

Erica looked down her nose at me, tapping her perfectly mani-cured fingernails on her binder.

"Remi," she said as if the word left a bad taste in her mouth. "That was quite a performance in the cafeteria the other day."

"Yeah," I giggled awkwardly. "We sure thought so."

"You got the whole team in on it, huh? They didn't mind being embarrassed like that?" Erica said smugly.

"Yeah, it was mostly their idea anyway," I replied, still trying to be nice, "And any excuse for the team to show off is a worthy cause for them. You remember how it was."

"Yes," Erica spat.

I winced. I probably shouldn't have brought up Erica's cheer-leading past.

"Don't you think it was lame and cheesy?" Erica asked.

"What?" I replied, even though I knew full well what she was talking about.

"Doing all that, a whole cheer routine, just to get Nicholas's attention?"

I blushed at his name and said, "Some guys are worth going the extra mile for!"

Erica smirked at that as if I had just touched on a point. She narrowed her eyes then and mumbled to me in a voice barely loud enough to hear.

'Hmm... might want to be careful. I don't think you're impressing him too much."

My eyebrows raised. Did Erica know something I didn't? I didn't know Erica even knew Nicholas. Oh, wait, that's right! She had a class with him!

"Why do you say that?" I asked hastily.

Erica looked back at her fingernails, picking at a loose gem as she spoke, her tone dripping with venom.

"He may have made a comment or two about how some girls don't have what it takes to pull off such a big spectacle."

I was floored. All the air was immediately gone from my lungs.

"Spectacle?" I managed to squeak out.

"Yup," Erica said cheerily, happy to finally have gotten a reaction out of me.

"He said that some girls don't understand how to be subtle and classy and just end up looking foolish trying to get a guy's attention."

"He said that?" I asked, trying to keep all emotion out of my voice.

"That's right. Directly to me. We were talking about a project in class and the topic came up... it was kind of hard to miss. I guess you could use a lesson on subtlety, huh, Remi?"

I felt lightheaded at that and dropped my books. Erica cackled as I hastily picked them up. I stood up staring blankly as Erica walked off in the opposite direction with a strut in her step. The next thing I knew, I heard a loud 'boom'. I quickly turned around and saw Erica sprawled across the floor looking humiliated as the students in the hallway erupted in laughter. She had slipped on a sheet of paper that had fallen out of one of my books. Hmm... I guess karma did exist.

# Chapter Seventeen

Our first few robotics club meetings were spectacular. We had a great turnout, six kids and two teachers. It might not seem like a lot, but for a new club, it was wonderful. Timothy was the club leader, but a teacher named Jeffery Humpheres pretty much led the group. Mr. Humpheres had a degree in computer programming and built robots in his garage. The whole club was thrilled to discover this, and he became our favorite club advisor.

Today's meeting, however, was more of a bumpy ride. We were troubleshooting some issues we'd been having with the robots and we discovered that we needed some new parts for them. Unfortunately, we would have to buy the parts online. But none of us had the money, in the club treasury or in our own bank accounts, to get all of the parts we would need. And we needed those parts. We all had our hearts set on competing in a local bot battle royale. To win in a battle royale, we needed only the best pieces.

"I really hate to say this, ladies and gents," Mr. Humpheres said with a sigh, "But I wouldn't count on the school for any additional funding. It'll all be going to the sports teams, as it usually does. And we are a new club! Maybe next year we'll have the parts to build a battle bot."

"Next year?!" we all exclaimed with a groan.

Mr. Humpheres, anxious to cheer us up, said, "Come on, guys, don't give up so easily. I can submit a request for more funding, at the very least. But I'd bet anything that all of the extracurricular funds have already been bookmarked for something sports-related. All of that money is spoken for by the end of October and here we are in March. Our options are making the money ourselves or make do with some of the scrap materials that we already have."

"How long would a request take?" a kid named Gary asked. He was a whiz with programming but wasn't the most sociable kid in the world. Still, he got to the heart of issues quickly and efficiently. I liked him.

At the end of the meeting, we all left feeling depressed and hopeless. Our hopes of winning a bot battle had been dashed upon the rocks of poverty. I'd been working on plans for a battle bot for nearly two years, and I knew for a fact that Timothy had designs older than that. Just between the two of us, we could build a bot that was sure to win! If only we'd get the chance.

"Hey," Timothy said quietly as the boys gathered their things from their lockers.

"Hey," I replied.

"Do you want a ride home?" Timothy asked

"Sure. Thanks," I replied. It would save me the walk.

"Cool. Come on."

We walked outside to the parking lot. I was tired, so we didn't talk much on the way home. As Timothy was driving, I got a text message. It was from my dad.

*We've been invited over to the Lucas's house for dinner. Are you going to be home soon?*

I felt an adrenaline rush seeing Remi's last name.

*ETA five minutes*

I replied quickly. It was a simple message. But my mind was racing as I shoved my phone in my pocket.

My dad knew that Remi and I weren't friends anymore. I mean, Remi's parents and my parents are still friends, they have been for years, but they usually did things together just the parents.

I'd spoken to my dad about my problems with Remi. But I hadn't told him about the book. I wasn't sure why. Maybe he'd think it was dumb. Or, worse in a lot of ways, he might think it was wrong. What would I do if the text by which I'd lived my romantic life for years was suddenly discounted by my own father? No, I never risked that. I told him only that I didn't want to hang out with Remi anymore. I let him assume what he would, a falling-out or just growing up. Either way, he knew to leave me out of any gatherings they had with the Lucas family.

Something had to be up.

Coincidentally, Timothy asked at that moment, "What's up?"

"I don't know," I said mysteriously. "I'll find out tonight and let you know."

Timothy shrugged.

"Is that your house?" he asked.

"Yeah. I'll hop out here. Thanks for the ride."

"Anytime."

I hurried up to the house with one thought on my mind.

What could Remi be up to now?

# Chapter Eighteen

I was trying not to scream at my mom. But I was failing miserably. I was leaning over the stair railing

"You did what?! They're coming when?!"

"Remi, calm down!"

"Do not tell me to calm down right now, Mom, seriously. How could you possibly think that inviting Nicholas over for dinner was a good idea! Especially after everything that has happened between us in the past few weeks!"

"I didn't invite Nicholas over, not specifically. I invited his father over and happened to include Nicholas in the invitation," my mom said, crossing her arms across her chest.

"That's the same thing and you know it!" I exclaimed, near tears. "How could you meddle in something like this?"

"I wasn't trying to meddle!" My mom replied calmly, "I'm helping. It always made me sad that you and Nicholas stopped being friends. He was such a good boy, such a gentleman. He was a good influence, too! Your grades were better when you two were friends."

"Because we were in middle school, Mom. It was insanely easy to get good grades in middle school! High school work is different; it has nothing to do with Nicholas!" I argued, my face flushed with fury.

"What went wrong between you, anyway?" my mom asked, ignoring my argument.

"I don't know," I admitted with a sigh.

"Well, if you are set on courting Nicholas then I'm going to take this opportunity to get the two of you together in one spot. Then maybe you can figure it out! At the very least, maybe I can get some information out of him," my mom declared.

"Mom, no! You're not going to interrogate him about me, are you? That's so embarrassing!"

"You performed in front of the entire school, openly declaring your love for this boy; I hardly think a few questions will be worse than that."

"Mom, please, call Nicholas's dad and cancel!" I begged.

"Absolutely not. They're coming, and you're going to be friendly and polite to them. Understood?"

I didn't answer, and I wasn't planning to. But my mom looked at me expectantly, waiting for some kind of response. So, I used a tried-and-true method, used by all teenagers at some point or another. I rolled my eyes and sighed deeply.

"Don't roll your eyes at me, young lady. Do you understand?"

I nodded but pouted.

"I'll bet Nicholas doesn't even come. His dad comes over here all the time and Nicholas never comes with him," I grumbled hopefully.

"Oh, he's coming all right. I made sure to tell Dale to bring Nick. I explained the whole situation to him," my mom said calmly.

"Mom, you didn't! Oh, please tell me you didn't. You'll make everything so much worse!"

I moaned and groaned as if I was dying. I didn't think my response was inappropriate, considering the situation. My social life was being murdered before my eyes and the murderer was my own mother. But my mom thought differently.

"Come down here right now," she ordered in a no-nonsense tone.

I trudged down the stairs like a convict sentenced to death.

"Wipe that pout off your face, young lady, or it might stick that way and Nicholas will never like you. Now, scoot and set the table. Your father will be home soon."

"I sure will!" my dad said, walking through the door at that very moment.

"Perfect timing, honey! Welcome home," my mom said, walking over and giving my dad a kiss.

"Perfect timing, indeed! I brought my lovely hardworking queen some flowers," my dad said, revealing a bouquet of lilies, my mom's favorite flowers.

"Aw, you big sweetheart." My mom blushed, took the flowers, and gave my father another kiss.

"Now, what's all this I hear about a dinner party?" my dad said, taking off his coat.

My mother had whisked the flowers away to put them in some water, and I saw my chance.

"Dad, you've got to save me!" I pleaded, begging for a rescue.

"Now, what's all this?"

"Mom invited Nicholas over to set me up with him, but I can't see him! I can't!" I groaned, pacing back and forth.

"Slow down, Remi. Why can't you see Nicholas? Your mother told me you really liked the guy."

"I did, but I don't think he likes me back! And I'm not ready to see him yet!"

"I don't understand you sometimes," my dad said, shaking his head, "You two used to be attached at the hip. Then you drop each other with no explanation? Maybe you two could use some time together. And some meddling from your mom! It's helped me out of a sticky situation a time or two."

My dad walked over and engulfed me in a hug. I didn't hug him back for a moment, because I was still mad, but it was impossible to resist his hugs for very long.

"Thanks, Dad," I mumbled into his chest.

"It'll be all right, pumpkin," my dad said. "It's just a couple of hours. Why don't you go upstairs and get all dressed up, just in case you change your opinion? It never hurts to look your best. Besides, it's fun to dress up sometimes. Right?"

"All right," I said, pulling away. "I did have a new makeup look I wanted to try."

"See? That's the spirit! You'll survive a few hours with Nicholas. I promise."

I smiled.

"Thanks, Dad," I said again.

"No problem. Off you go, now! I'll set the table for you."

I scurried upstairs. I put on a cute new pink blouse I had just bought at the mall, and a black skirt. Then I tried a new winged eyeliner that Mikayla had taught me at cheerleading. It looked super cute! I added some pale pink eyeshadow, which complimented the pink of the blouse. Then I added some blush to my cheeks. I finished off the look with lip-gloss and looked at my reflection, satisfied.

Nicholas or no Nicholas, I looked beautiful. Dad was right; it was fun to dress up every now and then. Just for fun. Not because I wanted to impress Nicholas. He probably wouldn't even come. Right?

I heard the doorbell ring from upstairs.

"Remi, can you get the door? I'm helping your mother in the kitchen!" my dad called.

"Sure!" I yelled back, already running down the stairs.

I took a deep breath when I saw the door. My heart had spet up, and my mouth was dry. I calmed myself down and slowed my breathing.

Then I opened the door with cool confidence.

The cool confidence was gone the minute I saw who was outside.

Nicholas was standing there on my doorstep. And I was immediately drowning in his gorgeous blue eyes.

# Chapter Nineteen

I swore in my mind. She was so stunning. I couldn't breathe, I couldn't think. She consumed my entire existence. There was nothing else in my world than her. Time was frozen. She was my past, my present. And oh, how I wanted her in my future. I loved her with every fiber of my being.

All I could think was, "I shouldn't have come. I really shouldn't have."

It was so hard not to just take her in my arms and kiss her.

"Sorry! Forgot the rolls," a voice said.

What was this, the voice in my head? Could it have a deep meaning, something to describe the love I was feeling?

Nope, it was my dad. Talking to Remi.

"Hey there, Remi. How have you been? Your mom's been telling me about your gymnastics and cheerleading escapades. It sounds impressive!"

"Thank you, Mr. Savage. How are you doing?"

"I am well, thank you!"

"Please, come in!" Remi said, opening the door for us.

I followed my dad into her house blindly. As the door closed behind me, I felt a pang of sorrow. I remembered coming in this door every day after school. I'd take my tiny sneakers off in this hallway and walk through that door into the kitchen for a snack. We'd do our homework through that door, in the living room. We'd race toy cars down this hallway.

I remembered the rainy days in the family room with Remi, days I had almost forgotten. We'd argue over what cartoons to watch and she'd make friendship bracelets. All the ones I tried to make ended up as knotted messes. But she liked them anyway.

I remembered the summer days at her kitchen table when her mom would give us ice pops and we'd run through the sprinkler in Remi's backyard.

I felt immense loss in the hallway of Remi's house. I hadn't even realized it before, but I had been grieving the loss of Remi. She had been my best friend. And now...?

Why had I ever shut her out.

Was it my fault that she wasn't in my life anymore?

"Are you coming, Nicholas?" my dad asked.

I nodded dumbly and followed him into the dining room.

I sat down at the table without daring to look at Remi. I couldn't. I wouldn't be able to hold myself back.

My dad joked around with Remi's dad about the football game. I could barely hear a thing over the sound of the blood rushing in my ears.

"Nicholas?"

I realized that the conversation had been directed toward me.

"Yes? Sorry," I said.

"You seem distracted tonight," Remi's mother observed.

"I'm just tired," I said.

"You've grown a lot since I saw you last," Remi's mom said, playing with her fork.

"Yeah," I replied.

"When did I see you last? It's been a while. Why don't you come around more often? You're welcome here anytime, you know."

If I had been paying closer attention, I would have seen Remi giving her mother glares from across the table. But I wasn't paying attention. I was trying not to look at Remi at all, because I knew that if I did, I would confess my love for her in a second.

"You used to come over all the time to do homework. I remember I helped you with that science project one time. What was that project about, Remi?" Remi's mom asked her.

"I don't know," Remi grumbled in reply, not looking up from her plate.

"It was a science project," I said, "About gravity."

"That's right! That was fun to hang out with you and help with it."

The feeling of guilt was rising steadily in my chest. Remi's mom had always been nice to me. But when I shut Remi out, I had shut her out too. At the time, it was a necessary casualty. Now I just felt bad about it.

"Yeah," was all I said in reply.

Remi's mom wasn't satisfied.

"You do seem distracted. Is anything bothering you? Anything you'd like to tell us about?" Remi's mom prodded.

I searched frantically for a change of subject. But my mind was suddenly an empty cavern. The only other thing I could come up with was the robotics club meeting I had just left.

I felt terribly awkward and I was panicking, trying to come up with some sort of reply as fast as I could.

The result was a mumbled, mangled mess. I rambled on about the problems with the robotics club for a good five minutes. I talked about how the school wouldn't give us any additional funds to make the robots, the contests we wanted to go to, the designs we had planned, everything. My face grew redder and redder as I spoke, and I barely stopped for air. There was some comfort in just talking, trying to avoid the silence and all of the overwhelming emotions.

That's when I heard her beautiful voice, and all the emotions came back in a wave.

"Why don't you do a fundraiser?" she asked.

It took me a solid minute to collect my scattered wits enough to compile a reply. And when I did get a response together, I had to rely on my sarcasm to carry it, which I'm sure sounded hurtful.

"Yeah, sure," I snapped in a panic, "What are we going to do? Run a bake sale? Those things almost always run at a loss. I know you cheerleaders always raise extra funds by having the senior girls run a car wash, but not all of us are hot chicks. I don't know why you even need extra money. The school gives you everything you could possibly need anyway. I'm not upset with you about it. It isn't your fault the school doesn't respect the STEM subjects."

There was dead silence at the table. I looked up, and everyone was staring at me. I looked at my dad, who stared at me, stunned. I'd never said anything like that, not to anyone.

Then I moved my eyes around the table. And I made eye contact with Remi.

That was the biggest mistake I'd ever made.

Her eyes were full of tears. I saw it on her face, in her eyes. She was done. With me, with trying... everything.

Doubt filled me. What had I done wrong? I had followed the book! She had to still want me. She had to! Why had she given up on me? Was I not worth the fight?

She looked down at the table. I saw something inside her just snap.

She didn't care anymore. She couldn't.

I'd hurt her one too many times. I'd pushed her too far away.

All the alarms in my mind were going off. I had to get her back! The book, I needed to reread the book. Maybe I had missed something! It wasn't true. My eyes were deceiving me. Maybe she was just tired. She still liked me! She still wanted me! She had to! After three years, she had to! I needed her.

The rest of dinner was small talk between the adults. I tried to start up a conversation with Remi a few times but tripped over every word I spoke. She replied politely. The tears were gone from her eyes and her voice was dull and empty. She ate all her food in near silence. I couldn't eat at all.

Dad nudged my arm at one point, telling me it was time to

leave. I followed him blindly to the door. Remi stood on the doorstep for a few moments.

I needed something... I needed to know that she still cared.

I touched her hand. Just a touch, just one. My mind was begging for more.

And why shouldn't I tell her the truth? Before I lost her forever. Maybe she'd forgive me for ignoring her, for pushing her away, for hurting her all those times.

Maybe, if I just told her the truth...

But then I caught myself. At this point, blowing Remi off was all I knew. It was how I handled any strong emotion I had for her. I didn't even know if I could love her now. I was so used to ignoring her.

It was a mistake. I knew that. But it was an instinctual reaction. Three years I'd been doing the same thing over and over, and in this moment of weakness, I did what I was used to.

I pushed Remi away again.

"I'm... sorry. See you around, Remi."

And I left.

I left her there, at the door. And she closed it behind me.

She never saw the one tear that ran down my cheek that night. And I never knew that she cried herself to sleep, ignoring her parent's attempts to apologize.

But I knew for a fact that I couldn't keep up this act for much longer. It was killing me inside.

I was killing myself.

# Chapter Twenty

When Remi and I were thirteen years old, I would go over to her house every day after school until my dad got home from work.

On this particular day, Remi's mom let us make smores in the microwave. They were Remi and I's favorite snack, and she had passed a spelling test, so it was a special treat.

"I know all the secrets to making the perfect microwave smore," Remi said with a giggle," Because one year my cheer team was supposed to go on a camping trip, but it got canceled because of the rain. So we ended up sort-of camping at the town's rec center!"

"Really?" I asked with a laugh.

"Really! Check this out," Remi said.

She melted the marshmallow in the microwave on a smore, then took two fingers and pulled out a tall piece of the sticky melted marshmallow. She held it there for a second, and the marshmallow hardened. Now the smore had a hard marshmallow tower sticking from the top!

"It's crunchy, see?" she said, taking a bite.

"Wow!" I had said.

When I tried it, I dripped a bit of chocolate on my shirt.

"Look," Remi giggled. "Here, let me help."

She hopped off the kitchen chair and got some paper towels. Then she came close to me, to wipe off the chocolate.

I could smell the fruity scent of her shampoo. I could hear her breathing. She was so close to me. I felt something for Remi, something new and unfamiliar. Something so strong that it overwhelmed and scared me.

I scrambled back.

"No, it's okay, I've got it," I stuttered, "I'll just go put a new shirt on at home."

Remi pulled back, staring at me, confused.

"At home? You're not going to stay and watch Pixar movies for a while?"

"No... no, I gotta go," I said.

"Oh, okay," Remi said with a shrug. She helped me put all my stuff back in my backpack and waved to me as I walked outside.

"See you tomorrow!" she called from the door.

I waved back, but the minute the door closed, my smile fell.

I remember the sinking feeling I had in my stomach as I walked home. I let myself in with the spare key, plopped my stuff down on the kitchen floor, and watched Pixar movies by myself in my living room.

That was the last time I'd been at Remi's house.

Every afternoon I'd let myself in with the spare key.

At first, I'd told Remi that I had homework. Then it was tutoring. Then swim team practice. Then I stopped making excuses.

Then we stopped talking.

That day making smores in the kitchen with my best friend... that was the beginning of the end.

And I never could think of that day without feeling the very same sinking feeling. It was only later that I found a label for it.

Loss.

# Chapter Twenty-One

Nicholas didn't like me back. I had no hope at this point.

Mikayla had called many times to comfort me, but her reassurance didn't help.

I was numb to everything now. Maybe I had moved on. Maybe I was just tired of trying. Maybe I finally realized the truth, that Nicholas didn't like me and never world. I didn't know.

Whatever the reason, my mind knew that I would never have Nicholas.

So, I wanted to say a proper goodbye.

I had decided to get Nicholas's robotics club the funding it needed. If the club meant that much to Nicholas, I would help him get into those contests with robots that had the right parts.

Then I would graduate. I would graduate knowing that I tried my best, and even when I was rejected, I was kind about it. I helped him when he threw me away. I was kind.

Maybe I was doing it for a sense of moral superiority. I'd like to think I did it to heal, even a tiny bit.

That was why I walked into the tenth-grade biology classroom to speak to Mr. Humpheres, the advisor to the robotics club.

"Hello?" I poked my head in the door. There was another teacher in there, organizing files on the desk.

"Hello?"

"I'm looking for Mr. Humpheres," I said.

"Oh. Check the teacher's lounge," they suggested.

"Thank you!"

I walked up to the teacher's lounge.

"Where's your hall pass, young lady?" a teacher in the lounge asked me.

I showed him.

"I'm looking for Mr. Humpheres," I said again.

"Check the physics classroom," the teacher said swiftly. "He spends a lot of his time there."

"Thank you!" I said, turning and hurrying to the physics classroom.

This classroom was one of the physics classrooms, but unlike the other physics classrooms, it also stored all of the robotics equipment. I walked in and looked around at all of the robotics equipment. There were bins of overflowing metal components. There were several toolboxes on the counter. One was open and had pliers sticking out. It was full of hex huts and different colored wires.

Then I found what I thought were the most impressive elements of the classroom. I saw three robots. One was small and looked like it may not be done. The other two were larger. They had wheels on the bottom and several arms and extensions protruding from the top.

I inspected one of them, looking at all the different elements. It looked impressive, even to my untrained eye.

Then I saw a sticky note on one side.

It was written in black ink on a yellow sticky note. It said,

*The third wheel needs to be replaced.*

I recognized that handwriting. It was Nicholas's.

I felt a sense of warmth. I was surprised to find that it wasn't tainted by hurt or longing this time. I could just be happy and proud of Nicholas's intelligence without feeling rejected.

At that moment, I grew rather fond of my new numbness.

Then a voice from behind me asked, "Are you looking for something?"

I turned and saw Mr. Humpheres there, a cup of coffee in hand, staring blankly at me.

"Oh, hello, Mr. Humpheres! I wanted to talk to you if you have a moment."

"Yes, I do. What can I help you with?" Mr. Humpheres said, putting his coffee cup on the desk.

"I heard that you're the supervisor of the robotics club?"

"That's right. One of them, at least. Did you want to join the robotics club?" Mr. Humpheres asked me.

"No, but I had an idea about how to get more funding. Nicholas told me that the club really wants to build robots for a competition or whatever, but you didn't have enough money."

"And you've figured out a way to solve that problem?" Mr. Humpheres asked skeptically. "With all due respect, if we teachers can't get the administration to spend more money on the club, how do you think you're going to do it?"

"That's just it," I started, "I can't. No one can. The school is always going to put more money into the sports programs, that's just how things are. We can worry about overturning the school administration's obsession with sports another day. I had an idea for an independent fundraiser. Clubs are allowed to do their own fundraisers, I looked it up! So, the robotics club doesn't have to rely on the school."

"What fundraiser?" Mr. Humpheres asked, interested.

"How about a car wash? The senior cheerleaders do one every spring to take us to competitions or get us new uniforms. It always brings in a ton! I'm sure we'd make enough money to get your robotics club to their competitions. And then some!"

"Are you offering to organize a car wash on the robotics club's behalf?" Mr. Humpheres asked.

"Yes, exactly!" I replied with a smile.

But Mr. Humpheres shook his head.

"I'm sorry. Remi, was it? The district funding bylines dictate that for independent club fundraisers, the club members themselves have to be involved. You're not a member of the robotics club, and I really don't think six boys who barely get outside at all would be willing to wash cars all day in this heat."

I frowned, my carefully crafted plans falling apart before my eyes.

"That doesn't seem fair. Aren't people outside of the club allowed to help?" I asked.

"They are allowed, but you can't organize it because you're not a member," Mr. Humpheres clarified.

I considered that for a long moment. There were obviously two solutions here. One, get someone in the robotics club to organize the event, with me just 'helping'. But I didn't know anyone in the club besides Nicholas. And I certainly wasn't going to ask for his help with this. Or two, I could become a member of the robotics club. But I didn't know anything about robotics and, quite honestly, couldn't care less.

This farewell gesture for Nicholas was turning out to be much more complicated than I had expected.

But hey. I put in all that effort when I thought I could have him. I might as well put in the effort to say goodbye.

I took a deep breath and looked the puzzled teacher straight in the eyes.

"Mr. Humpheres, I'd like to join the robotics club."

# Chapter Twenty-Two

I stared at Remi at lunch. I admit it! I barely took my eyes off her for the entire lunch period. I was searching for a sign, something to give me hope again.

As it would turn out, I didn't have to wait long.

Remi met my eyes, winked, and smiled at me with that adorable smile of hers. I audibly sighed. My heart raced, but I didn't let my enthusiasm show.

Still, I had to give her something. I decided on the slightest of smiles, and Remi's smile grew just a tad.

There was something between us, still. But it wasn't like before. It was warmer. There was less longing from Remi's side and less desperation from mine. She was comfortable where she was, and I could feel it.

But did that mean she was comfortable without me?

I stared at her again. She was the center of attention, as usual, talking to all of her cheerleading and gymnastics friends. I wasn't surprised. She grew into the leader of any group she was with. She was a natural leader. Not in a bossy way, either. She led by example, always taking time for other people's problems and helping the team work together smoothly.

Usually, she would be laughing and chatting with her group

about movies, books, school, or guys. They would all giggle and whisper amongst themselves light-heartedly.

But today something was up. Remi was sitting in the middle of the table. She usually sat on one end so she could see everyone at once. And she was leaning forward, talking excitedly. Was she planning something with her friends?

I wondered what they could be up to now. Oh, could it be another ploy for my attention? My heart soared for two seconds as I considered the possibility, then sank back to earth as I realized.

She was probably talking to her friends about cheerleading stuff. She wouldn't pull her friends into two big and grand gestures. Especially now...

I sighed into my cup of chocolate pudding. Then I remembered I hated chocolate pudding. Remi had distracted me from the real world once again.

I dumped my lunch tray and went about the rest of my day. I focused as well as I could in my classes but was grateful when the bell rang, and I could escape my thoughts in robotics club.

"Good afternoon, Mr. Savage," Mr. Humpheres greeted me as I walked in the door.

"Afternoon, sir."

"Hey, Nicholas." Timothy gave me a fist bump as I sat down.

"What are we working on today, sir?" I raised my hand and asked.

"Actually, I wanted to talk to you. Is everyone here?"

We all looked around, making sure that everyone was, indeed, there.

"Good. Now, I'm sure you all know about our financial struggles. I may have stumbled across a solution."

"Really?" Timothy asked, his eyes lightening up.

"Yes. Well, maybe. But first I would like to introduce you all to our new members."

We stared at each other, confused. We had struggled to get even the few club members we had. No one else had wanted to join in months. Who were these newcomers?

I leaned over to Timothy.

"Who suddenly wants to join?" I asked.

"We do," came a voice from the doorway.

I looked up in complete shock. Remi and four of her cheerleading friends were standing at the door! My mouth fell open in amazement before I could catch myself. Remi saw it and smiled coyly.

"We want to join the robotics club and we have some ideas to help you raise money for those gadgets you need."

Remi and her friends strutted into that physics classroom as if they were on a fashion-week runway. And from the way the other guys were staring at them, they might as well have been.

The other robotics guys stared at Remi and her friends openly, eyes wide. And the girls stared back, the attractive, popular queens that they were. They might as well have been from another planet. I thought all the other nerds in the room were about to have a collective heart attack.

Remi broke the silence.

"The girls and I had an idea about using a car wash to make money for the robotics equipment. The cheerleading team does one nearly every year, right guys? It works great!"

Everyone just stared at her. I did, too. My eyes were wide in disbelief and I didn't even try to hide it. A million questions were flooding my mind in a hurricane of confusion.

I had no idea what was going on, or why she was acting this way. But I intended to find out.

# Chapter Twenty-Three

The girls and I set up the car wash in front of the town mall. They weren't thrilled about it at first, but I managed to win them over. And we got a lot of the other cheerleaders to join in, too! We'd all gone shopping together and got matching t-shirts and shorts so we would all stand out. The boys refused to wear them at first, but we convinced them eventually.

The spot I picked was the same place the cheerleaders used every year. The owner of the property thought a fundraiser for a robotics club was slightly strange, but I had managed to convince him. Now we were all working together to set up on the side of the parking lot.

We had a blast setting up, spraying each other with water from the hose. By the time the guys showed up, we were all thoroughly soaked.

We took a collective breath as the guys got out of Mr. Humpheres car. The past few days in robotics had been an awkward mess. The girls were nice, of course, but I don't think the guys knew what to do with them. I doubted if any cheerleader had ever spoken to them before.

The thought made me laugh.

"Morning, boys!" I called to them as they walked up hesitantly.

"You guys can set up the robots over here, where it's dry," Mikayla suggested.

The grand plan was to have a robot battle going on during the car wash. The robotics guys weren't thrilled about washing cars all day, so we compromised. We would all take turns playing with the robots and washing cars. That way, we would all get a break to rest in the shade.

"Sierra, why don't you go ahead and start filming?" I asked one of my cheerleading friends.

Sierra had a huge following on social media. She was basically an influencer. I had recruited her to get the word out about our car wash and to film the robot battle.

"Cameras are rolling!" Sierra said with a giggle, turning her phone's camera on the boy setting up the first robot.

The poor kid flushed every shade of pink and nearly dropped the robot.

I laughed to myself again. These nerds had no idea how to handle my friends. I supposed that it was up to me to bridge the gap between the cheerleaders and the nerds.

"Timothy!" I said, addressing a boy I knew was close friends with Nicholas. I had seen them hanging out a lot and had made it a point to learn his name.

Timothy turned to me, looking surprised that I would speak to him.

"Great day for a car wash, huh?" I said, trying to make conversation.

"Um... yeah," he said.

I waited a moment for him to pick up the conversation, but he looked like he was grasping for a subject, so I tried again.

"Thanks for helping out."

"I mean... it is for our club... so..." He was drowning again.

I grimaced internally but reminded myself that small talk wasn't everyone's cup of tea. Time to bring out the big guns.

"Didn't you design one of these robots?" I asked.

The kid's face lit up like a Christmas tree.

"Yeah, I did, actually! I've been working on a design like this one for a long time now. I built one like it a few years ago that won an award at a robotics show in the city. Of course, for today, I made some minor tweaks so it would fight more strategically. But not too strategically, you know. The goal is to give the audience a show, not to win immediately."

"Like you would win immediately, anyway!" the boy setting up the other robot interjected.

"Shut up, David, you know mine would win," Timothy replied with an eye roll.

"Would not! Mine would. I spent years perfecting the design. No other battle bot could defeat it!" David protested.

"Please, your bot would be putty in the hands of my bot."

"Acid putty!"

"That's not a thing!"

"Sure it is!"

"Is not!"

"We could make it be, then!"

"Make acid putty? Why on earth would we do that?"

"To prove you wrong, idiot!"

Mikayla coughed. Both boys stared at her like deer in headlights.

"You guys, the car wash starts in ten minutes. Let's set up first and have the battle once there are actually people to watch?"

"Okay," said Timothy.

"Okay," said David.

"My money is on Timothy's robot! Someone better keep track of how many battles it wins, because it will be more!" Bethany, another of my cheerleading friends, exclaimed.

"I'll take that bet! David's will obviously win more battles. Five dollars?" Mikayla jumped up and replied.

"You're on!"

"I'm putting ten dollars on David's!" Sierra declared, half into her phone and half to us.

The rest of the guys and the girls gathered around, inspecting the bots and placing their bets.

I stood to one side, watching the parking lot.

A small part of me really wanted Nicholas to come. He didn't say he would, but he hadn't said that he wouldn't, either. Not that it mattered; we would raise the money either way. He would still get his parts. He could still go to those contests. He would have fun with his friends.

It was still a goodbye.

But I wouldn't have minded seeing him.

Then the first car drove up.

"Guys, quit with the bots! Time to get started!" I yelled.

Everyone froze for two seconds, then ran for the hoses, buckets, sponges, and soap.

"Remi, heads up!" Mikayla threw a sponge at me.

I caught and, with a laugh, turned to our first customer.

# Chapter Twenty-Four

That day, the day I went home from Remi's house, was the beginning of the end of our friendship. I tried to smother my feelings that afternoon with Pixar movies, but it was useless. So, I paced around my bedroom, wondering what the matter with me was.

I'd never been so uncomfortable around Remi before. I had started to notice it weeks before. I couldn't take my eyes off her, in school, after school. I always wanted to be around her, but being around her made me uncomfortable.

I didn't understand it, and it kind of scared me. Why did I feel like this? What changed between us? Remi and I had been best friends since we were babies. Our parents were friends long before I even existed! I couldn't even remember a time when Remi wasn't in my life! She had always been there for me.

So, why were things different now? Why did things change? She doesn't seem to feel like I do. How do I even feel? Why do I feel so jittery and embarrassed around her?

Then the lightbulb when off in my mind.

It was because I had never wanted to kiss her before.

I sat down on my couch, trying to grasp this concept.

All of this was because I had *feelings* for Remi! She wasn't just my friend anymore. She was a pretty girl that I'd like to kiss.

Until this point, I'd only seen her as a best friend, or a sister. Now, it was a crush. And that made things weird.

I got up slowly and walked to the mirror we had in the hallway. I meticulously inspected my appearance, scanning to see what chance I had with Remi.

The chance I had was fairly small. I had acne, I was short, my voice would crack at inconvenient times... the only thing Remi could see in me was our friendship.

In short, I would be friend-zoned.

I sighed at my reflection, and he sighed back. There was no way Remi could ever like me back. If I tried to explain how I felt, she would reject me. It was inevitable.

My eyes fell to the floor just thinking about it. I couldn't bare Remi's rejection. It would break my heart beyond repair. Then I would have to see her every day next door! I couldn't. I couldn't lose her, not like that.

But maybe...

Another lightbulb! An idea! Something to save me!

I would avoid Remi, just for a while. Just until the acne went away. Just until I was worthy of her. Then she would be mine. Then she would like me back!

It was a brilliant plan. At least, it was to my thirteen-year-old self. So, that's what I did.

I didn't go over to Remi's house in the afternoons again. I joined the science club. I joined the swim team. I got a tutor to help me with my homework. My parents were thrilled by my grades, my science fair awards, and swim team trophies. I made new friends that I sat with at lunch, who I talked to in the halls, just to avoid Remi.

She would try to talk to me. I would escape as fast as I could. She would wave to me on my way home. I wouldn't wave back. She would call me. I let it go to voicemail. She would text. I left her on read. She would skip down the sidewalk, stroll up to my door, and ask my father if I could come out to play. I would make an excuse, or I wouldn't be home.

But I would watch her. I saw every gymnastics competition she won. I was happy for her when she passed those hard math tests. I celebrated her every success in secret. All of this as I waited to be worthy of her.

The night she had a gymnastic team bonfire, I was watching through the window. I realized that I didn't know most of her friends. I always used to know Remi's friends. She'd tell me all about them. Now I only recognized one.

Then some guys showed up with pizza and sodas. My interest was immediately piqued. All the girls squealed and cheered, greeting them with surprise and delight. They were welcomed into the party enthusiastically. I watched as they paired off, boyfriends and girlfriends sitting together until Remi was the only one sitting alone.

I admit it, I was glad that Remi was sitting alone. She couldn't have a boyfriend. I was practically her boyfriend! Or, at least, I would be!

All of my delusions melted away as a handsome young man sat next to her. I knew him. His name was Matthew. He was on the chess team, so he was smart. He played basketball, so he was strong. A lot of girls liked him. A lot of girls would give anything to have him. He was sitting next to my Remi.

I wanted her to get up.

"Get up, Remi!" I mumbled, "Please. Walk away. Or push him away! Do something!"

She didn't do anything. No, that wasn't true. She did the *wrong* thing. She *smiled* at him at started talking with him!

My whole world was flipped upside down.

I was letting her slip away. But I didn't know what to do. I didn't think that there was anything I could be done. I was just an acne-covered science geek. And I didn't even know how to be around her anymore. I couldn't even be her friend. Not like this.

Not when I want so much more from her... And she'll never want that with me.

I pulled away from the window and sat on my bed until Remi's friends left. I saw her flash her lights three times before she went to bed.

*On, off.*
*On, off.*
*On, off.*
I stared up at my ceiling. She flashed them again.
*On, off.*
*On, off.*
*On, off.*
I didn't move. Remi didn't try again.
That was the last night we flashed our goodnight signal.

# Chapter Twenty-Five

The car wash was a resounding success! We had so many cars that there was a line going down the street. A lot of the drivers had gotten out of their cars and walked over to watch the robot fights, which were also an amazing success.

We had a few moms show up at the beginning. All of my friend's parents or grandparents had shown up to get their cars washed, but they didn't stay long. We were surprised at how many of the robotics guys' moms came. They stayed forever, taking pictures and bragging about their sons. The guys were embarrassed as anything, but we liked their moms.

Finally, they all left, and we got some regular customers. When the customers got more frequent, we started up the robot battles.

The cheerleaders and robotics club guys alike had taken sides for the robot battle of the century. They all took turns piloting the robots and each time a robot one, the winning party cheered and marked the win down with an expo marker on the side of a bucket. A few car drivers had stayed even past their car wash to watch the battles unfold.

David's robot had been christened the Terminator. Timothy's

robot had been nicknamed the Red Destroyer. The teams had been made. The lines had been drawn in the soapsuds.

It was war.

"There's no way you'll beat me now!" Bethany squealed at Nathan, another robotics club member.

"No way? Watch this."

Nathan manipulated the robot into a semi-flip and pounded Bethany's robot into the ground.

"The Terminator is the winner!" David exclaimed, lifting Nathan's hand into the air.

All of the Terminator fans exploded, while the Red Destroyer team groaned. Nathan walked the walk of glory up to the bucket, then was given the great honor of making another tally line on the bucket. The Terminator was up to twelve. The Red Destroyer was at thirteen.

While the war was raging on the battlefield, the members of both sides worked together to get cars washed. A lot of soap was thrown into people's faces and it didn't take long for everyone to be wetter than the cars they were washing. Whatever team lost the most recent battle did most of the work, but everyone helped out equally. Before long, the water-proof pouch that held the money we made was full to bursting.

I was on team Red Destroyer with Timothy's design. We'd done well so far. But I hadn't piloted the robot yet. I always passed up my turn. I didn't really know what I was afraid of. Maybe nothing. My mind was just on other things.

Mainly, a thing named Nicholas. He hadn't shown up yet. I didn't think he was going to. It made me slightly sad if I was obvious with myself. Maybe I had intimidated him. Maybe he thought I was trying to come on to him again. He hadn't said anything at the robotics meeting when my cheerleading friends and I showed up with my bright idea. Not that he looked upset, he didn't. He just looked... shocked. All of his friends were excited, if hesitant, about the idea.

Maybe it was just because the dinner at my house didn't go well.

I hadn't expected my mom's reaction after Nicholas and his dad left. As I wiped some soap off a pick-up truck, I thought back.

"I'm... sorry. See you around, Remi."

And he left.

He left me there, at the door. And I closed it behind him.

I nearly broke down at that moment. But I held myself together. I walked back in and helped my mom clear the table. And my mom told me honestly what she thought.

"Remi?"

"Yeah?" I said, not daring to look into her eyes.

"Nicholas still cares about you."

That did it. I put the plates on the table and burst into tears. My dad was the first one to hug me, with my mom not far behind.

"Honey, I'm so sorry. What happened?" my dad asked, clueless as he was.

It made me giggle as my mom glared at him. She stroked my hair to calm me as my dad held me.

"I'm sorry, Remi. I wouldn't have invited him over if I had known it would upset you this much," my mom said.

"No, it's okay. I needed to know," I gasped through my sobs, "Please, Mom, what did you mean? He still cares about me?"

"He does," my mom said with a sigh, "I don't know if his feelings are romantic in nature or not, but he still cares. He misses you, I'm certain. I saw it in his eyes, in the way he stole glances at you, trying not to stare."

"Then why has he been so distant?" I begged my mom for answers as my dad held me tighter.

"It could be that he doesn't understand his feelings, sweetie, or maybe he does understand them, and he just doesn't know what to do with them," she said.

"Your mother is right. A lot goes on in a guy's mind when he likes a girl, especially one as beautiful as you are," my dad said.

I giggled.

"But you didn't blow Mom off for years, did you, Dad?" I asked, staring up at him with tears running down my cheeks.

He wiped away my tears with a napkin.

"No, I didn't. But all guys do stupid stuff to impress girls. I dated another girl for two weeks in an attempt to make your mother jealous. And it worked!"

My mom snorted.

"Only because the girl figured out and told me!"

"Still worked." My dad grinned, giving my mom a kiss.

I laughed and pulled away from my dad's hug, wiping away the last of my tears.

"Thanks, Mom."

I cried myself to sleep last night. I needed to release some emotions. And the next day, I'd forced myself to get out of bed and go about my day. I could survive without Nicholas. I would have to.

But it still hurt that he wasn't here.

"Remi! You've been washing that same spot for ten minutes. I think it's clean now!" Sierra said with a giggle.

I awoke from my daze and laughed with her.

"I guess you're right. How's the livestream going?" I asked.

"Great! Say hello to the camera, and the six hundred people watching!"

"Six hundred people!?" I shouted, attracting the attention of several bystanders.

"That's right. Six hundred and twenty-four to be exact. And our numbers keep growing! I guess people like watching nerds and cheerleaders try to wash cars, with a good old-fashioned robot battle going on as well." Sierra laughed.

"That's wonderful! Great work, Sierra. Keep it up!"

I went back to washing and Sierra went back to filming the robot battle. And I made a decision. I would have fun with the car wash whether Nicholas was here or not. I didn't need him to hang out with my friends and have a good time! Sure, I was disappointed that he hadn't shown up when the whole reason we did it was for him and his robots. But I didn't need him.

"Remi! Are you taking a turn? The Red Destroyer needs you!" Mikayla called.

I looked over to see another Terminator victory.

"I don't think I..." Then I stopped. Why not play with the robot? One battle wouldn't hurt. The other girls had all tried it.

I strutted up with false confidence, fully convinced that I was about to get destroyed. Mikayla handed me the controller, and I crouched down by the bot.

"Players ready?" Timothy asked.

David, who was piloting the Terminator, nodded. I took a deep breath and nodded too.

"Fight!"

I started laughing immediately. I couldn't get the thing to even walk! I was completely awful at it. I knocked my own robot over at one point and was hitting myself in the face.

The whole group started dying of laughter. All the car drivers were near tears with laughter. The car wash was abandoned. Everyone had gathered around to watch me make a fool of myself. And I loved it! Even David joined in, abandoning his controller and making up a cheer routine for me.

"Go, Remi, go! Destroy your own bot!"

The little robot was convulsing on the battlefield as I desperately tried to get it to stand upright again. The other bot stood there, thoroughly confused.

Everyone was bent over with laughter, including me.

It was a wonderful day.

# Chapter Twenty-Six

I slept in on Saturday morning. I turned off my alarm clock and slept until the light shining through my blinds woke me up naturally.

I sighed and stared at the ceiling for a while, thinking about what I was going to do that day.

I knew that it was the day of Remi's car wash. But I wasn't sure that I wanted to go. Or that I *should* go.

I'd been incredibly moved that Remi would go out of her way to help me and the robotics club. It really made me think that she cared about me, my interests, and my problems.

But at the same time, I didn't want Remi in the robotics club. The robotics club was my sanctuary, my escape. It was the one place where I could get away from my problems and just geek out with my friends. It was the one place where I could truly forget about Remi for a while. Now, she was there! She would be on my mind all the time now. I would be close to her nearly every day.

She had infiltrated my world, my whole life. If she was around me all the time, how could I keep pretending that I wasn't interested? I couldn't.

I couldn't ignore Remi anymore.

I pulled *True Love Needs Persuasion: Making Any Woman*

*Fall in Love with You* off my nightstand and flipped through the dog-eared pages, scanning the notes I had made in the margins and the highlights I had drawn on the pages.

"It's never really safe to let a woman know you want her," the book spoke through the voice in my head, "but eventually you need to respond to a woman's advances on some level. Otherwise, how are you ever going to spend time with her or enjoy her company? Spend some time with the woman you want to fall in love with you. But take caution! Remain as emotionally distant as you can."

I put the book down again with a sigh. I was getting tired of being emotionally distant. I was getting tired of avoiding Remi. It was starting to hurt worse than the possible rejection.

Maybe I would go to the car wash after all.

I pulled myself out of bed, putting on a t-shirt and jeans. Remi's friends had gotten the whole team matching t-shirts, but I hadn't taken one. I kind of wish now that I would have.

I got a quick breakfast and walked outside.

"Good morning, Nicholas!"

I looked up sharply. It was Remi's mother, gardening in their yard.

"Good morning, Mrs. Lucas. How are you doing today?' I asked politely.

"I'm doing very well, thank you! Are you off to Remi's car wash?"

I flushed. For some reason, I felt guilty and uncomfortable talking to Remi's mom. I knew that Remi's mom had no idea that I was keeping Remi at a distance on purpose, and that made things awkward.

"Um... yeah. It's a fundraiser for my robotics club, you know," I stuttered.

"I heard." Remi's mom got up and walked over to the fence that separated the sidewalk from Remi's yard.

"You know," Remi's mom started, "Remi has been trying to rekindle a friendship with you for a while now."

"Yeah." I coughed, my throat suddenly dry. "Look, I'd better go."

"All right," Remi's mom said with a sad smile. "Be safe."

"Yeah," I said, and ran off.

I rode my bike down to the mall parking lot where the car wash was. I went fairly slowly, my mind on other things.

Maybe I should just give up the playing hard-to-get game. It was dumb, now that I was thinking about it. Remi had been trying so hard. She had done so many wonderful, sweet, and thoughtful things for me. Maybe it was time I gave it up and started doing sweet and romantic things for her, too. I certainly had plenty of ideas.

I rode into the parking lot and dismounted my bike. I walked it over to the car wash, which was set up at the edge of the parking lot under the shade of a couple of trees.

I saw Remi. She was laughing with her friends and the other guys in the robotics club. She was nearly doubled over laughing, her hands on a robot controller. David had her robot pinned, but he was cheering her on anyway, which only made her laugh harder.

They looked like they were all having a wonderful time.

But was she flirting with other guys? I stopped to watch for a moment. It certainly looked like she was flirting!

I grew angry.

The second I wasn't around she ran off, looking for attention from someone else. Ugh, this was exactly what the book said would happen!

I was furious at this point. At Remi for what I supposed was a betrayal, and at for myself for second-guessing the book even for a second. I never could have doubted it. It had served me so faithfully for so many years. And the moment I even think about doing anything against it, Remi flirts with my friends!

My face was red with anger, so I took a second to control my emotions.

I had temporarily fallen, but I was back now. I was ready to follow the book to the letter. Every chapter, every page, every word. I would obey it completely.

I took a breath, the anger I had felt falling to resolve.

I would ignore Remi again. I wished that I didn't have to, but it was her own fault. She was back to getting the silent treatment until she wanted me again.

I stopped to consider this. Maybe the silent treatment wouldn't work this time? She seemed to have moved on...

I took another deep breath.

All right. Ignoring Remi wasn't enough anymore. It was time to take drastic measures.

It was time to enact step three.

# Chapter Twenty-Seven

I watched Remi and the car wash crew for a long time. Probably too long. But I didn't know how to approach her. I wasn't sure if I was ready for the drastic step I was about to start.

Then she caught my eye.

"Nicholas!" she said, standing up from the robot battle.

She waved me over cheerily, beckoning me into the fun. I knew that she was trying to be nice, trying to be friendly. But I was determined now.

I squared my shoulders and walked over to her.

"I wasn't sure you'd come," Remi started to say, but I walked right past her.

I caught her staring at me, confused, out of the corner of my eye. It made me smile slightly to know that I caught her off-guard.

I picked up a bucket full of soapy water and a sponge and walk to the nearest car.

"Good morning to you as well," Timothy said sarcastically.

"Sorry I'm late," I replied, squishing the sponge into the warm water.

"Late? Dude, we've been here for hours. I didn't think you were coming."

"Sorry," I apologized again.

"Hey, Nicholas! Glad to see you're finally doing some work!" David called.

"Hey!" I replied, "Couldn't let you guys have all the fun!"

"Sure, sure," David said with a laugh.

"So, what's up?" Timothy asked, his voice hushed.

"What are you talking about?" I asked, turning to him.

Timothy looked me up and down slowly.

"You're acting weird. Is this about Remi again?" he asked.

"No!" I insisted.

Timothy stared at me for a few more minutes in uncomfortable silence.

"Fine, yes," I admitted with a sigh.

"Aha! I knew it. What's up now?" he asked.

"Just step three," I mumbled, more to myself than Timothy.

"Am I supposed to know what that means?" he asked.

"No, no. Never mind. Just something I need to work out," I said.

"All right, then." Timothy shrugged and went back to scrubbing the mud off of some middle-aged soccer mom's van.

Step three. I had always planned on skipping that step. I rarely even read over the chapter, and I reread every part of *True Love Needs Persuasion: Making Any Woman Fall in Love with You* nearly every day.

But I could see the text in my mind.

"Step three."

I could hear the book speaking in my mind as I mentally read the words on the page.

"Another way to get a woman's attention is to make her worried. More specifically, worried that she could lose you. Nothing lures a woman in more than the promise of a rival. Flirt with her friends, take a few girls on dates and be sure that it gets back to your target woman. Also, be open to another woman flirting with you. Women want men all the more if they know that the man is wanted by other women. Women tend to accept the opinion of other females around them, so if other women think you are attractive, your target woman will, too."

I always considered this part of the book cruel, manipulative, and toxic. Also, it could very easily go wrong.

But at this point, I had burned all my bridges. I was months from graduation, my time was running out, and Remi seemed to be further away than ever.

If Remi was so disinterested that she was flirting with other guys, it was time for drastic steps. I had suffered so much already, that suffering could not be in vain. I had to do this. I had to put step three into practice.

It was the only way I could think of to win her back. It was what I had to do to secure her affections.

I picked up my bucket and walked over to a new car, where one cheerleader was cleaning by herself.

"Hey," I said with a friendly smile.

"Hey!" The girl returned my smile.

"Bethany, isn't it?" I asked, holding eye contact and maintaining my smile.

"Yeah, it is!" she said, her smile brightening. "And you're Nicholas?"

"That's right!" I replied.

I glanced over. Remi was not even trying to hide the fact that she was staring at me. It was time to commit.

"So, what's a beautiful young lady doing cleaning this car all by yourself?" I asked, putting my arm on the side of the car over Bethany's head.

She giggled, scrubbing the car nervously.

"I don't know, I guess I was hoping you'd come to join me," she said quietly, blushing.

I moved in closer.

"I'm here now, aren't I?" I asked, purposely lowering my voice and adding a wink to sell the act.

"Yup," she squeaked. Then, collecting herself, lowered her voice as well.

# CHAPTER TWENTY-SEVEN

"Maybe you could help me with the top? I can't quite reach."

As Bethany said this, she reached her hands to the top of the car slowly.

"I guess I could help," I said, putting my hand on top of hers without needing to stretch.

"Wow, you're so tall..." she mumbled, staring into my eyes.

Suddenly Bethany stiffened. Her eyes locked onto something behind me.

"Um..." She coughed, threw me an apologetic glance, and slunk to the other side of the car.

I turned around quickly, wondering what had gone wrong.

Remi was standing there, her arms crossed. She had a disapproving, disappointed look on her face.

"We aren't here to flirt, Nicholas. If you're going to help, then help. If you're going to be all romantic, then go get a room."

"Um..."

"I'm going inside."

With that, Remi stormed off into the mall. I watched her go, wondering if my plan had thoroughly succeeded... or massively failed.

# Chapter Twenty-Eight

I just needed a break. I was trying to be mature. I was trying to move on, I really was. But seeing Nicholas flirt so hard with Bethany stung just a little too much. Especially since I was trying to be nice to him, and he completely ignored me!

I went into a clothing shop called the Galaxy Boutique. It was owned by a long-time friend of my family, Mrs. Francis. Her husband had died many years ago, and she had even lived with us for a while. I knew her as a grandmotherly figure and, when I was younger, a babysitter. She had moved out and started the clothing store when I was eight, but I still kept in touch.

She didn't know everything about Nicholas and me, which was how I liked it. I could tell her, or not tell her, anything I liked. She would always support me without prying or meddling.

"Mrs. Francis?" I asked, walking toward the back of the store.

"Remi? Is that you?" came a sweet, quiet voice.

I smiled in spite of myself.

"Yeah," I replied.

"Well, come on back! I'm taking a little break. Things have been so busy today! Would you like some lemonade?"

I walked to the back and was engulfed in a hug.

"It's so good to see you, dear, so good. What brings you by

today? Sit down, sit down, let me get you a glass of lemonade," Mrs. Francis said, waddling around hurriedly.

"I can only stay for a minute," I said with a sigh, taking a seat and resting my head on the counter.

"What is wrong?" Mrs. Francis said, reappearing suddenly with a cup of lemonade in hand.

"Did Mom tell you about the car wash we're doing today?" I asked, sipping the drink.

"Yes, she did call and say something about that. I would take my car to get it washed, but I've been so busy today! It must be all the traffic your car wash is bringing in. Good for business!"

"Well, I'm glad it helped someone," I said with a pout.

"Oh? Oh." Mrs. Francis slid into a seat beside me, filling my slightly empty glass back up to the rim.

"Tell me everything."

"It's just... I did it for this one guy. Nicholas. I had a crush on him for a long time. Like, years. But he's always ignored me. Recently I tried harder to get his attention. A lot harder. It's a long story, but he rejected me. Mom even tried to set me up with him by inviting him to dinner! I'm trying to get over it now. I did the car wash to get him and his club parts for their robots. It really meant a lot to him. I knew that. I thought it would be a nice way to move on. So that I wouldn't have any bad feelings about him, you know? It would let me forgive."

"Of course, of course!" Mrs. Francis said, nodding.

"But it didn't end up like that. I mean, I'm having a lot of fun with it. Really, I am! I like robotics club and the guys and hanging out with my friends is always a blast. But... well, Nicholas didn't even come for the first couple of hours. And the whole thing is for him!"

"Oh, dear," Mrs. Francis said, thoroughly enjoying my drama.

"Oh, but it gets worse," I said, very energetically telling my story now that I had a sympathetic and impartial audience.

"Tell me, tell me," Mrs. Francis replied.

"The minute he got here I went up to say hi to him. Do you

know? I was just trying to be friendly! But he walked right past me like I was invisible and started flirting with one of my friends! Not cute, playful, friendly flirting either, the messy stuff."

I took a long drink of my lemonade and put my head back on the counter.

"Oh, deary," Mrs. Francis said. She rubbed her hand in circles on my back, comforting me.

"I'm sorry. That sounds awful."

"It's not so much that he was flirting with her even... it was being ignored," I said with a sigh.

"I understand. It's never fun being invisible. Especially to a guy you like."

"I don't like him anymore, that's for sure. Or, at least, it's obvious that he doesn't like me. I guess I can move on now."

"I'm sorry your farewell car wash didn't turn out as you expected. But at least you're raising money for that club, right? You did a good deed with this. Not just for Nicholas, but also those other kids in the club," Mrs. Francis said comfortingly.

"That's right!" I said, lifting my head. "The livestream!"

"You're doing a livestream?" Mrs. Francis asked.

"Yeah, Sierra is! She's a friend of mine. Look, see!"

I pulled out my phone and opened the livestream. I was greeted by a view of the robot wars.

"My, doesn't that look exciting!" Mrs. Francis chuckled. "I might have to close up for a while and come watch. Oh, that one is winning!"

"Yeah, go Red Destroyer! That's my team. You should be on Red Destroyer's team, too, it's the best one."

Mrs. Francis and I watched the stream for a second more. Then I noticed something.

"Wait, what's this?"

I clicked on the link below the livestream and I was taken to an online shop. The banner on the top said, "Donate to get our Robotics Club the tools we need to continue building our amazing fighter robots!" The list of supplies we needed was underneath, with their prices and a place to donate.

"All of the items are funded!" I exclaimed, surprised and delighted.

"You got all of the supplies you need?" Mrs. Francis asked, equally excited.

"Yeah! And we didn't even have to use the money we made off the car wash! This is amazing! People are amazing! They donated all of this!"

"That's wonderful! Cheers, to the robotics club." Mrs. Francis raised her glass of lemonade.

I raised mine as well, clicking it against the side of hers.

"Cheers!"

"See, this whole thing wasn't all bad," Mrs. Francis said after we both took a sip.

"No, not bad at all," I said with a smile. Then, my smile fading, I whispered, "But I did it for him... it was all for him. And he didn't even care."

# Chapter Twenty-Nine

I kept looking out for Remi when she disappeared inside, but she didn't return. I washed the cars on autopilot, staying in a place where I could see the door.

Where had Remi gone? What was she doing? What was taking so long? Who was she with? Was she safe? The more I thought, the more worried I grew.

Remi had seemed so disappointed in me. She wasn't even that mad! Mad I could have handled. She didn't yell or anything. She just scolded me.

I began to realize that I might have taken things too far.

My eyes grew tired of watching the door and my nerves grew tired of jumping every time it opened. Thirty minutes went by and there was no sign of Remi. Shouts kept coming from under the tree where the robot fights were happening. So, I turned to watch them.

My stomach tied itself in notes as I made another realization. I had been jumping to conclusions, thinking Remi was flirting. Throughout the course of the day, the other girls played with the robots and laughed with the guys. They were all just having fun and being friendly. I'd been too blinded by my own jealousy to see what was happening. Remi wasn't trying to flirt at all. She was enjoying herself.

How could I have thought that she was flirting when she'd been doing everything she could to get my attention!

I wanted to pound my head into the side of a truck until I got some sense knocked into me. I had to do something to make it up to her! I had to fix things. My determination grew the longer Remi was gone. I was two minutes from going after her when she came back to the group.

"Guys, guys, guys!" she exclaimed, running up.

Everyone turned to stare at her, and she made the exciting announcement in a breathless voice.

"We did it! All the parts are paid for! Sierra, check! I just looked it up!"

Sierra checked the donations from her phone.

"Remi is right!" She squealed in delight, "We did it! All of them were paid for by our livestream viewers!"

It took a second for the others to realize what that meant.

"So... we don't have to use the money for the car wash to pay for the parts?" David asked.

"No, all the parts are already paid for!" Remi explained again, laughing.

"What are we going to do with the car wash money then?" Timothy asked, standing with a soapy sponge in his hand.

"For traveling expenses, more parts, new computers, whatever we want! Don't you see?"

That's when the news sank in.

"No way!"

"That's great!"

"We did it, guys!"

Suddenly everyone was everywhere at once, high-fiving each other and trading hugs.

"All right, all right everyone," Remi said when the celebration had died down slightly. "We've still got to clean this all up. Let's pack it up for the day. Great work, gang!"

The robotics club began cleaning up, grateful to rest their

tired legs and wipe off their soap-covered arms. I watched Remi pack some of the robot equipment in a box and struggle to lift it. I was over to her before I could think.

"Can I help?" I asked, extending my arms for the box.

Remi hesitated, looking shocked that I was speaking to her.

Then the awkward box began to slip out of her hands and she hurriedly said, "Sure, here."

I took it and struggled to position it in my arms.

"Where does this go?" I asked.

"Mr. Humpheres's car. This way, come on."

Remi led the way, and I followed closely behind. She opened the trunk for me, and I slipped the box inside.

"Thanks," Remi said.

"Thank you for putting this together today," I replied, "It was great."

Remi looked even more surprised.

"I'm sorry if I didn't seem... um... thankful earlier. I am and it was great. You're great."

I knew my face was bright red at this point, but there wasn't a whole lot I could do about it.

Remi didn't respond. She just stared at me. So, obviously, I had to panic.

I started rambling, "I just... I don't know... I don't always act the way I should and I'm sorry."

*Nicholas, just shut your mouth.*

Thank goodness the reasonable part of my brain decided to speak its piece then. I clamped my lips together to avoid another outburst. Not even my illogical ramblings could fix the damage to this conversation. I needed to leave this train wreck of a situation before anything else could happen. Exit line, exit line...

"Yeah, I'm sorry," I mumbled.

I hung my head, staring at my shoes in shame. In another second, I would have scurried away. I'll always be grateful that I didn't.

I felt something wrap around me. It was Remi! Remi's arms...

she was hugging me! I froze, stiffening. She didn't let go. I mentally pinched myself to check if I was dreaming. No, not a dream. A hug. A real hug. From Remi.

I hugged her back. Tightly.

"I've missed you, Nicholas," Remi whispered in that angelic voice of hers.

That brought me back to earth. I took a breath and got myself together.

"I've missed you, too," I replied softly.

# Chapter Thirty

When I pulled away from Nicholas, his face was fiery red. It made me smile. It was nice to see the real him again. Not the distant and emotionless jerk I'd seen in the past months. The quiet, nerdy, kind of awkward but completely adorable Nicholas.

I could see him shifting his weight from foot to foot. He tried to rush off, but I grabbed his hand. I wanted him to stay. But did he want it, too?

"Nicholas, do you want this or not?" I asked, rather sharply. I wasn't trying to be mean. I needed to know for sure.

He cleared his throat and said, "I... I don't know how to answer that yet."

I nodded and dropped his hand. He ran to his bike, jumped on, and pedaled away. I smiled as he left. That was the most open he'd been with me in years. Maybe we had at least a friendship ahead of us, maybe not. Either way, I was all right with it.

"Gather up, kiddos!" Mr. Humpheres sang. I laughed. He certainly was in a good mood now that we had all the parts we needed, and money to spare.

"Who wants to go to Hal's Diner for pizza and ice cream to celebrate your success? You've earned it!"

The team cheered, and I joined in. Pizza and ice cream sounded perfect after a day of hard work.

When we got to the diner, the guys got a table and all the girls scooted into a booth. We ordered and ate, chatting about the day.

"So, what did Nicholas want?" Sierra asked.

"What?" I asked, putting my slice of pepperoni pizza down.

"I saw you and him talking... and hugging," Sierra relayed the information to the group with a satisfied smile on her face.

"No way!" Mikayla said, dropping her spoon into her strawberry sorbet in surprise. "Remi! Tell me everything."

"There is really nothing to tell," I admitted with a shrug, "We just talked. He did apologize for blowing me off earlier."

"That's a step in the right direction! And you hugged him?"

"Yeah," I said with a sad smile.

"Remi, this is wonderful! Why aren't you more excited?" Bethany asked.

"It was wonderful, talking to him. I don't think it was anything more than that, though. I don't think I want it to be more than that. I've been through so much with Nicholas... I'm finally ready to let go. Move on. We're graduating in a couple of months, right? I can't follow him around forever."

"Wow, this is a switch!" Mikayla exclaimed, "Just a couple of weeks ago you were obsessed with him! Haven't you wanted him for years? What happened to change that?"

"I guess I got tired of getting my heart stomped on."

"Good for you!" Sierra said, raising her glass of soda.

"Yeah, good for you! You deserve so much better anyway," Bethany agreed.

"A toast!" Mikayla declared, raising her own glass, "To Remi! May she find someone better who won't stomp on her heart."

"I'll drink to that!" I said with a chuckle, clinking my glass on Mikayla's.

"Cheers!"

"And a toast to the robotics club! May we build the best fighter bots and win whatever contests we go to!" Sierra said.

"Cheers!"

We all clinked glasses again.

"I know we didn't join the club for the robots, but I have to admit, I had a lot of fun piloting them today. And I especially had fun winning the last battle of the day... and the tiebreaker! The Red Destroyer forever!" Mikayla said with an evil laugh.

Sierra and Bethany groaned.

"That reminds me, Bethany, don't you owe Mikayla five dollars?" I said, taking a sly sip of my drink.

"Ugh, fine. I'll get it to you at school Monday, Mikayla," Bethany groaned.

"Thank you very much! And Sierra, I seem to recall that you bet ten dollars?"

Sierra sighed and slid the money across the table. Mikayla picked it up with a smile.

"Thank you! A pleasure doing business with you."

I laughed and high-fived Mikayla.

"You're right, though, Kayla," I said, "I'm having fun in the club, too."

"Yeah, same," Bethany agreed.

"Me too. I didn't think I would, but it's a cool club. Maybe we can convince the rest of the team to join too! Then we could outvote the guys and we could pick the competitions we go to!"

"Ooh, they would hate that!" Mikayla laughed.

"We could go to a really dumb competition just to get on their nerves," Sierra said manically.

"I did read an article about a competition that was leprechaun-themed. Contestants are required to dress up like leprechauns!"

"They would *hate* that! Imagine them in little top hats and buckled shoes!"

We burst into an uncontrollable fit of giggles.

"What are you girls plotting over there?" Timothy called, his eyes meeting Mikayla's.

"Nothing!" we said in unison, resulting in more giggles.

"Mikayla, are you blushing?!" I whispered sharply when Timothy looked away.

"What! No." Mikayla denied it, but she surely was.

"Ooh, someone has a crush! Timothy, is it?" Sierra seized my observation and ran with it.

"Oh please. Would someone give Sierra a gold medal in the conclusion jump?" Mikayla said teasingly.

"Your gold medal, milady." I gladly obliged, offing Sierra the gold foil from Bethany's frozen yogurt container.

"I accept this medal with honor. Thank you, one and all! I promise to live up to my title." Sierra raised her yogurt foil high, and we all saluted it without thinking.

"Oh no, they've started a yogurt cult," came a voice from the boy's table.

We all nearly died of laughter.

I remember that night vividly, even years later. I watched my friends laugh and I thought about how happy I was. I decided that no matter what happened with Nicholas, I wasn't going to lose that happy feeling. I was going to have fun with my friends. I was going to enjoy my last year of high school. And I was going to have fun in the robotics club.

As I watched, I couldn't help but notice that Timothy kept glancing over at Mikayla. The minute he would look away, she would glance over at him. The smile on my face grew bigger, but I hid it in my ice cream.

I guess opposites really did attract.

# Chapter Thirty-One

The summer before I turned twelve, I did my first competitive gymnastics competition. I'd done junior competitions before, of course, where everyone got a participation prize and candy at the end. This one was different. There would be real judges who would give real marks. Every participant would be scored, and the top three would win trophies.

I was both excited and terrified. I'd practiced my routine every day for weeks, so I knew it inside and out, but I was afraid that I would blank midway through the competition. I wasn't worried about stumbling or messing up, not on most of the routine anyway. It was the flips that really scared me.

Flipping made me anxious ever since that afternoon in the basement. I'd taken a few weeks off to recover, and in that time the fall replayed so much in my mind that it engraved the feeling of fear. My coach had been very understanding, pushing me slowly but surely to try flips again. My routines were floor routines, and beam routines without a lot of flips.

That day, however, I did have to do one flip.

"You'll be fine, Remi," my coach tried to reassure me.

I scanned the crowd for my parents, nervously chewing on my

hoodie's string. Coach pulled the string out of my mouth and gave me a hug.

"You'll be fine, okay? I promise. Just keep loose. If you feel like you're going to fall, just roll out of it, okay? Take it slow. But whatever you do, don't tense up. Remi?"

"Yes, ma'am," I replied.

"Good. You got this, okay?"

"Yeah," I mumbled.

"Say it."

"I've got this," I said quietly.

"Louder?"

"I've got this!" I declared.

My coach smiled. At that moment, we heard my name being announced.

"Okay, kid. Go get 'um!"

She gave me a little shove toward the mat. I stumbled forward, peeling off my hoodie to reveal my leotard. I took a deep breath and got ahold of my nerves. Then I stepped onto the mat.

I stood on the two strips of bright red masking tape that marked my starting place and waited for the signal to begin. As I did, my eyes searched the audience for my parents again. I saw them, sitting in the front row. They waved when they met my eyes and I smiled at them. I noticed something else, as well. Lots of people in the audience were wearing yellow. Some were in yellow t-shirts, some in sweaters, and there was even one woman was in a yellow dress. I was surprised. None of the team's colors were yellow. It didn't look like an official uniform. The people weren't even sitting together. It must have been a coincidence.

It was a wonderful coincidence. Yellow was my favorite color. I smiled. It felt like the universe was trying to give me the confidence I needed. It worked, too.

The signal came for me to begin, and I was flipping and twirling away. I flew through my routine like a fairy, muscle memory overtaking my anxiety.

It was time for the flip. I couldn't hesitate or I'd be off the beat. I took a quick breath and just did it. The next thing I knew, my feet were back on the group. I'd landed it perfectly. The routine was over, and the audience cheered. I bowed quickly to the judges, then again to the audience, before scurrying off the mat.

"You did amazing, Remi! The flip was flawless. Great work!"

Coach gave me my hoodie and a high-five as I arrived, breathless, in the locker room.

"Did you see?" I asked, delighted in myself, "Did you see the whole thing?"

"Yes, the whole thing," my coach replied, pointing to a tv in the locker room that showed the competition still in full swing.

"I landed the flip!" I said, still high from the adrenaline.

"And you landed it beautifully. Now sit down. Where's your water bottle? Here. Deep breaths. You did great, Remi. Your parents are here tonight, right?"

"Yes, coach," I replied.

"Okay. If you'd like you can go wait with them until the end of the competition. Just be back here ten minutes before awards so we can take a team picture!"

"Sounds good! When is Mikayla going, do you know?"

"Three more gymnasts, then her. About fifteen minutes. Go on, get a snack and go watch!"

I did as my coach instructed. I got candy and popcorn from the concession booth and hurried to meet up with my parents.

"Remi, you were amazing!" my dad said, hugging me tightly.

"We're so proud of you, honey," my mom agreed.

"How did the flip look?" I asked anxiously.

"Like... a flip? How was it supposed to look?" my dad asked.

My mom swatted him on the shoulder.

"It looked perfect, honey. I'm so proud of you. Finally getting over your fears!"

"Maybe not completely." I giggled nervously.

"Do you know when your friend is competing?"

"About five minutes!"

We all settled in and watched the rest of the competition. Mikayla aced her routine as well, and my voice was hoarse at the end from cheering. The other gymnasts were good as well, which made me nervous. I hadn't thought about the actual scoring part of the competition. I had been so anxious about my routine. Now that it was over, I couldn't help but wonder. Had the judges liked my routine? Had they liked Mikayla's? How had we scored?

"Don't be nervous, honey, I'm sure they loved you!" my mom said, giving me a kiss on the cheek as I left to rejoin my team.

"Thanks!" I called as I hurried away.

"Remi!" Mikayla beckoned me over and I ran to give her a hug.

"You did so good!" I exclaimed.

"Me?! You did so good!" she replied. "Did you see my routine?"

"Yeah, I was sitting with my parents," I said.

"All right, good work today, guys!" my coach said, gathering the rest of the team together in the hallway. "You did great. Now, we're all going out there to stand for the awards ceremony. If your name is called, go up, get the award, and walk back to the group. Okay? Everyone got it? And whoever wins, we're going to be happy for them, right?"

"Yes, coach!" we chorused in unison.

"Good. Let's get out there!"

We ran out and stood in a line on the mat. There were six other teams standing around us. I hadn't realized there were so many kids participating. With each gymnast going one by one, it was hard to tell. And our team had arrived late because all our gymnasts were scheduled toward the end of the competition.

They read the awards for the trampoline and power tumbling divisions. Those had mostly older kids in them. We all clapped and whistled for them. Then it was our turn!

Mikayla and I held each other and crossed our fingers. First place was called. Neither of us won.

"Second place... Remi Lucas!"

I walked up to the platform with the biggest smile on my face. I could hear Mikayla cheering her lungs out for me.

"Good job," the guy said, handing me the medal and my scoresheet.

"Thank you!" I replied and strutted back to my team on cloud nine.

Mikayla high-fived me as she passed. It took me a moment to realize that she was going up to claim the third-place prize! I cheered as loud as I could when I got back to the group. When she came back, we were jumping up and down and hugging each other from the excitement.

My parents took Mikayla and me out for ice cream to celebrate. We went over our scoresheets and picked the parts we needed to work on.

"We'll get first next time, for sure," I declared.

"We can't both get first, silly," Mikayla said with a laugh.

"I'll bet I get first, first!" I replied.

"In your dreams!"

The whole drive home, I stared out the window of the car, watching the lights go by as if I was the main character in a movie. I saw the lights on in Nicholas's house when we pulled up.

"Mom, can I run over and show Nicholas my medal?" I asked.

"Sure, honey. But be quick! You need to get to bed," my mom said.

"Thanks!"

I jumped out of the car and ran over to Nicholas's house. I knocked on the door, and he answered.

"Nicholas, guess what!" I said, jumping around the porch.

"What?" he asked.

"No, you have to guess!" I insisted.

He sighed but guessed anyway to make me happy.

"Did you... get a puppy!"

"No!" I laughed.

"Did you... bring me candy?"

"No! Try again."

# CHAPTER THIRTY-ONE

"Did you... win a million dollars!"

"No, Nicholas! But I won something else. Look!"

I held up my medal with pride.

"Woah, Remi, that's awesome!" Nicholas admired my medal.

"Thanks! And guess what else? I landed the flip!" I said, not waiting for him to guess a second time.

"You did!? Good job, Remi! That's so awesome!"

"Thanks!" I said, blushing with happiness. "I was really nervous, but I did it anyway!"

"Good for you!"

"Yeah, but it was only because a lot of people in the audience were wearing yellow. It's my favorite color, you know. It gave me luck!"

Nicholas laughed at that. "You know luck isn't real, right? It's just something people pretend is true to make themselves feel better!"

I was much too happy to listen to Nicholas's reasonable arguments. My mood could not be squashed.

"Maybe you're right. But it sure made me feel better!" I said, swinging my medal from my fingertips.

Nicholas grinned at me.

"I'm glad."

"Okay, I've got to go to bed now. Goodnight, Nicholas!"

I ran off with a wave goodbye, leaving Nicholas smiling after me in the doorway.

I thought about that night a lot after that. I got better at gymnastics, and I won a lot of competitions, but I was never quite as happy as that night. Maybe it was because it was my first time. Maybe it was because I had conquered my fear. Maybe it was because I'd impressed Nicholas. Or maybe life hit me hard after that, and I missed being that happy little kid.

I thought about that night a lot after that. It made me smile every time.

# Chapter Thirty-Two

My dad was late getting home from work. It was the third time this week. Not that I minded. Being alone in the house gave me the chance to get some work done. Still... it was awfully quiet.

Nights like these made me think of Remi. I used to go to her house when my dad was late. It was loud at Remi's house. There was always something going on. Her mom would have friends over, or her dad would play games with us. It was always quiet at my house in the afternoons.

Just another reason to want Remi back in my life. Just another reason to work to make her fall in love with me.

I got made myself an omelet for a snack after school. Dad would probably bring some fried chicken and ice cream when he came. He usually did that when he was late. It was his way of apologizing, I supposed. For what, I didn't know. He couldn't help being late. Maybe he was apologizing for the quiet.

I sat down at my computer with my omelet. I thought about calling Timothy to see if he could come over. I remembered just in time that he had his sister's piano recital tonight. I didn't mind. I had some programming to do, anyway. I ate my omelet as the computer booted up. I opened the program I was working on and got to work, talking to myself as I did so.

"Blah... whatever... oh, that's wrong. Fix that... velocity equals distance divided by time..."

I always tried to drown out my thoughts of Remi in code and math. It usually worked. My computer was my escape, my sanctuary. Except for today. Today it was a distraction. Her image was hung in the front parlor of my mind, so whenever I thought of anything, she was the first thing I saw.

I kept replaying the day over and over in my mind. I'd done so many things wrong, so many things against the book. I don't know what I was thinking.

My emotional outburst to Remi at the car was unacceptable according to the book. I was beginning to wonder if I actually cared about the book anymore. Remi liked me. I liked her. Why couldn't I just be with her?!

I sighed, staring at my computer screen without seeing it.

I knew why. I knew perfectly well why. I was terrified of losing her.

I'd seen my father be the perfect husband. Romantic, supportive, he would have hung the moon for her. She left. Remi would, too. She would leave me unless I did exactly what the book said.

It hurt. Every day it hurt, pushing Remi further and further away. I was nearly numb to it by now. I had to keep going. I couldn't let her leave. I needed Remi. I needed her to love me unconditionally, for the rest of her life. We were perfect together. We were soulmates! I was willing to do anything. The book had worked so far. It would continue to work.

I was so tired of being patient. So, so tired.

I turned away from my computer for a moment and flipped through the book. I always kept it close to me in case I needed advice.

"If women are sure of where they stand with you, they can't

fall in love with you. It is imperative that you remain unpredictable and mysterious," the book spoke through the voice in my head once again.

Another quote, another reminder that would echo in my mind for weeks. Yet another lesson that seemed to push Remi further away. I was getting sick of it all.

I had taken things too far, flirting with Remi's friend as I did. Even I could admit that. I'd made a mistake and let my feelings get the better of me. But after my emotional display, I had to go back to keeping her at a distance.

I typed harder and faster. I found myself working on a different program. A special program. One I was making for Remi. She would probably never see it. I don't know how I would ever give it to her without ruining my plans. It made me feel better, anyway.

I worked hard on the program. It was some of my best work. Maybe I'd use it someday. On a college application, or maybe I'd use it for a job. Regardless, I would pour all my feelings for Remi and my skill at coding into the project. I would see how emotions and knowledge would blend.

I worked until I heard my dad come in the back door.

"Nick?" he called from downstairs.

I saved the program and closed my laptop. As I did, I looked out at the window over my bed. I saw the light in Remi's room go off.

"Nick! Are you alive up there?"

"Yeah!" I replied.

"I brought butterscotch ice cream and fried chicken! You want some?"

I smiled slightly.

"Yeah. I'll be down in a moment."

"Alrighty!"

Another day of longing for Remi, quiet, working with computers, finishing off with chicken and ice cream. I'd get up tomorrow, and it would be the same thing all over again. Sometimes, the consistency comforted me. Sometimes, it made me feel in control.

Tonight, all I felt was exhaustion.

# Chapter Thirty-Three

I had Mikayla come over on Sunday afternoon to hang out, just us girls. She came over a lot, but lately we'd both been so busy that it felt like a treat.

"Hello there, Mikayla!" my mom greeted her at the door.

"Good afternoon, Mrs. Lucas. How are you?"

"Fine, fine. Come on in! I've got a tray of cookies in the oven. They'll be ready in about fifteen minutes."

"Great! Just enough time to paint our nails," Mikayla said with a smile.

"Kayla, are you coming?" I asked from the stairs.

"Right behind you!"

We hurried up to my room and Mikayla hopped on my bed.

"I bought a new pink nail polish, but I hate it on me. Do you want to try it?" Mikayla asked, pulling a nail polish bottle from her purse.

"Sure, thanks!" I said, taking it. "Do you want to try that navy color? You said you liked it on me yesterday."

"Sure."

We painted our nails and discussed the usual topics, school, cheerleading, and gymnastics. Then Mikayla brought the conversation down a different route.

"So, how are things with you and Nicholas? We haven't talked about him in a while."

I shrugged.

"I'm not really sure. He ignored me at the car wash, then flirted with Bethany, only to turn around, give me a hug, and say he missed me. I'm honestly over the rollercoaster he's put me on, Kayla."

"Yeah, I heard about it from Bethany. She said he weirded her out."

"She didn't seem weirded out. She seemed into it," Remi said bitterly.

"Come on, Remi."

"She did! She was flirting back and everything."

"Really?" Mikayla said, sitting up.

"Yeah. I was literally four feet away. I saw the whole thing," I said with a sigh. "I thought she was my friend."

"Don't judge her too harshly. It is pretty obvious he's trying to push you away, after all," Mikayla said apologetically.

"You're right. What did Bethany tell you?" I asked.

"She said that Nicholas was being super sketchy about the whole thing. She said he stood there and stared at you for like, a long time. You didn't see him when he first rode up on his bike, because you were running the robot. Anyway, she said that he just stared at you playing with the robot for around five minutes. Then he walked over to her and flirted with her, but he kept sneaking little looks at you. She said it looked like he was hoping you were watching."

"Oh, please," I snapped, "You believe that story? She got caught flirting with the boy she knows I like. She's just making excuses! She doesn't want me mad with her!"

"I know, I would think that too. But I saw some of it, too. He was watching you, Remi," Mikayla said seriously.

"What're you saying?" I asked, starting to believe my friend's story.

"I think he did it to make you jealous," Mikayla said.

"You're kidding."

"Why else would he? Look, Remi. I've never seen him flirt with any other girl. Ever! Like, through all the years I've seen him at high school! Have you?"

"No..."

"So why do you think he just decided to right then?"

"I don't know," I said, defeated.

"Okay, believe me, or not. But from what I can see, he's trying to make you jealous," Mikayla said, finishing up her nails.

"That blue looks good on you," I mumbled.

"Thanks."

I finished the pink on my fingers and blew on the nails to dry them. Mikayla surprised me then by changing the subject again.

"What do you think of Nicholas's friend?"

"Which one?" I asked, even though I knew exactly which friend she was talking about.

"Timothy. Brown hair, brown eyes. Genius with computers. Sits beside Nicholas in the robotics club. That kid?"

"Yeah, yeah. I don't know. He seems nice enough. He was hard to beat at the robot battles."

"True," Mikayla said dreamily.

"What do you think of him?" I prodded.

"Oh, I don't know. You're right... he seems nice," she said.

"Do you like him?" I asked teasingly.

"No, I don't," Mikayla said. I wasn't convinced.

"Maybe you should call him. Ask him to come over for a while."

Mikayla looked in my eyes.

"Can I?" she asked.

I was surprised. I hadn't expected her to agree. But I knew my mom would be fine with more guests, so I shrugged.

"Sure, why not? Have him come over so the best friend, me, can see if he is worthy of you," I said with a smile.

"Shut up." Mikayla laughed, nudging me on the shoulder. Then she asked again, "Really, I can invite him over?"

"Sure! Go ahead, call him right now. See if he's free."

Mikayla grabbed her phone. Just as she was about to dial, she paused.

"Okay, but if I'm inviting Timothy over, you've got to invite Nicholas," she said.

"No way." I laughed.

"You have to! Otherwise, it will look like I want Timothy to come over just for me. And it would be two girls and one guy. That would be weird! It would be better if I could say that Nicholas is coming, and he might want to as well. Come on, Remi! Please?"

"No way!" I repeated.

"Please, oh please? Do this for your best friend? Your best friend who loves you? Your best friend who danced in front of a full cafeteria of her friends for you? You totally owe me!"

I hesitated. I did owe Mikayla for everything she had done to try and get me together with Nicholas. I could at least try to get her together with Timothy.

"Fine," I said with a sigh. Then, as Mikayla's face brightened, I added, "But I'm not calling him. I'll give you his number. You call."

"Fine with me!" Mikayla said, smiling. "Wait, how do you have his number?"

"My mom gave it to me," I admitted reluctantly, "His dad gave it to my mom in case of an emergency."

"Gotcha," Mikayla said with a twinkle in her eye. I groaned. I knew that I would be teased later about getting a guy's number from my mom.

"Hey, Timothy!" Mikayla said, her voice bright and cheery.

I couldn't hear what Timothy said on the other end, but it must have been good because Mikayla blushed.

"Thanks. So, I was wondering. I'm over at Remi's house. You know her, Remi Lucas, from the robotics club? Yeah, that's her. Anyway, I'm at her house. We were wondering if you wanted to come over? We're asking Nicholas, too, and since you two are friends... yeah. Yeah, that's right. Do you want to? If you're not doing anything. Um, I don't know. Let me ask."

Mikayla took the phone from her mouth, covered the speaker with one hand, and whispered to me.

"What are we planning on doing?" she asked.

I shrugged and said, "We can grill burgers and hang out. Play games, maybe."

Mikayla turned back to the phone.

"Grilling burgers, games, hanging out... the usual stuff. Are you free? Great! Okay, I'll text you the address. Okay, see you soon!"

Mikayla hung up and squealed, "He's coming!"

"I'm so happy for you and your future children," I said sarcastically, "Now text him the address so he knows where to go."

Mikayla texted him quickly, then said, "Give me Nicholas's number."

I hesitated.

"You promise you won't do anything embarrassing with it after this?"

"What? Would I do that?" Mikayla asked with suspiciously innocent eyes.

"Yes, yes, you would! Promise you won't?"

"Okay, I promise. Give me the number!"

I gave it to her against my better judgment. She called him immediately.

"Hey, is this Nicholas?"

I couldn't hear the response.

"Okay, this is Mikayla. I'm a friend of Remi's."

Silence as Mikayla listened.

"Yeah, okay, well, I'm over at Remi's house. We're having Timothy over to grill burgers, hang out, and whatever. Do you want to come? I know you and him are friends."

I sat nervously as Mikayla listened again.

"Okay, see you soon!" she said and hung up.

"He's coming?" I asked, my heart fluttering.

"Yup!" she said with a grin. "He'll be here soon. We'd better get ready!"

# Chapter Thirty-Four

I'd been invited over to Remi's house. It was a significant step, to say the least. At least, I thought it was. I mean, *she* hadn't exactly invited me. Her friend had. Nevertheless, it was a step in the right direction.

But how did Remi's friend get my phone number?

I mentally shrugged away the question. I had bigger things to worry about. I was standing in front of my front door, wondering when I should go over. I could walk over right at that moment, but would that be too soon? Did they mean later tonight? Were they setting up? Did they need help setting up? Should I offer to help?

I paced in my front hallway. Finally, I decided to just head over. I locked the door behind me and walked as briskly as I could to Remi's door. I knocked with no answer. When I knocked again, Timothy answered the door.

"Hey!" he said, smiling at me.

"Hey," I replied, surprised. I had been mentally preparing for Remi to open the door and was slightly thrown off to see my friend.

"Everyone is out back," Timothy said, beckoning me into the house.

"Everyone?" I asked.

"Yeah, Mikayla and Remi," Timothy explained. "Come on!"

I followed him inside, through the house, and out the back door. Mikayla and Remi were hanging out near a smoking grill.

"Hey, Nicholas!" Mikayla greeted me first with a smile and a friendly wave. "Glad you could make it!"

"Thanks for inviting me," I replied, but my eyes were on Remi.

She didn't seem to know how to react. After a minute she gave me a tiny smile and beckoned me over.

"Do you want a burger?" she asked.

"Yeah," I replied.

She pulled one off the grill and put it on a plate for me.

"Buns, ketchup, and stuff are all over on that table over there. Sodas are in the cooler. If you want water, it's inside; you can just use the fridge. You remember where that is, right?" she asked.

"Yeah," I said again. Then, in a feeble attempt to make a joke, I said, "Unless you've moved it up to your room since I last came over. You were planning to do that as a kid, remember?"

"Oh, that's right!" Remi said, her smile widening. "I wanted to be closer to the chocolate my mom had in the freezer. I can't believe you remember that!"

"Nicholas has a memory like a steel trap," Timothy said, interjecting himself into the conversation. "At least, most of the time. Don't you, Nicholas? He remembers every embarrassing thing I've ever done and reminds me of it on a daily basis. But when it comes to our literature homework, I believe his usual excuse is 'I forgot'."

"Shut up," I replied, reaching over to grab Timothy's soda can.

He jumped to avoid my hand, spilling the drink anyway. I laughed and he glared at me.

"Waste of a perfectly good can," he grumbled, "Now I have to get another one. The turtles thank you, Nicholas."

"The turtles!?" I exclaimed.

"Trash ends up in the ocean, Nicholas. And the turtles think it's food! They eat it. They eat it and *die*."

I shrugged. "Not my fault that turtles are dumb."

Mikayla gasped in mock horror, then laughed. Timothy stared at her until she awkwardly turned her laugh into a cough.

"It's no joking matter," Timothy said seriously.

"That shirt is no joking matter. Where did you get it, your grandma?" I asked.

"My grandmother is dead," Timothy replied.

"Ah, makes sense. That shirt looks like something died in it," I retorted.

"Your face looks like you got hit with a cattle prod," Timothy snapped.

"What even is a cattle prod? How is that an insult?"

"Ah, so you're dumb as well as ugly."

"Okay, okay boys, that's enough. Back to your corners," Mikayla said.

She reached over and touched Timothy's arm slightly. I watched him soften as he looked at her. At first, I was happy for him. They really seemed to have a connection. Then I felt a twinge of jealousy. Timothy connected so easily with Mikayla. It seemed so natural, so effortless. Why couldn't I have that with Remi? Was I making everything difficult for no reason?

"Do you want to sit down, Nicholas?"

I turned as I heard Remi's voice. She was gesturing to two lawn chairs in the corner of the yard. I looked back over at Timothy, who had gathered a plate full of food and had retired to the edge of the yard to sit, eat, and talk with Mikayla. They were laughing and eating together in blissful isolation.

"Sure," I replied, walking over to sit with Remi.

I hoped and prayed that it wouldn't be awkward. And, more than that, I hoped and prayed that I wouldn't say anything dumb and reveal myself and my emotions to her. Or, worse still, do something to humiliate myself and push Remi even further away.

What if I said something that made her never want to speak to me again? I was on the verge of panic.

Remi seemed to sense my worry and discomfort. She started the conversation herself, without waiting for me to speak.

"I'm glad you came."

"Yeah," I replied, and immediately panicked again. I couldn't come up with anything to say, so I commented on the layout of the backyard.

"You took down the swing set. You used to have it over there, right?" I pointed to the place in the yard that once held the swing set. Now it was a patch of flowers that Remi's mother was apparently growing.

"Oh, yeah. We took that down years ago. I don't swing much anymore."

It was a joke. I could laugh. Nope, my lungs were too constricted by this conversation to laugh. The best I could manage was a strangled giggle. Remi looked at me, worried. I wanted to punch myself in the face.

"How's school?" I asked. It was the dumbest of dumb questions, but I had to say something or risk choking on my own breath.

I hadn't touched the food in front of me yet. I was worried it would get stuck in my constricted throat and kill me. Did I look strange, not eating the food in front of me? I didn't want to seem impolite and I really didn't want to waste it. Remi had cooked it, or her parents had; either way, it would be rude not to eat it. But my throat was too tight to swallow my own spit let alone a burger. I had to relax. I focused on my breathing. In and out nice and slowly. It worked, a little. I felt calmer and I could feel my heart rate slowing.

"... he's a good teacher and everything, just not my style. But as long as you get a good grade in the class, right?" Remi finished, turning to me.

I froze again. I had been so focused on trying to breathe that I forgot Remi was talking.

"Right," I choked out.

"Do you not like the hamburger?" Remi asked.

Red alert, red alert! She had noticed! I would have to eat now. I prayed to whatever gods were listening that I could get a bite through my throat. If Remi had to watch me choke to death, I would die of embarrassment.

"No, it's good," I said. I forced a bite into my mouth.

I chewed for as long as I could without it being weird and swallowed hard. Thanks to any and all deity beings, the food traveled safely down into my stomach.

"Good, I'm glad. Hey... do you remember when we were little, and Dad would grill hamburgers and hot dogs for us? We'd always beg him to let us flip them over because they would steam and sizzle. You liked the noise, didn't you?"

"Yes, I did. I still do," I said, taking another bite of the hamburger. I ate it naturally this time, my mind consumed by Remi's words.

"And then we'd go inside and do homework, and if we got all our homework done before your dad got home, we could watch a movie. Remember? We'd race to see who got it done first. I always won. "

"No, you most certainly did not! I always won!" I insisted.

"No, you did not! I got all of mine done first like every day!" Remi argued.

"That's only because you had less than me!"

"It still counts!"

"Does not!"

"Does too!"

I opened my mouth to reply, but Remi burst into an uncontrollable fit of laughter.

"What?" I asked, genuinely curious.

"We're having the same argument we had when we were eight," she said, still laughing. "Have we really not matured at all? Even a tiny bit?"

"I guess not," I said, laughing too.

The tension had been broken between us. My throat loosened without me noticing. I began to breathe normally, and I ate my hamburger without thinking about it while we talked about the past.

"Remember that one time that we went to the zoo together? And we named all the animals? Then one of the zookeepers told us the animal's name and you got so upset because you wanted that elephant to be named... what was it?"

"Florence!" Remi said with a giggle. "Yeah, I remember that! I was so upset. Your dad didn't know what to do, it was hilarious! Poor guy. I wanted him to tell the zookeeper that its name was Florence."

"Then he got you ice cream to cheer you up," I remembered. "Then we got our faces painted."

"That's right! It was a significant improvement. You've got to paint over that ugly face of yours more regularly," Remi teased me playfully.

I laughed. "You're one to talk. You could fit a large cargo ship in the space between your front teeth."

"You could sail that ship in the sweat stains on your shirt."

"Hey, now that's just mean!" I replied, still laughing.

"No, what's mean is you forcing the world to look at that face of yours every single day."

"Is this why I came here?" I asked, "To be roasted by everyone around me? Because if so, I do believe I shall leave. My dignity and honor have been threatened!"

"Oh, has it now?" Remi said with a posh accent, "I didn't know you had any dignity and honor, to begin with!"

"Naturally a peasant like yourself wouldn't know anything about dignity and honor," I replied, sitting up straighter and using the same posh accent.

"Peasant, you say? My good, or not-so-good, sir, I'll have you know that I am a woman of noble birth!" Remi declared.

"Well, I'm the son of a duke," I countered.

"I'm a countess."

"Is that higher than a duke?" I asked.

"Naturally!"

"Then I'm also heir to the king's throne!" I added.

"Yes, you are the heir. Right behind me!" Remi said with a smug grin.

"So, a fight to the death for the throne it is!"

"Name your weapon!"

"Knives?" I suggested the first thing that came into my mind.

"No, too callous and vulgar. How about a duel? Pistols, at twenty paces?"

"Were pistols invented at this time period?"

"Which time period?" she asked.

"Whatever time period has kings and dukes and whatever," I explained.

"They still have them today, Nicholas," Remi said.

"Oh. So yes, the answer would be yes, they have pistols."

"So, pistols then?"

"Agreed."

"Um... guys?" Mikayla said, staring blankly at us.

Remi and I exchanged glances and burst into laughter. We hadn't realized that we were speaking so loudly, or that Mikayla and Timothy could hear our nonsensical ramblings.

"Never mind, Kayla," Remi said, waving her friend away.

Mikayla went back to talking to Timothy, who had also been staring at me.

"We're too weird for them, I guess," I said.

"You're probably right," Remi agreed. "We are pretty weird."

"In a good way, though."

"Oh, naturally."

Remi took a sip of her soda, and I took another bite of my burger. We sat in comfortable silence for a moment before I broke the quiet.

"Are you still cheerleading?" I asked.

"Of course! It's my passion," she replied.

"Good. You were always good at it," I said.

"Thanks. I know."

"So humble, too," I teased. She smiled.

"Are you planning on continuing to do it in college? And compete and stuff?" I asked.

"I hope to. Yes, I'm planning on it. I've got a long way to go before I'm ready for that level of competition, though. And I've got a very short period of time to learn it all."

"You could take a year off after you graduate," I suggested.

"I don't want to, though. I don't want to still be in college when I'm old. I want to get it done as fast as I can and get on with the rest of my life," Remi said.

"Why?" I asked.

"Why not?" She shrugged.

"Because... well, what about the college memories? If you're rushing through it, you'll miss out!"

"On what? Parties? You know I don't do those kinds of things, Nicholas. It's just not my thing."

"Not just parties. You could make lifelong friends there, and-"

"I plan to! But the focus will be on my studies." Remi sighed, then said, "Besides, what do you know about lifelong friendships?"

Ouch. That one stung a little bit. I took another bite of my burger in the awkward silence that followed.

"Sorry..." Remi said. It was more of an invitation to speak that an actual apology. I took the invitation.

"Don't be. I haven't exactly been the best friend for you lately, have I?" I asked.

"Lately? Try years," Remi snapped. I could tell that she regretted it as soon as the words left her lips.

"No, Nicholas, I'm sorry. Don't listen to anything I say, okay? I'm just... tired, I guess. I don't mean to be cruel," Remi mumbled.

She did look tired.

"It's all right, really. You're right, I don't know anything about lifelong friendships. I don't know anything about anything. You were always the smart one, anyway. Remember?"

Remi smiled at me again. That smile could solve all the world's problems, I would swear on it. It solved all of mine.

She didn't answer my question. Instead, she reached out her hand and put it on mine. I took her hand in mine. For once, I didn't think. I didn't think about the book or the plan or anything. I just took her hand and didn't pull away.

And for one brief minute, all was right with the world.

# Chapter Thirty-Five

I said goodbye to Remi as soon as Timothy said he had to leave.
I didn't want to linger after he had left. It turned out that I
left a little while before him because he stood around in the
hallway talking to Mikayla, inching ever so slightly toward the
door. Remi threw me a couple of glances, non-verbally asking if I
had noticed Mikayla and Timothy. I nodded to her and shrugged.
I had noticed, but I wasn't sure what was going on. Timothy
hadn't said very much about it to me. I would be sure to ask him
next time I had a moment alone.

I made it to the door before Timothy. Remi opened it for me.

"Thanks for coming," she said, stepping aside so I could exit.

I walked out the door and stood on her porch.

"Thank you for inviting me. The burgers were delicious," I
said.

"Thank you. It... it was nice. Talking with you," she said
slowly. I could tell that she was choosing her words carefully. I
picked mine just as meticulously.

"It was nice talking with you, too. Catching up and all..."

"Yeah."

"Well, goodnight," I said, not wanting things to get awkward.

"Goodnight, Nicholas."

I turned and walked away, forcing myself not to look back. I practically flew back to my house. Once I had stepped inside and closed the door behind me, I let out a sigh of utter bliss.

For one night, I hadn't forced myself to do anything, or be anything, or push Remi away. I enjoyed her company and, I hoped, she enjoyed mine. We had spoken civilly, like the old friends we used to be. For a while, all the drama and problems between us had vanished and we were the kids we used to be, just hanging out in Remi's backyard. It was so, so wonderful.

I walked up the stairs and sat on my bed as I so often did, waiting for her light to go out. I half hoped that she would do our goodnight signal, but her light went off without it. I didn't mind. Nothing could ruin my joyful mood.

I turned off my own lights and lay back on my bed. I closed my eyes, then opened them again, waiting for them to adjust to the sudden loss of light.

It was so wonderful, being near Remi. It was so refreshing, just talking and reminiscing with her. So many of my childhood memories had been buried under years of patience and distance. I had just begun to realize how much I'd forgotten. How much I'd lost when I left my friendship with Remi. How much I had chosen to lose. I had chosen it. That's the part that hurt the worst. But it wasn't like I had any other options.

I love her so much. I couldn't lose her. I knew that I was doing all the right things. I knew it was hard, and I knew that I would get through it. But it was amazing to have a brief respite in the eye of the storm to breathe and remember. I was reminded for the millionth time just how much I loved Remi.

And I fell asleep with that thought on my mind.

The next morning, I was woken up by my dad leaving for work. I pulled myself out of bed and got ready for the day. I didn't usually mind school too much. I wouldn't say I liked it, I just tolerated it more than my friends. They hated it with a burning passion. Today, I related to their feelings. I would rather have been anywhere but on my way to school. Preferably, I would be back in bed.

But no, I had to go to school, so I could get good grades, so I could get into college, so I could get a job, so I could be successful... and then what? Some days it just felt like I was a hamster running on a wheel. Going and going, always striving to get ahead and be better, but never getting anywhere.

Any happiness I had received from the previous night had disappeared. I had woken up on the wrong side of the bed which I titled reality. It was just one of those days.

I grabbed my bag and walked out the door, locking it behind me. I checked my phone. Dad had texted me.

"Hey, buddy," the text said, "I'll be late tonight. I'll bring home food, okay? Don't do anything I wouldn't do!"

I sighed and put my phone away. I knew my dad worked hard, and I knew he loved his job. Still... the texts always said he would be late. He never texted to say he was coming home early.

I grabbed my bike, which was waiting patiently by the fence for me. I put my feet on the pedals and away I went on the usual path to school. But just before I rode off my driveway into the street, I saw Remi come out of her house.

She looked beautiful that morning. The rising sun was flashing through her hair and it seemed to make her glow as she walked down her driveway. She was wearing a light blue shirt. Blue was my favorite color on Remi. It complemented the color in her eyes.

I wanted to leave my bike behind that morning. I wanted to run and catch up with Remi. I wanted to walk her to school as I had so long ago. We would walk together and talk about our week, and everything would be exactly like it used to be, if only just for a while. That's what I wanted.

But I got on my bike. I pushed the pedals down, riding off my driveway and building up speed. I saw Remi out of the corner of my eye as I whizzed by. Every day I flew past her on my bike without a backward glance. I should have been used to it by now. Spending time with her last night made me think that things could be different. It made me remember a time when Remi was beside me through everything when she was always in my life. She seemed to remember too. She seemed to enjoy hanging out with me.

No. Not, she only liked me because I was keeping her confused. The second she understands how I feel, I'll be boring to her. I hate to do it, but I love her too much. I've worked too hard for too many years to lose her now.

"Nicholas!"

I pulled up to school and ran over to where Timothy was waiting for me.

"Thanks for coming over last night. I know it must have been awkward for you. It would have been weird if I was there by myself," Timothy said as we walked to our first period class.

"No problem. It wasn't awkward at all, surprisingly. It turned out to be a very nice evening," I replied.

The next couple of class periods went by smoothly. I let myself forget about my problems for a while and focus on my schoolwork. For a while, I didn't think about Remi. But when lunch came around, it became impossible to ignore her.

Remi came up to my lunch table and sat beside me.

"Hello, Timothy! David, Nathan," she greeted my friends.

They stared at her, wondering what she was about to do. The dance in the cafeteria had shown everyone in the school that Remi was willing and able to create a public spectacle at any moment. I also stared at Remi as she pushed a plate of smores in front of me.

"Do you remember the last time we made smores?" Remi asked with an unrecognizable tone in her voice.

I swallowed hard. Everyone was glancing at us, waiting for Remi to do something crazy. I hated being the center of attention, so a large part of me wanted to leave. But I didn't want to seem like a jerk like I had the last time Remi did something to get my attention in the cafeteria. So, I picked up a smore and took a bite.

Once I finished chewing, I said, "I remember."

"That was the last day we were friends."

The venom in Remi's voice turned the smore to concrete in my mouth. I nearly choked and had to drink nearly all of my water bottle before I could breathe properly again.

Remi tilted her head to watch me.

"Are my smores that bad?" she asked in a sickly-sweet voice, her tone like poison dripping off a candy apple.

"You never told me what I did wrong, you know," she went on, now nearly whispering. "What did I do wrong, Nicholas? You can tell me. Why did you stop being my best friend?"

# Chapter Thirty-Six

Freshman year of high school was the worst year of my life. On paper, it should have been the best. I had just turned fourteen, which was an actual teenager. Thirteen was a baby teenager, now I was fully a teen. I was the lead cheerleader in my squad. We were competing around the country. That summer I had won three first-place medals and numerous medals for other places. I was learning new tricks every day and perfecting my old ones until I could do them in my sleep. I had the most wonderful best friend in the world, Mikayla, who I was just starting to get really close with. We had gone shopping for back-to-school together and had bought a whole new wardrobe of cute clothes and accessories.

We showed up on the first day of high school looking like Hollywood movie stars. We quickly figured out where all our classes were. So very lucky for us, we both had the same classes! It was an adjustment to figure out how to move quickly between classes and work out how to open our lockers. But we quickly did, even going so far as to decorate our lockers with cute matching blue and yellow decor. Our teachers were nice, and we didn't find the coursework too hard. And the very best thing of all, Mikayla and I tried out for the cheerleading team. We both made it!

Yes, on paper freshman year of high school should have been the best year of little Remi Lucas's life. It seemed like she had everything she wanted. But she didn't.

I didn't mention a few things. Let me go back. The first day of high school, I waited for Nicholas outside my house. I missed the bus waiting for him. My mom had to drive me, and I was thirty minutes late to my first class. I found out later that he had left early.

The next day I waited. Not as long, and I got on the bus without him. I knocked on his door that day after school. No one answered. I knew he was home. He was always home at that time. But he didn't answer.

The third day I waited. I was worried he was mad at me and ignoring me for some reason. After being late a second time, my teacher called my mom. She, in turn, called Nicholas's dad. He told her that Nicholas decided not to walk with me or take the bus with me anymore. He said that Nicholas wanted to ride his bike to school and back.

I stopped waiting for him.

The first day of high school, after school was done for the day, I ran home to tell Nicholas all about it. We had always done this with all our other grades. I didn't think anything would be different. I ran up and knocked on his door, as I always did the moment I got home. He didn't answer. I rang the doorbell. No answer. I went home and told my mom all about my day.

The next day I knocked again. No answer. I didn't even try the doorbell.

The third day I didn't bother going over at all. My mom called Nicholas's father again to see if Nicholas was planning on coming over after school to do homework like he always had. Nicholas's father said that Nicholas had decided to stay after school for some extracurriculars.

I stopped knocking.

I tried to sit with him at lunch. Once. He got up and moved to another table without a second glance or a word in my direction. Mikayla noticed me on the verge of tears and invited all the girls she was sitting with to move with her. They all sat by me that day and, by the end of lunch, I had a wonderful group of friends to sit with at lunch.

I stopped trying to sit with him at lunch.

I called him. I texted him. I tried to talk to him and be friendly to him in the hallways at school. I waved if I saw him on his bike outside his house.

He never called back. He didn't text back. He shut down every conversation I had with him in the hallways, leaving as fast as he could. And he pretended not to see me when he was outside.

My mom said to give him space, so I did. I backed off. I stopped calling, stopped texting, stopped talking, and stopped waving. I still smiled at him, of course. But he never smiled back.

For all of my freshman year of high school, I gave Nicholas space. I learned a lot that year. I made a lot of new friends. I grew as a person. I learned my first cheer routine. I won more gymnastic contests. I went to my first camp retreat with the cheerleaders. I had sleepovers and birthday parties. My family went on vacation with Mikayla's family. I lived a wonderful year of life and experienced all the wonders that it brought me.

And I didn't speak a word of it to Nicholas.

It hurt. We had always been a part of each other's lives before. We had shared in each other's joys and sadness. It used to be that every day we would talk about what had happened at school. We knew all of our secrets. Our families went on vacation with each other.

Now, every day I talked to Mikayla. She knew all of my secrets. My family went on vacation with her. It was great. She was a wonderful friend.

I just missed Nicholas.

I'll always remember one particular day. It was the day I realized that I had lost him, not just temporarily, but for good. It was the last week of high school. I had given him space for months. I was ready for us to be friends again. I had so much to tell him!

That particular day, I had just gotten word that I had passed all my finals. My first finals! I was so excited.

I saw him outside getting on his bike. I was just going outside anyway, to walk over to Mikayla's house.

"Nicholas!" I called, waving and smiling brightly.

He turned and stared at me like I was some strange creature that had crawled out of the sewers.

"Nicholas!" I called again, walking over to him.

He broke my eye contact and looked at his shoes. Then, in a sudden motion, he pulled himself up on his bike and whizzed by me.

I watched him pedal away down the road. I watched until his back disappeared. Only then did I realize that my hand was still raised as if waiting for a wave in reply. I lowered it slowly, the smile vanishing.

I decided not to go to Mikayla's after all. I decided not to do anything that day. My parents took me bowling to celebrate my finals. I had fun with them. Really, I did.

I still cried when I got home. Call me a dumb teenager, go ahead. I was. I was a young, dumb teenage girl who just realized that she had lost her best friend.

I didn't even try that summer. I spent all my time at gymnastics camps and the mall with my friends. I lived my life without him but always thought about him. I started to wonder if it was my fault. I wondered if I had done something to drive him away.

I decided that I must have. I must have done something so horrible that he could never forgive me. The guilt ate me away inside. I spent more and more time away from the house, running from the ruins of what I assumed I had destroyed. I hung out with Mikayla and my friends, worked on gymnastic routines and even went out with my parents. It all made me feel wanted and happy.

But at the end of the day, I had to go home. I had to watch Nicholas's light go out. I had to miss the goodnight signal. I had to miss Nicholas.

# Chapter Thirty-Seven

It might have been a cruel thing to do. I would admit that. But I had given Nicholas space for years. I had waited for him. I had worked for him. I had done everything but beg for him to be back. I didn't need him. I didn't need his friendship. I just needed the answer to one question. One question, so I wouldn't have to wonder for the rest of my life. I needed to know what I had done that offended Nicholas that he had cut me out of his life forever. I first had to remind him of what we had with the smores. Then I had to know.

I watched him choke on his bite of smore with an emotionless mask on my face. Inside, I was trembling. Finally, after what felt like an eternity, he caught his breath. He took a moment, seeming to collect himself, then turned to look me in the eyes.

"I'd rather not talk about that. Why... why don't we just see what happens now?"

That wasn't good enough for me.

"Do you want something to happen now?" I asked stoically.

He didn't answer. Not directly. He pushed his plate of smores back over to me. I took it and got up to leave.

"Remi?"

I stopped but didn't turn around.

"Are you coming to robotics today?" he asked.

I answered without turning to look at him.

"Yes. I'll be there."

"Okay."

I walked to the back of the cafeteria and threw the plate of smores in the garbage. I turned to head back to the table I had been sitting at with Mikayla, only to find my friends had gathered their things and were behind me.

"What did he say?" Sierra asked in a low, serious tone.

"Nothing. Exactly what he's been saying for years. Absolutely nothing."

"I'm sorry, Remi," Mikayla said, "I guess sometimes you just don't get closure."

"I guess not," I replied.

"Come on. Why don't we all go hang out in the library for a while?"

I smiled. My friends knew exactly what would cheer me up.

"Thanks, guys. But I'd rather be on my own for a while if you don't mind."

They nodded sympathetically and disappeared to their various friend groups, leaving me alone. I dragged my backpack to the library and plopped down on one of the large beanbags in the back. I opened a book called *The Candymakers*. It was one of my comfort books. My dad used to read it to me before bed. I wished I could carry it with me everywhere, but it was just too thick for that. So, I did the next best thing. I sat right by it on the shelf when I came to the library. That way, whenever I needed it, it was right there.

"That bad, huh?"

I jumped. I had been so consumed by my story that I didn't realize someone had walked up to my beanbag. Not just someone. Nicholas.

"What?" I asked.

He pointed to the book in my hands.

"Isn't *The Candymakers* your comfort book? Was your day that bad?"

"It was, thanks to you," I snapped before even thinking. I regretted it when I saw a glimmer of sadness spread across his face

"What are you doing here? Don't you have precalculus this period?" I asked.

"Mr. Jameston is absent today. Sick, I guess. The sub said we could hang in the library for the hour," Nicholas explained.

"Well, hang somewhere else. I'm reading," I said, burying my face back in the book.

"Can I read with you?"

I looked up at him, non-verbally saying, "Seriously?"

"Believe me, I wouldn't if I didn't have to. I know you like your quiet when you're reading. But that beanbag chair next to you is the only place left to sit," Nicholas said, raising his hands defensively.

"In the whole library? Really," I said in disbelief.

"Look around for yourself, sherlock."

I did and reluctantly admitted that he was right. Precalculus was a big class and all the tables were taken by either them or the kids in study hall.

"Fine," I said, gesturing to the seat beside me.

"Thanks," he said and took it. He opened a book titled *1984*.

"George Orwell?" I asked.

"What?" he said, looking up.

"The book. Is it by George Orwell?"

"Oh," Nicholas said, flipping the book to check the author. "Yeah."

"I read *Animal Farm* by him. It was good," I said.

"I haven't read that one. This is great though."

"I'll have to try it."

"I'll have to reread *The Candymakers*," Nicholas said.

"I guess we should switch sometime."

"I guess."

We both fell silent. For a few minutes, it was awkward. We

both wanted to talk to each other, to say all the things we wished we could say. It wasn't the time, nor the place. The library was a place to read. So, we read. We read in blissful, comfortable silence.

Before we even realized, the hour was up and the precalculus class was leaving.

"I guess I'd better go," Nicholas said, still coming out of the daze his book had created.

"Me too. I'll see you in robotics?"

"I'll see you there."

We went our separate ways, to our separate classes and our separate worlds. It would have been nice to have more of a conversation with Nicholas, but for now, I was happy with the silence.

# Chapter Thirty-Eight

I wasn't sure what to think or how to feel after the meeting with Remi. I guess it might have been in shock or it could have been relief. It was more a sense of wonder, a surreal feeling of peace. There had been so much I wanted to say. There was so much I couldn't explain. It was as if none of that mattered for an hour. I enjoyed spending time with Remi. It was amazing just to be close to her.

"You seem happy," Timothy observed as I sat next to him in history.

"I saw Remi in the library," I said.

"Saw her, or talked to her?" Timothy asked.

"A little of both."

"What did she say?" Timothy asked, intrigued.

"Nothing much. We read together."

"That's it? Just read?"

"Yeah."

Timothy sighed into his history book as the teacher began the class.

"You're infuriating, you know that, right? Just tell the girl you like her already. It's been my advice from the beginning. You'd be a lot happier if you did!"

"I know," I whispered, "Believe me, I know."

"For what it's worth, I think you two would be a nice couple," Timothy said with a shrug.

"Thanks."

I sat and tried to focus on history as we learned about the Spanish Inquisition. My mind was on Remi, as usual. I couldn't wait until robotics class.

As it turns out, I didn't have to wait very long. The rest of the day went by smoothly. My mind was distracted by homework and tests, giving it a brief respite. But the break was over the moment I walked through the doors of the robotics club.

"Hey, Nicholas!" David called.

"Hey," I replied, sitting down next to him. Timothy, who had followed me from our last period class, took the seat next to Nathan.

"Where are the girls?" Timothy asked.

"You mean Mikayla?" Nathan teased.

Timothy flushed and said, "That's not what I meant. They're just usually here by this time."

"Sure, Timothy, sure," David said.

"I think they have cheerleading practice today," I offered.

"Of course, Nicholas would know. Simping much, you two?"

"Shut up, Nathan," Timothy replied.

"Aw, are the boys missing us?"

We all looked up to see Remi and her friends walk in.

"Good of you to join us, ladies. Take a seat," Mr. Humpheres said.

"Sorry we're late," Sierra said, "And we can't stay very long. Cheerleading practice was moved to today, and it starts in fifteen minutes."

"Well, hurry and sit down then. We'll jump right into it."

Mikayla took the seat next to Timothy, which I noticed made him blush a considerable amount. The rest of the girls took seats at their own table. There was an empty chair near me, and I was hoping Remi would take it, but she sat with the other girls.

"All right. Good work, gang, on the car wash. Thanks to all of your hard work, and Sierra's social media following, we've got all the parts we need for the battle robots, and plenty of money left over for travel expenses. We'll be attending every contest I can book us in!"

We all let out a cheer and burst into rowdy applause. Sierra stood up and gave a little bow, and we applauded for her as well. After all, without her idea of a livestream and her viewers watching us, we would never have received all the parts we needed.

"All right, all right, settle down. We've only got the girls for a couple of minutes, so let's settle down and get straight to work. David and Bethany, will you help with the boxes?"

We oohed and awed as the parts came out of the box. I saw Sierra wiggling with excitement and whispering to Remi.

"Okay, now that everything is unloaded, we can get to work. David and Timothy, were you two the ones with the designs?"

"That's right," Timothy said.

"Yeah, and mine is better," David replied with a smirk.

Timothy scowled at him, but before an argument could ensue, Mr. Humpheres interrupted.

"Why don't we try to make them both the best they can be? Those designs worked pretty well in the ring at the car wash. Did anyone remember to take notes on their performance? Did anyone note the two robot's strengths and weaknesses?"

We turned to stare at each other. No one had thought that far ahead. We were just having fun with the robots.

"I recorded the livestream..." Sierra said hesitantly, "Maybe we can look over it to see the strengths and weaknesses?"

"Perfect. Timothy, David, you two are the team captains here. You go get that recording from Sierra before she has to go. Then look it over. Carefully, do you understand? Figure out where the robot is unbalanced, where it can perform better, and where we need to add an additional defense or attack. Then we'll run those changes by the other club members. These two robots will be our glorious creations, sound good? They must be the best."

"Yes, Mr. Humpheres," David and Timothy replied, standing up and walking over to Sierra, who already was scrolling away on her phone.

"No need," I heard Sierra whisper to them, "I texted it to you. Watch it at home, when you have a spare few hours and a bag of popcorn."

"Thanks," they whispered back, returning to their seats.

"As for the rest of you, pair up. The robots suffered some damage from the car wash war. Before we can make them better, we must fix them up. Or, more specifically, you must fix them up. I have a very alluring crossword puzzle to complete. Holler at me if you need me."

Mr. Humpheres retreated to his phone for his afternoon's relaxation of online crossword puzzles and politics podcasts. I looked around for Timothy, my usual partner. I was surprised to find that he and Mikayla were already huddled over the Red Destroyer, working with its wheels.

"Can I do it?" Mikayla asked, pointing to the part of the wheel Timothy was adjusting.

"Um... sure," he stuttered for a moment, then handed her the tools.

"Show me how?" Mikayla asked with a smile.

I chuckled a little to myself, watching Timothy turn various shades of pink. He pulled himself together and reached over Mikayla's shoulder to show her what to do. She purposefully leaned back, into Timothy's arms. His smile grew huge as he explained what to do.

"I guess this is the only seat left."

I heard Remi's voice and turned sharply. It took a second for her sentence to register in my mind and another second for me to formulate a response.

"No, there's not. There are chairs over there, and there..."

"I was referencing what you said in the library, dumbbell. Do you want me to sit with you or not?"

"Oh," I said, staring blankly at her. "Oh. Yes, sit. Please."

"Thank you," Remi said and sat down next to me.

She opened her arms, revealing part of David's robot's engine.

"Something in it broke during the final battle of the day," she explained. "David is working on the arms so it's our job to get it up and running again. Can you do it?"

"I think so. Put it down, let me see."

Remi put the parts on the table, and I scooted my chair closer, inspecting them. Just then, a timer on Sierra's phone went off.

"Guys, time for cheerleading. Come on, we're going to be late enough as it is, coach will scream if we're any later!" Sierra exclaimed, standing up.

"Oh," Timothy said sadly as Mikayla stood up.

"I'll see you later, guys!" Mikayla said with a wave, but her eyes didn't leave Timothy.

"I'll expect to see you ladies at the next club meeting... early!" Mr. Humpheres said.

"We'll be there!" Sierra said.

"Early!" Bethany promised.

"Remi, are you coming?" Mikayla asked, turning to Remi, who had remained seated beside me.

"No, I think I'll skip this practice and hang out here for a while. With all the work I put into the car wash and everything, I feel like I have to stick around for a while and see the guys put our parts to good use!" Remi said.

"Coach will be super mad..." Sierra warned.

"Forget it, Remi, I'll cover for you," Mikayla said with a wink. "But you'd better not miss the next one!"

"I won't!" Remi replied, smiling broadly at Mikayla.

The girls hurried from the room and headed outside to the football field for practice. Remi watched them run outside through the window for a moment, and I watched her closely. I couldn't decide what she was thinking, and before I could consider it further, she turned back to me.

"David was telling me about an idea he had for the robot," she said in that beautiful voice of hers.

"Oh? What idea?" I asked, trying to pay attention to what she was saying. It was hard to focus on her words when my thoughts kept drifting to the adorable half-smile she wore like an accessory.

"He thought it would be cool and maybe helpful in a battle for the robot to have some kind of rocket launcher on the arm," Remi said.

"A rocket launcher? What does he want it to do, launch the other team's robot into space?" I asked.

Remi giggled, and I flushed.

"No, not that kind. Something that could launch rocks or something," she explained.

"Rocks?" I questioned again. "How on earth would that be any good in a fight with a metal robot? Unless your goal is to make cool plinking noises as the rocks bounce off him, I don't think they'll have much of an impact."

Remi laughed again.

"I guess David thought the other teams would make their robots out of glass," Remi said.

"Either that or David as a very different experience with rocks than the rest of us," I replied.

"He might! Why don't you ask him?" Remi suggested.

"Hey, David!" I called, taking her advice.

David jumped and looked up from where he had been focusing intently on the robot's engine.

"Do you have a bad experience with rocks?" I asked.

"What?" David responded, completely befuddled.

"Rocks. Do you have a bad experience with rocks?"

By now the rest of the team had taken notice of our conversation and had stopped what they were doing to listen in.

"No?" David answered my question hesitantly as if he wasn't sure of his own rock-related memories.

"Then why do you want to add a rock launcher on the robot?" I grilled him again.

David sighed. "All I was saying was that it might be cool if the robot shot something out of its arm! I didn't mean rocks specifi-cally, that was just the first thing to come to mind."

The rest of the robotics team lost interest in our conversation at this point and resumed work on their various mechanical parts. Mr. Humpheres looked up from his crossword puzzle and inter-jected his thoughts.

"Don't make anything that could launch and hurt someone, boys, okay? I don't want to be sued for a robot attacking a person... not again."

I turned to question the last part of Mr. Humpheres sentence, but he had pulled his headphones back on and had resumed his crossword puzzle. So, I redirected the conversation back to Remi.

"We could add a launcher into the arm, then figure out what to launch later. We can adjust the weight parameters once we decide what to launch, but we could get the frame on there today. If you wanted to work on that right now, I don't know if there was something else to work on..." I suggested.

"No, working on this is fine. I'll go get the parts we'll need," Remi said, standing up.

"Do you know which ones?" I asked.

"Of course! I'm not a complete idiot, you know," she said with a smile.

"You could have fooled me," I replied, teasing her.

She threw me a dirty look and strolled up to the front of the room for the parts. I went to a table on the side of the room and grabbed some of the tools we would need. When I turned back, Timothy gave me a meaningful glance. He looked from me to Remi and raised his eyebrow. I pretended not to understand, and he rolled his eyes. I sat back down at the table with a contented smile.

"Got the stuff," Remi said, putting the supplies down on the table.

"Ah, so you're not as dumb as you look," I said. I immediately regretted the words, but Remi laughed.

"Nope, not a mirror, sorry."

# CHAPTER THIRTY-EIGHT

"Did you just call me dumb?" I asked, pretending to be offended.

"If the robot part fits," Remi replied.

"Hand me that part there, then, and we'll make it fit. Here, I should think," I said, redirecting the conversation to the robot in front of us.

"Yeah, I think so. Hey, maybe we should test the launcher on cotton balls. There's a ton over in that jar," Remi suggested as I tinkered with the parts.

"Why cotton balls?" I asked.

"They're continent and around the size of the stuff we will be launching. Right?"

"Sure, go grab 'um."

Remi stood up and walked over to Mr. Humpheres.

"Mr. Humpheres, can I use those cotton balls?" she asked.

Mr. Humpheres paused his podcast, looked up from his crossword puzzle, and blinked twice.

"Those? Sure, I guess," he said.

"Thanks!" Remi grabbed the jar and returned to the table.

"Hey," Mr. Humpheres said and Remi froze.

"What's an old English word meaning 'before'?" he asked.

"Ere," Remi replied and sat down.

Mr. Humpheres nodded his thanks and returned to his podcast.

"Woah," I said, "Impressive, Lucas. Where did you learn that?"

"Lucas?" Remi said with a scoff, "So, I'm one of the boys now, am I? Going by last names? All right, Savage, for your information, my dad used to be obsessed with them. I know all the basic questions and answers. Vocabulary in middle school literature class was a breeze."

"Oh, I remember that! Your dad would ask us questions about toys or movies and sometimes would tell us about a cool word he learned," I said, recalling times I had spent with Remi's family.

The smile flickered on her face as she said, "Yeah. I do remember that."

She dropped her eyes from mine and fiddled with a cotton ball. I hurried to complete the launcher, bitterly regretting bringing up anything about the past. But Remi quickly put an end to my regrets.

"It was nice, wasn't it?" she asked.

"What was?"

"Those times when you would hang out at my house after school. You and me doing homework together. The afternoon snacks my mom made us, and the Pixar movies... you were a huge part of my childhood."

"And you were a huge part of mine. They were nice... Really nice," I said, choosing my words carefully.

"Thank you," Remi said quietly. "For those memories."

"... no problem," I stuttered. I didn't know what to say.

"Come on, that looks good enough to me. Let's load that launcher on the arm already," Remi said, changing the subject.

"I don't think it's quite ready..."

"Come on! David will change it anyway; you know how he is with his robot's design. I want to get a good couple of cotton ball shots at the back of Timothy's head before I have to leave," Remi insisted.

I shrugged. "All right then!"

We pulled the robot's body over to us and attached the launcher as David was re-installing the repaired engine.

"What is that...?" he asked, suspiciously.

"Just a cotton ball launcher," Remi replied.

David's eyebrows raised.

"Why would we want the robot to launch... you know what, I don't want to know. Never mind. I'll just be over there working on some designs."

Remi giggled as David walked back to his table, sat down, and opened his notebook of design ideas.

"I guess he doesn't see the brilliance of our cotton ball launcher," she said.

"I guess not," I said as I attached the launcher to the robot.

"There," I sighed, taking a step away from the table. "That looks secure enough to me. Maybe not to launch anything heavier than a cotton ball, but-"

"We can work out those details later. Right now, we must launch a cotton ball at the back of Timothy's head," Remi announced.

"Why?" I asked. "What did he ever do to you?"

"He is a necessary casualty of war, Nicholas. Many good men must die for the sake of one good cotton ball launcher," Remi said seriously.

"What are you even talking about?" I asked.

"Man the guns, Nicholas!" she ordered, moving to stand behind me.

I obeyed the order and took aim with the joystick. The arm moved as I knew it would and, with it, the launcher.

"Take aim!"

I reluctantly aimed at the back of Timothy's head. It was as Remi had said. A necessary casualty of war.

"Fire!"

I pressed the button on the controller. The mechanics worked perfectly, and the cannon shot the tiny ball of cotton ammunition into the air. It struck Timothy dead-center. He turned around, confused to see what had hit him.

He saw Remi and me standing behind the robot and grew even more confused.

"Why is Remi saluting?" he asked.

I turned to see Remi standing with a serious expression and a stiff salute.

"A noble man has fallen today," I explained, "For the sake of science."

"They're insane," David called over to Timothy.

"Oh, yeah, I knew that," Timothy said and turned back to his work.

I chuckled and Remi swatted me on the shoulder.

"Excellent work, Private Nicholas," she said.

"Private? And what are you? A captain, I suppose," I replied, crossing my arms across my chest.

"No. I'm the admiral."

"Admirals are for the Navy, dimwits!" Nathan injected himself into the conversation from across the room.

"What's the top rank in the Army then?" Remi called back.

"General?" Nathan answered with a shrug.

"I'm a general, then," Remi said, returning to our conversation.

"General Remi it is, then."

Remi smiled at me and I looked down at my feet to avoid blushing.

"All right, next target, Private Nicholas," Remi said, reloading the launcher with another cotton ball and picking up the controller. She stared at it for a second, then looked at me.

"How does the launcher work with the controller?" she asked. "Which button?"

"This one. Here," I said, reaching over to show her which button.

Remi pushed it and the cotton ball flew into the air, before falling harmlessly back down onto the floor.

"Be sure to pick all of those up!" Mr. Humpheres called from his desk, beginning to regret giving the cotton balls to Remi.

"Will do!" Remi responded with a giggle. "I guess I need a refresher course on the controller. Show me?"

Remi turned and stared up at me with those beautiful eyes of hers, and I found that I was unable to breathe.

"Um... sure," I stuttered out.

Before I even knew what was happening, my hands were on top of Remi's, showing her how to work the controls. And I was the happiest man alive.

# Chapter Thirty-Nine

Robotics club was a lot of fun. I was glad I skipped out on cheerleading practice. It would cost me in jumping jacks and miles around the football field, but it was worth it. Oof, I winced just thinking about the punishment coach would inflict on me.

"Are you okay?" Nicholas asked.

"Yeah," I responded with a smile. "I was just imagining the exercises Coach is going to make me do next practice. He doesn't like any of the team members skipping practice."

"Sounds rough," Nicholas said, "Worth it though, right?"

"For the cotton ball launcher? Totally!"

"All right, kiddos, that's enough tinkering for today," Mr. Humpheres said. He stood up and stretched, and I swore the cracking could be heard in Canada.

"Time to pack up and head home. Wrap all breakable projects in bubble wrap please, there is a roll in that tote over there. Not that one, Nathan, the green one. There you go. Anyway, wrap anything that could get broken in the back of my car in that bubble wrap, and if I catch any of you popping my bubble wrap, I'll ban you from the club!" Mr. Humpheres finished, glaring at

David who had just finished popping a very satisfying row of bubbles.

David put the bubble wrap down slowly, wide-eyed.

"Would you really ban someone for popping the bubble wrap, Mr. Humpheres, sir?" Timothy asked, his voice hushed and worried.

"That depends. How much did you pop, Timothy?"

Timothy flushed and I giggled as I watched him push a sheet of popped bubble wrap under the table.

"Do you want to wrap up the cotton ball launcher in bubble wrap?" Nicholas asked.

"Yeah... how about we use that sheet under Timothy's desk?" I suggested.

Nicholas looked to see the sheet I was talking about, then smiled at me.

"Good idea."

He went to grab it and wrap the cotton ball launcher while I cleaned up the rest of our table.

"Okay, okay, enough cleaning, you guys! Get out of here, the bus is going to leave," Mr. Humpheres said, shooing us from the room.

I watched Nicholas grab his backpack and head out into the hall. I followed him closely. He walked out of the school and was about to hurry away but I called him back.

"Nicholas!"

He turned and I caught up with him.

"Hey... I usually walk home with Mikayla but she went already because practice got out early. I don't like walking home alone. It's a long way and there are strangers... I could get kidnapped, you know?"

"Do you want me to walk you home?" he asked.

"Please," I asked nicely.

Nicholas didn't say anything in response, but he did nod, so I headed toward home and when I looked back, he was walking beside me.

We passed the same old buildings I passed every day. I had forgotten what it was like to pass them with him. I had grown used to talking to my friends on the way home. We passed the place my friends and I would split up to go our separate ways. Nicholas was still right beside me.

"Remember when we were late getting home because we stopped to play in that alleyway, and you lost your favorite ball?" I asked quietly. It was more of a question to myself, to my own mind. Nicholas answered anyway.

"Yeah. Your parents were mad."

"Yeah. You took all the blame," I replied.

"I didn't want you getting into trouble."

"Well, I didn't get into any trouble, thanks to you. They still don't know," I said with a laugh.

Nicholas smiled slightly.

"Ah, so the mask does break," I mumbled.

"What mask?" Nicholas asked, the smile crumpling into confusion.

"Never mind. It's not important," I said, waving him away.

We fell silent for a while; the only sounds were the cars driving by and our sneakers on the sidewalk.

"I'm sorry," I said suddenly.

"For what?"

"Embarrassing you. That day, that show I did in the cafeteria. It was dumb, and it must have been humiliating for you. It was wrong of me to put you in that position. I'm sorry," I said.

Nicholas stopped for a moment. I didn't stop to wait for him to recover from his surprise. He caught up with me again in a second.

"Thank you. I appreciate your apology," he said. "And I'm sorry for running out. That must have been embarrassing for you."

"It was just an awful idea all around," I said and tried to force a laugh.

"Yeah," Nicholas said, and we fell quiet again.

Desperate to fill the silence, I said, "I was just desperate for your attention. Kid stuff, you know. I've grown out of it." I cringed as I said it.

"It wasn't that long ago," Nicholas said hesitantly.

"Yeah, you're right," I sighed, "I don't know why I said that."

Nicholas considered this for a moment, then replied.

"But you are right. You have changed. Matured."

"Thank you."

And again, silence. But this time it was more comfortable.

"Do you realize that this is the first time we've been alone together in years? Even when you came over to the backyard, Mikayla and Timothy were only a few feet away," I said after a while.

"That's true," Nicholas said.

We had reached our houses by this point. We stopped in front of mine, as it came first on the block. Part of me wanted to rush inside. Part of me wanted to hug him. I wasn't sure what my next move should be.

But this time I didn't have to make a move. This time Nicholas took charge. He pulled me into his arms and kissed me.

My heart exploded with fireworks and my mind was full of expletives. It had taken me years to get over Nicholas and now, in a ten-second kiss, he had my heart again. I knew it was dumb. I mean, he had rejected me over and over again! But I had wanted him for so long. I had dreamed about this moment for so many years. It might have been a dream, but it was a wonderful one. And I never wanted to wake up.

I sunk into his arms, surrendering to be entirely his.

# Chapter Forty

So, that was what I had been missing. All those years of waiting, watching, worrying, wondering... all of that time lost when I could have had this. When I could have had heaven. Why had I done it?

For this, I answered myself. But would I have gotten Remi without all the manipulation? Would I be in the same place? Would Remi be in my arms now without the book? Or would I have had her, and lost her, long before now?

I had made my choices. I had played by the book's rules. Sometimes they seemed to work. Other times they only seemed to push Remi further and further away. Every day apart from her was pain. Every moment we were separated felt like an eternity. But eternity was over. Remi and I were standing at the edge of the waterfall that was space and time. Reality was at our feet, waiting to obey our commands. There was nothing, no world, no life, nothing other than Remi in my arms. But I couldn't help but wonder if I could have had it sooner.

Regardless. I had her now. She was mine. The time of trial and anguish had ended. Now it was time to enjoy paradise. I was done with the tricks and the games. I would throw out the book, and forget it ever existed. What was once a large part of my life was now all but a distant memory. The journey led me to my final destination. Nothing in life would be greater than this, than her.

I only wanted to hold Remi like that forever.

She pulled away and pressed her forehead into mine. I could smell her conditioner and I loved it. I kissed the top of her head, happier than I had ever been in my life.

"I've wanted you for so long..." Remi mumbled, her voice trembling.

"I'm sorry I kept you waiting," I replied, holding her tighter.

"But... you're going to let go, aren't you?" she asked low and quietly.

"No, no. I never want to let you go," I mumbled into her hair.

I felt her relax into me. It was the best feeling in the world. I wanted to lead a parade, throw balloons in the air, laugh, cry, do something. No, no, I didn't want any of that. I just wanted to hold Remi until the world ended.

I pulled away, mumbling something about needing to get inside before my mom started to wonder where I was. Nicholas nodded and hoisted his backpack back over his shoulder.

"I'll see you tomorrow, then?"

I don't even remember what I said. I couldn't hear anything over the blood rushing to my ears. My mind was a cloud of amazement and joy.

I turned and practically flew up the steps and into my house. When the door was shut behind me, I leaned against it like a princess from a romance novel and sighed deeply. I dropped my backpack without a thought and ran through the front hallway.

"Mom! Mom! Where are you?" I yelled, scurrying around with giddy excitement.

"Remi? Is something wrong? I'm in the kitchen!" my mom called from the kitchen. I followed her voice.

"No, nothing is wrong but guess what!" I squealed.

"What, what happened? Did you have a good day at school? Did something good happen?" my mom asked, looking up from the carrots she was cutting.

"Nicholas kissed me!" I blurted out.

"What? What happened? I thought you two weren't even friends anymore?" my mom exclaimed, thoroughly confused.

"We weren't! I mean, sort of. I didn't think we were but then we started talking again and now apparently he likes me because he kissed me... that means he likes me, right?" I asked, suddenly doubting myself.

"Yes, that means he likes you, Remi," my mom reassured me.

"Oh good," I sighed, relieved.

"So, are you two a couple now?" my mom asked, picking up the knife again and chopping up the carrots.

"I don't know. I don't think so. I mean, he hasn't said anything about it. To be honest, he hasn't even told me he liked me in so many words. But he *kissed* me, Mom," I finished with a contented smile.

"I'm happy for you, honey." My mom smiled with me. "Why don't you help me make the stew for tonight and tell me all about it!"

I washed my hands off before I started chopping potatoes for the stew.

"I really moved on from him in the past couple of weeks," I said, "I was focusing more on my friends, school, cheerleading, and gymnastics. I thought I had moved on completely but now... well, I haven't. And I'm glad I haven't! Because he likes me back!"

"I'm very happy for you. But don't forget your friends. Or school, cheerleading, and gymnastics for that matter! Those things are important, Remi. Boys will come and go but a GPA lasts forever. Or, until college admissions at least."

"I know, Mom," I replied, "I won't. I'll still work hard on school and stuff; you know I will. But now I'll have the best of both worlds! I'll have Nicholas, too! Oh, and I'll get to spend time with him and sit with him at lunch! And did I tell you, he's in the robotics club? So, I'll see him there, too!"

"That's lovely, sweetie."

"What's lovely?" my dad asked, walking into the kitchen.

He stole a carrot from my mom's cutting board and popped it in his mouth. My mom scowled at him and gave him a playful smack on the arm.

"Nicholas kissed me," I said, sharing the blessed news with a gigantic smile.

"Oh, he did, did he?" my dad asked, turning to look at my mom.

"Don't look at me like that, she's your daughter," my mom said, shrugging.

"Aren't you a little young to be kissing boys?" my dad asked, crossing his arms and faking a glare.

"Dad," I groaned, "I'm a senior in high school!"

"I know, it's just hard to see my little girl growing up," my dad said.

"Aw, I'll always be your little girl," I said, putting the knife and potatoes down to give my dad a hug.

"Honestly, it's about time something happened between you two," my dad said as he hugged me. "You could do a lot worse than Nicholas."

"Thanks, Dad," I mumbled.

I spent the rest of my evening feeling over the moon, and that night, I went to bed feeling incredibly joyful. I put on my very favorite pink and yellow pajamas because this was a special occasion. I also got out the secret supply of fruit gummies to eat while watching romantic comedies on my phone late into the night. I only allowed myself to do this when something truly wonderful happened in my life or if something truly terrible happened and I needed cheering up. Tonight was a wonderful night, and I deserved PJs, candies, and romcoms.

I bounced up and down on my bed, thinking over the events of the day. I was so happy about what happened with Nicholas, of course, but I was also thrilled that my parents approved of my relationship or whatever I had with Nicholas.

But what did I have with Nicholas? Until today, I thought there was nothing between us, or even less than nothing. I thought he hated me. He had rejected me time and time again... why did he like me now? What changed? I had even seen him flirting with Bethany. Did he even really like me, or was he leading me on?

No, no, I couldn't think that. I needed to stop overthinking it. He kissed me. He likes me back. I sighed, turning over on my side. I stared at the potted plant I kept by my bed. I didn't know what kind of plant it was. I had gotten it for Christmas with a vague instruction packet that told me to water it every three days. Its name was Jerry. Jerry was a good listener.

"Am I finally going to have a relationship with Nicholas?" I asked Jerry. "I've wanted it for so long. It seems slightly coincidental that right when I move away from him, he makes a move like this. But I suppose, we have gotten the chance to talk more in the last few weeks. Could that have changed something?"

Jerry had no answers. I sighed and stared at the glow-in-the-dark stars I had stuck on my ceiling.

"I can't get my hopes up," I told myself, "He's been so on and off, hot and cold. But I can see where things take us. I can hope just a little bit."

I leaned back over to my nightstand and grabbed my phone. After scrolling a bit to see what my friends were up to, I decided to follow an age-old relationship tradition. I searched up Nicholas's social media accounts to stalk him. A lot of his posts were about the robotics club, or his friends, which was nice.

"Wait, why am I stalking him, Jerry?" I asked.

Jerry had no idea, as he was a plant, so I decided to enlighten him.

"Nicholas kissed me. That means he likes me. That means I can add him on social media," I explained. Jerry seemed impressed at my logic.

I sent Nicholas friend requests on all my social media accounts. Then I put my phone down for a moment to go brush my teeth, leaving Jerry behind to guard it. When I came back, Nicholas had accepted all of my requests.

"Yes!"

I twirled around my room for a moment, feeling like a Disney princess. Thankfully, I stopped before woodland creatures came to clean my house. Mom wouldn't appreciate a squirrel folding the laundry. Mom was picky about the laundry folding.

"Time for bed, Jerry," I said.

I walked over and turned off the lights.

"Oh, I almost forgot!"

I flicked the lights on and off for our goodnight signal. Then I hurried to the window to see if Nicholas had seen. There was no response. Maybe he wasn't home yet, or maybe he wasn't in his bedroom, or maybe he was on his phone and didn't see. Whatever the reason, it didn't affect my mood at all.

I fell asleep with a sense of pure bliss. The peace I felt allowed me to fall asleep early but if I had stayed up just an hour and thirty minutes more, I would have seen Nicholas flash his lights.

# Chapter Forty-One

It took a moment in the morning for me to remember. But when I did, the happiness spread across my body like honey. It was as if I was waking up in a dream. I pinched myself to check. No, it wasn't a dream. I was living my wildest daydreams. The universe had decided to bless me with everything I had ever wanted. Perhaps it had been the long years of hard work and patience that brought Remi to me. Then again, maybe it was one night's wish on a star. Who knew? Who cared? Remi was mine and all was right with the world.

I stood and stretched, getting the day with the vigor it deserved. Dad had already left for work, so I got myself a banana for breakfast. I grabbed my backpack, dropped my backpack, remembered that I forgot to zip the zipper up last night, took a quick stop to put everything back in my backpack, and was out the door in no time!

Remi was just walking up the path from her house. She had her hair in a neat braid, which was good because the day was especially windy. I could tell that she was tired. Could it be that she didn't sleep well?

"Remi!" I called, opening the fence in front of my house and letting myself out onto the sidewalk.

"Good morning!" she said cheerily. "I was waiting for you!"

"Were you?" I asked with a chuckle. "I should have known last night would only encourage you."

Her smile flickered, then collapsed in on itself as she asked quietly, "Does that mean you don't want me to be encouraged?"

I opened my mouth to say yes out of pure instinct. Thankfully, I stopped myself at the last second. I had Remi. I had won. There was no need for games. There was no need to keep her at a distance anymore. She was mine.

It felt real at that moment. The realization hit me like a tidal wave, and I felt unspeakably happy. This was love. This was true happiness. This was the meaning of life and reality. But now was not the time for an existential debate. Now was the time to reply to Remi.

I took her hand. She looked up and met my eyes. I let myself dive completely into the bottomless pool of my emotions. I pulled her close to me and kissed her on the forehead.

"Be encouraged," I said.

Remi smiled and blushed, which caused an entire migration of butterflies to take flight in my stomach.

Then she reached up with her small, soft hands and caressed my cheek. I thought I was going to pass out right on the sidewalk from happiness.

"I'll give you a ride to school, if you want," I mumbled.

"On your bike?"

I nodded, gesturing to where it was chained to the fence.

"If you'd like."

"I would. I'd like that very much," Remi said with a smile.

"All right then," I said.

It physically hurt to step away from her, but I tore myself from her side just long enough to unchain my bike. I climbed on it and balanced my feet, one on the pedal, one on the sidewalk.

"Hop on," I said.

Remi smiled and climbed on the bike behind me. She

wrapped her hands, toned and strong from gymnastics and cheer-leading, around my waist. I could hear her breathing.

"Are you ready?" I asked.

"Yup, let's go!" she replied.

I pushed off the sidewalk with my foot and started pedaling. It was the same route I took every day, but it felt magical that day. The sun was brighter somehow. The sky was bluer, the grass was greener, and Mr. Fillinger was grumpier as he sprayed me with his garden hose. Remi laughed, wiping the spray from her eyes, and it sounded like the tinkling of little bells. I didn't even mind the potholes in the road that morning. Nothing could have made that day anything less than the best day ever. Nothing could have popped my balloon of joy.

Remi's arms tightened around my waist as we went faster down a hill. I slowed down and stopped at a road crossing, and her hands came from my waist to my shoulders. They clung there for the rest of the ride, giving me shivers down my spine from pure bliss. The wind shifted at one point, coming from behind us, and blew a few strands of her hair across my cheeks. I caught the scent of her perfume, strawberries and lime.

The bike was flying. It was. Remi and I were part of the beautiful blue sky. We road my bike between the clouds. Our happiness would never end. My joy would never go away. It was eternal. Life was eternal. I was eternal. Or maybe none of that was true. It didn't matter. Nothing mattered but Remi and now I had her.

I was the luckiest man in the world.

# Chapter Forty-Two

"Mikayla!" I hissed at Mikayla.

Mikayla had, until this point, been innocently talking to a girl named Francesca about a history project they were doing together. Now, she turned to me with alarm.

"Girl, what? You scared me half to death!"

"I have something very important to tell you," I said, in the serious voice my friends and I used only when we had very important and usually time-sensitive gossip to share with the group. It was a code to drop what you were doing and listen. So, Mikayla sighed and turned to end her conversation with Francesca.

"Sorry, girl, Remi needs something apparently. I'll text you later about the project, okay? I don't mind doing the research if you do the display. But I'll text you about it."

"Sounds good," Francesca said with a smile to Mikayla and a curious glance in my direction.

"What is so important that you had to interrupt me, Remi?" Mikayla asked skeptically.

I grabbed her and pulled her to our desks close to the back of the classroom.

"Nicholas kissed me," I blurted out.

Mikayla stared at me blankly for a moment before the news registered in her mind.

"He did what?!" she exclaimed.

"Shh!" I insisted, looking around to see the rest of the class staring at me. I lowered my voice and tried again.

"I know, right? I couldn't believe it myself!"

"When did this happen?!"

"Last night!" I said, Mikayla's surprise only making me more excited.

"What?! And you didn't tell me last night!?"

"It was late, I didn't want to wake you!"

"Wake me?! You didn't want to wake me? Remi, the guy you've been after for literally years kissed you and you didn't want to wake me?! Text me, girl!"

"All right, all right, I will next time," I promised.

"How did this happen?" Mikayla asked, baffled, "I thought he hated you!"

"So did I! Or, at least, I thought he wasn't interested in me. Over the past few weeks, we've been on more civil terms. We even had a few pleasant conversations."

"And why is this the first I'm hearing of this!?"

"I didn't think it meant anything!" I whispered as more kids came into the classroom. "It was mostly small talk! And you were there when he came over, that was the only major conversation we had. The point is it took me entirely off guard!"

"When was this? After I left robotics? It better not have been after I left robotics! I will punch something if I missed the kiss by going to cheerleading!" Mikayla said.

"No, he walked me home. We stopped in front of my house and he kissed me!" I said, feeling the happiness of that night all over again.

"That's awesome! What was it like? Short but passionate? Long and sweet?"

"Short and passionately sweet, I would say," I described.

"Where were his arms?"

"Around my waist."

"Best place, honestly."

"I know," I squealed.

"What did he say?"

"He was like 'I'm sorry I kept you waiting. Now I never want to let you go,'" I related with a deep sigh.

"Well dang, girl!"

"I know, right? And guess what."

"There's more?" Mikayla gasped.

"Yes! This morning I was waiting for him outside, you know, because I wanted to see what he would do," I said hurriedly.

"Of course, naturally." Mikayla nodded.

"Anyway, he was all like do you want a ride to school? So of course, I said yes."

"Wait, wait, can he drive?" Mikayla asked.

"He can, but he doesn't have a car. His dad drives to work early so he rides to school on his bike."

"How do you fit on the bike?"

"It's got a spot in the back for backpacks and stuff, but people can sit on it, too. It's not the most comfortable thing in the world, but it was worth it," I said.

"Okay, I'm with you, go on."

"Anyway, so I climbed on the back of his bike and I wrapped my arms around him, and we rode to school like that," I said, sighing for probably the hundredth time that day.

"So, does he like you now?" Mikayla asked, still confused.

"Yes! Maybe? I'm not entirely sure. I mean... he hasn't exactly said that he likes me. But he hasn't said that he doesn't like me. And he kissed me, so that means something, right?"

"Yeah," Mikayla said hesitantly. "I would talk to him, though. He's been a mysterious mess ever since I've known him. I would get the full truth out of him. Get him to say how he really feels with words, you know?"

"You're right. I need to hear the words before I can date him," I said.

"Wait, you're still going to date him? After everything he did? All the times he rejected you?" Mikayla asked.

"Of course! I still love him. You know that."

"I thought you were getting over him, though."

"I was! But now..."

"I get it," Mikayla sighed, "Now that he likes you back everything is different. Good for you, girl, I'm happy for you."

"Thanks," I said, contented.

"All right, class, let's get started!" our teacher said.

Mikayla and I slid into our seats and searched our backpacks for our books and notebooks.

"When are you going to see him again?" Mikayla asked in a whisper.

"I don't know," I replied, "Maybe in the hallways. Maybe at lunch."

"Are you going to sit with him at lunch?" Mikayla inquired, sounding slightly hurt. "What about the girls' table? We'll miss you."

"Yeah, I know," I said. I hadn't considered where I would sit at lunch until that moment.

"Would it be okay to ask Nicholas to sit with us?" I said finally.

"Wouldn't that be weird for him? If he's the only guy at the table?" Mikayla observed. She had a fair point. "Why don't you ask if Nicholas and his friend want to sit with us?" Mikayla suggested.

"Which friend?" I asked. Then, I realized. "Oh, you mean Timothy!"

Mikayla flushed, saying, "I mean if he wants to sit with us. Only so Nicholas wouldn't be alone."

"Sure, Kayla, sure," I said with a giggle. "Not for any other reason?"

"No, no other reasons."

"Sure," I repeated with a smug smile.

Mikayla opened her notebook and pretended to take some

notes. I shook my head and mentally reminded myself to tease her about her crush later.

"I think I will invite them both," I whispered after a moment of consideration, "Thanks for the idea."

"No problem. And if you see Nicholas before lunch, you have to tell me everything! Just tell me everything in general. I need updates!" Mikayla ordered.

I laughed quietly.

"Of course."

As it would turn out, I didn't see Nicholas in the halls before lunch. I looked for him, or Timothy, or any of the boys in the robotics club. I saw Nathan for a split second as he turned the corner, but I didn't feel like running after him. I would see Nicholas at lunch, and I didn't want to seem too clingy. But still, I looked for him.

# Chapter Forty-Three

I didn't see Remi in the halls before lunch. I looked for her, for Mikayla, or any of the girls on the cheerleading squad. I saw Sierra for a split second as she turned the corner, but I didn't feel like running after her. I would see Remi at lunch, and I didn't want to seem too clingy. But still, I looked for her.

I felt like I was living a dream. School seemed both meaningless and infinitely important. It existed only for me to see Remi in the halls, at lunch, in robotics, or at cheerleading practice. I was fully intending on going to watch her practice when she had a cheerleading practice next.

I was still working on a very special computer program for her. I wasn't ready to tell her about it yet. It wasn't perfect. And it had to be perfect for my perfect Remi. I would give it to her when it was ready, and not a moment before. I had to work on it in study hall on the library computers because mine had been incredibly slow the past couple of weeks.

With these thoughts in mind, I walked aimlessly through the halls, still searching for Remi. I knew I had about two minutes to get to my next class, and I intended to spend one minute and fifty-eight seconds looking for Remi. It would be worth it if I caught just a glimpse of her.

"Get to class!" a hall monitor called to me.

I didn't hold it against him. Obviously, the middle-aged man had never felt true love's call. Otherwise, he too would be strolling the halls in search of his one true love.

"Now, Savage!" the hall monitor called again.

I checked my watch. I had fifteen seconds to get to class. It was time to call this quest for the time being. I would see her at lunch, and I had to be content with that. With a sigh, I walked as fast as I could to my next class.

As I walked into my third period class, my eyes locked on Timothy, who was sitting calmly doodling in a notebook.

"Timothy!" I said, hurrying over and dumping my stuff next to my desk.

Timothy stared at me blankly.

"I kissed Remi," I blurted out.

"Awesome," Timothy said. "With tongue or nah?"

"Not this time," I admitted.

"Next time then."

"For sure."

Timothy gave me a high-five and went back to doodling dinosaurs fighting robots in his notebook.

"Are you guys a couple now?" he asked after a moment.

"Yeah, I think so," I said confidently. Timothy was less certain.

"Has she said so?" he asked.

"Well, no," I reluctantly admitted.

"Have you said so?"

"No."

"Have you asked her to be your girlfriend?"

"Not really..."

"You need to ask her, my dude," Timothy handed down his wise advice.

"Yeah, you're right," I said, realizing this fact. "But how? And when?"

"Don't ask me," Timothy said with a shrug, "But you'd better make it good. After all the stunts she's pulled to get your attention, the bar is high, my friend. It's your turn to pull out all the stops."

"You're right!" I mumbled.

Dozens of lightbulbs were going off in my mind. All those plans and daydreams of things I would do when I had Remi... all of that was possible now! Not just possible. I needed to do it all now. I had Remi. Now I could show her my affection. Now I could do all the wonderful things I had planned for years.

"What are you thinking?" Timothy asked.

I blinked out of my thoughts and turned to him.

"I know that look. The wheels are turning," Timothy said with a sigh, "What did your book say to do now?"

"Oh, no. This isn't the book's problem anymore. It's mine. And I've got a few plans of my own," I said mysteriously.

"Good for you, go write your own book. Call it 'How to Get a Girl to Do Crazy Dance Routines in the Cafeteria for You'. An instant bestseller," Timothy said sarcastically.

"Maybe I will! And I'll bet you would read it, too."

"I would not," Timothy scoffed.

"Not even to get Mikayla to do the same thing...?"

Timothy flushed and I laughed.

"All right, how about this. You help me with Remi, and I'll help you with Mikayla."

"I'm not planning on waiting for years to get Mikayla, thank you very much," Timothy said, doodling teeth on a plesiosaur.

"You won't have to. I won't give you any advice from my book unless you want it. Whatever you want to do, I will help with. I'll just be a friend."

Timothy looked up from his plesiosaur.

"Really?"

"Really," I confirmed with a nod.

"Sounds good, then. I'll help you with Remi and you help me with Mikayla. But no more games."

"No more games," I agreed.

We turned to where our teacher was pulling up the day's PowerPoint presentation and got ready to learn. But neither of our minds was on the lesson. Timothy's mind was with Mikayla and mine was with Remi.

# Chapter Forty-Four

Remi was waiting in the hallway outside the lunchroom for me when Timothy and I were walking to lunch. She greeted me with a huge smile. She started to walk over to us, then stopped, as if wondering what to do.

I approached her and hugged her close to me. She giggled and hugged me back tightly.

"Get a room, you two," Timothy said. Mikayla laughed a little too hard at his joke, then blushed when he met her eyes.

"You two get a room," I teased, which made Timothy blush as red as Mikayla.

"Do you and Timothy want to sit with us at lunch?" Remi asked, putting her hand in mine.

"Sure," I said. "Timothy, sound good with you?"

Timothy nodded. I knew he hadn't heard me, though. His eyes hadn't left Mikayla's face.

We all went in and sat at a table together. It wasn't my regular table, with the guys from robotics, and it wasn't Remi's usual table with the girls from her cheerleading and gymnastics. It was a table all to ourselves at the back of the cafeteria. We got a few strange looks from our friends as we passed, and I knew that I would have some explaining to do later. Tomorrow I would probably go back and sit with the guys, maybe bring Remi with me if she wanted. But just for today, it was fun for it to just be us.

Remi must have shared my thoughts, because she said, "This is cool! Kind of like a double date."

After she said it both she and Mikayla looked over at me. There was something strange in their glances, but I couldn't pick up on it. After we all sat down with our lunches, I decided to bring it up.

"Is there something wrong with a double date?" I asked Remi quietly.

"No, nothing wrong," she replied.

"So why were you and Mikayla staring at me...?"

Remi sighed and I knew I was in trouble.

"It's just... this is like a date, right?"

"I mean..." I said, choosing my words carefully, "We are at school, and this is the cafeteria, so it's not really a date..."

"But if it was a date, it would be a date, right?" Remi asked sharply.

I was confused. Was this a trick question?

"Yes? If it was a date... it would be a date. So, yes?"

"Good!" Remi said, immediately brightening.

I internally shrugged. I guess whatever I had said was the right answer.

"What about you, Timothy?" Mikayla asked.

Timothy stared at her, looking like a deer caught in the headlights, with cookie crumbs around his mouth.

"If this was a date, would it be a date between us?" Mikayla asked hesitantly.

"What are you even saying right now?" Timothy asked.

Mikayla scowled. I shook my head. He was doomed.

"I'm *saying* that if this was a date, it would be a date in real life, right?"

"I don't understand," Timothy said.

"If it was a date, would it be a date!?" Mikayla demanded.

I tried to help by mouthing 'say yes' to Timothy, but he didn't look over at me at all. He stared at Mikayla like a rabbit watching an oncoming car.

"Um... no?" he guessed.

Remi and I were watching this train wreck unfold with curiosity, unable to look away.

"Why not! I thought... you do like me, don't you?" Mikayla asked sadly.

"Yeah, I like you," Timothy said sheepishly.

"So, why wouldn't our fake date be a date?"

"Because it's fake?"

"Our relationship is fake?!"

"What relationship?"

"What relationship?!"

"Kayla, I think..." Remi started, but Mikayla silenced her with a glare.

"Oh, he's dead," Remi whispered to me.

"Yeah, I knew that from the start," I whispered back.

"Now that I'm hearing it, it was a bit of a ridiculous question, sorry about that," Remi said.

"That's all right. I answered right, didn't I?"

Remi giggled. "Yeah, you did."

"I thought you liked me. I like you!" Mikayla exclaimed.

"I like you too, but what does this have to do with fake dates?" Timothy asked.

"If our fake date was real, that would mean you want to go on a date with me!"

"Are you even speaking English?"

We turned to talk to each other while Mikayla and Timothy were arguing.

"Mikayla just wanted me to figure out how you really felt about me," Remi said quietly.

"Oh? Kissing you wasn't enough?" I replied with a grin.

"Well, you have to admit, you're pretty confusing sometimes," Remi said.

"I will admit that. So, what would you like me to say?" I asked.

"I don't know, honestly," Remi said with a shrug.

"I'll tell you what," I mumbled, "Why don't we walk over to the library so we can talk properly?"

"Sounds great," Remi said.

"Timothy, we're going to the library," I said.

He didn't respond. He was too focused on Mikayla, who was still angry at him.

"Kayla? We're going to the library, okay? See you later?"

Mikayla didn't respond. She was too focused on Timothy, who was still clueless.

Remi and I stood and gathered our things quietly, slipping away from the argument and out the door, stopping only to throw our lunch trays away.

"You know, I was jealous of them at one point," I admitted to Remi as we walked through the empty hallway.

"What? Why?" she asked.

"They got along so well... so smoothly. And they both knew they liked each other so quickly. It didn't seem fair to me."

"They're just different people," Remi said with a shrug.

"That's true. I was just upset, I guess. It was always so hard with you."

"Why?" Remi asked.

"Why was I upset?" I clarified.

"No, why was it hard? I've had feelings for you for years, Nicholas. You could have told me you liked me at any time. Or not even that, if you had given me any encouragement at all I would have been yours," Remi said quietly.

"I know."

We walked into the library and smiled at the librarian. It was always good to keep the librarians on our good side. We swore they were part of a secret Illuminati that was brainwashing the students with romance novels. Either that or they were picking the romance books based on their personal choices. Chilling either way.

"Where do you want to sit?" I whispered.

"Somewhere in the back," Remi replied.

"What about that table?" I said, pointing toward a table in the back, near the mystery section.

Remi nodded and walked over to sit down. I took a deep breath and smiled, reminded for the hundredth time today that Remi was mine. It was real.

"Are you coming?" she asked.

I nodded and sat down across from her so I could look into her eyes.

"You are beautiful, you know that?"

Remi blushed and I smiled. She was so adorable when she blushed.

"Really, you are," I said seriously.

"Thank you," Remi replied. "You're not half bad yourself, mister."

"What did you want me to tell you, Remi?" I asked, keeping my voice low.

"Tell me you like me. Like, actually like me."

"I'll do more than that," I said, mentally committing to what I was about to say. I reached across the table and took Remi's hand.

Then, looking into her eyes, I said, "I love you, Remi Lucas."

Remi flushed redder than I have ever seen her, and her eyes were shining as she met mine.

"I love you, too, Nicholas Savage. I've waited so long to hear that from you."

"I'm sorry I kept you waiting. But the waiting is over now. I'm here for you, always. I promise I won't keep you at a distance anymore."

Remi laughed, but it looked like she was about to cry.

"Does that mean you're going to come over after school to watch Pixar movies again?" Remi asked.

"Only after we finish our homework," I replied with a soft smile.

Remi squeezed my hand and laughed.

The bell rang, the sound echoing through the library.

"I guess I'd better get to class," Remi said reluctantly.

"Me too. But I'll see you at robotics today, right?"

"I have cheerleading... but I'll be there tomorrow?"

I was severely disappointed, but I comforted myself with the thought that I would see Remi at robotics tomorrow.

"You can still walk me home if you would like...?"

"I would love that," I replied with a huge smile. "I'll meet you out front after school?"

"Sounds great. I'll see you there," Remi said, grabbing her backpack, standing up, and waving to me as she walked out.

"This is the greatest day of my life," I whispered to myself.

# Chapter Forty-Five

"Ah, Remi! Good to see you at cheerleading practice for once," Coach said as I ran up, still trying to adjust my uniform.

"Sorry for missing a day, Coach," I apologized.

"That's all right, Remi. It's just good to have you back. Take your position! We're running through the whole routine today."

"Remi!" Mikayla beckoned me over. "I was worried you would be late, and Coach would make us all run laps!"

"Glad I could spare you," I said with a laugh.

"Come on, ladies! Two, three, four!"

We grabbed our pompoms and began the routine.

"Whoo! Go Remi!" a voice came from the bleachers.

"Who is that?" I asked Mikayla, as I was unable to turn around during the routine.

"Who?" Mikayla asked, trying to look over her shoulder and stay on the beat at the same time.

"Yeah, go Remi!" the voice came again.

"That! Who is calling my name?"

"Mikayla and Remi, less talking, more moving!" Coach yelled.

Mikayla did her spin and faced the bleachers for a moment.

When she was next to me again, she whispered, "It's Nicholas!"

"What?! But he's in robotics club!" I whispered back, but Mikayla was already on the other side of the formation.

"All right, enough! Stop, stop!" Coach yelled, waving to stop us. "Bethany, your pacing is awful! Ladies, take five."

The team moved toward the bleachers, where our water bottles and backpacks were. I looked up, scanning the seats for Nicholas. There he was! He was here!

I ran up the steps to greet him. He stood, smiling at me with that adorable grin of his.

"What are you doing here?" I asked, reaching over to give him a hug.

He pulled me close to him, saying, "I wanted to come to see your practice. It's been years since I've seen you cheer. You've made a lot of progress."

"I should hope I've made progress since I was thirteen!" I said.

"Has it really been that long?" Nicholas said, holding me tighter.

"All right, you can let go now," I said, laughing. "I've got to get back down there."

Nicholas let me go, took my hand, and kissed it.

"You may go now," he said quite regally.

I blushed and tried to cover my flattery with an eye roll.

"Thanks for coming, Nicholas. Really."

"Anytime, princess."

Oh dear, oh no, there is no way I could focus on my cheerleading routine now.

"Is that my nickname now?" I asked sheepishly.

"Only if you like it."

"Remi!" Mikayla yelled from the field.

"I'll see you after practice?" I asked.

"Of course! I still have to walk you home," Nicholas said with a wink.

I scurried down the stairs like a frightened bluebird.

"What was that all about?" Sierra asked.

"Nothing," I said, brushing a wisp of hair behind my ear.

"Didn't look like nothing," Bethany said, walking over to me.

"Ooh, Remi, can I tell them?" Mikayla whispered, not quietly enough, as it would seem, as the rest of the team caught on quickly.

"Tell us what?" Sierra asked.

"Remi? Can I?" Mikayla pleaded with me.

"Sure," I relented with a sigh. "Why not?"

"Nicholas kissed Remi!" Mikayla said with a delighted squeal.

The team went wild.

"No way!?"

"I thought he hated her?"

"Are you two officially dating now?"

"Did he ask you out?"

I smiled, soaking up the attention, even if I didn't have all the answers. I thought back on all the support my teammates had given me over the years. They had been so supportive of me and Nicholas. This was a win for them, seeing me happy.

"Girls? Excuse me, am I interrupting your drama session?" Coach said.

"Sorry, Coach," I apologized.

"I mean, you did give us a five-minute break," Sierra mumbled.

"What was that?" Coach snapped in Sierra's direction.

"Nothing, Coach!" Sierra backtracked quickly.

"Nothing, indeed. That's it, all of you can share your drama while you're running laps around the track."

The team groaned and moaned but lined up to run laps around the field.

"Sorry, guys," I apologized to the team.

"It's okay, Remi. It'll give us a chance to hear all the details," Sierra said with a grin.

"You can talk while running?" I panted, gasping for air.

"Don't worry, I can. I'll fill everyone in," Mikayla said with a smile, hitting her stride.

The other girls matched her pace and Mikayla told them all the details. All the ones she knew, at least. I jogged along, smiling as the girls shot interested glances in my direction from time to time. I didn't participate, though. I kept my eyes on Nicholas, smiling at me from the stands.

"Remi!" Bethany waved me over.

I jogged behind a couple of girls before I was next to her.

"What's up?" I asked.

"I was wondering, what are you going to do for your next stunt?" she asked.

"What do you mean?" I wondered between gasping breaths.

Bethany ran a little faster than I was used to. Bethany noticed me struggling and slowed her pace.

"Ever since the cafeteria, we've all been wondering what you're going to do next!"

"I don't know if I will do anything," I admitted, "Now that Nicholas and I are... well, we're practically together. I don't think I need to do anything else to get his attention."

"Are you kidding? You need to do it now more than ever! You've got to keep guys feeling wanted, you know?" Bethany said.

"I have to say, Bethany is right," Sierra chimed in.

"Right about what?" Mikayla asked.

"Bethany thinks Remi should do another crazy stunt to show Nicholas how much she cares about him," Sierra filled Mikayla in.

"Oh, awesome! What are you planning, Remi?"

"Um... I don't know. I don't want to do anything like the cafeteria again," I said.

"But you have to do something big and public, right?" Sierra said.

"Yeah, you have to, Remi!" Mikayla said.

"Do I?" I asked hesitantly.

"Come on! It's our senior year! Why wouldn't you?" Bethany asked.

"I don't know, I don't want to embarrass him again. But... I see your point. I'd like to do something else, just to show him that I care," I said.

"Can we help?" Mikayla asked.

"I'm not sure. I don't even know what I should do... wait! I've got an idea!" I exclaimed, a lightbulb going off in my brain.

"What, what?" the girls asked.

"Sierra, you volunteer in the office during study hall, don't you?" I asked.

Sierra nodded.

"Yeah. Mrs. Vella usually has me organizing files and typing up field trip permission slips. But the volunteer hours look good on college applications, so I don't complain. Why?"

"Come closer and I'll tell you."

So, the cheerleading team and I planned my next big performance. I just hoped Nicholas would like it.

# Chapter Forty-Six

I was honestly excited to walk Remi home that evening. It gave us a chance to be alone together and to talk. It was just like it used to be, talking about our day, our friends. Just sharing life together.

"How was your day?" I asked.

"It was good," Remi replied with a smile. "Are we biking home?"

I had forgotten that I was holding onto my bike.

"I thought I would walk it home," I said, "It would give us a chance to talk a little."

"Okay. Did you have something you wanted to talk about?" Remi asked as we walked away from the school.

"Nothing particular. No, I take that back. I have years to catch up on. What has been happening in your life since we last talked?"

"Since I was thirteen? That's been a while, Nicholas," Remi said.

"I know. And I can't apologize enough about keeping you waiting."

"Why did you?" Remi asked. "If you don't mind me asking."

"Not at all. You deserve to know," I admitted.

Then I hesitated. I had already decided not to tell Remi about the book. It would only cause problems. But what was my excuse?

"I guess I didn't know how I felt. I was trying to figure it out. And talking to you these last few weeks... what you did at the car wash... it helped me figure it out," I said.

"Did I completely embarrass you in the cafeteria?" Remi asked, cringing.

"No," I laughed, "Not at all. I actually liked the attention. But it *was* a little overwhelming."

"Yeah, I can imagine," Remi said with a tiny laugh. It made me smile. I loved hearing her laugh.

"I might do something else like that in the future," she said suddenly.

"Oh?" I asked. "Another lunchtime performance, just for me?"

"No, not that again. But something else, just to show you I care about you."

"I look forward to it," I said, putting my arm around Remi.

She took my hand and pulled my arm tighter around her, which gave me chills.

"I was thinking..." I started but paused to make sure she was paying attention.

"Yeah?" Remi asked.

"Where would you like to go for our first date?"

Remi's nose scrunched up as if she was trying to hide her smile.

"I don't know... are you planning on asking me out?" she asked coyly.

"You know I am. But you've got to give me some ideas. Would you like to see a movie? Or go get dinner somewhere? Would you want a more formal dinner, or perhaps a picnic somewhere? Are you up for a hike? Would you prefer indoors or outdoors?"

Remi looked surprised. "You've certainly put a lot of thought into this," she said.

I laughed to myself. I'd been planning our first date for years but, of course, I couldn't tell her that.

"You have no idea," I replied.

Remi thought in silence for a moment as we walked.

"Outdoors, I think," she said at last. "But maybe not a hike. Nothing formal, that's all I'm saying. I don't much like fancy restaurants and stuff."

"Neither do I," I replied, honestly grateful that she held my same opinion. "Outdoors it is then. Are you doing anything tomorrow night?"

"Tomorrow is what, Thursday?"

"Friday, actually, today is Thursday," I answered.

"Oh, I'm actually busy that night," Remi said.

"Oh. What are you doing?"

"Something with you!" Remi exclaimed, reaching down and grabbing my hand tightly in hers. She swung our hands, smiling at me.

"You're such a tease," I said, not realizing my voice had gotten lower.

Remi flushed a bright red and held my hand closer to her.

"So, are you going to tell me what we're doing?" she asked.

"You'll have to wait and see," I said mysteriously.

We stopped at Remi's house. She turned to leave, then stopped.

"Do you want to come in? I have a lot of homework, but we could do it together. Like we used to?"

"I would love to."

Remi grabbed my hand again and we walked up to her house together.

"Remi, is that you?" her mom's voice came from upstairs as we went in.

"Yeah! And Nicholas is here, too!" Remi replied.

"Nicholas! Is he? Is something wrong? Did he lose his key?"

"No, he's just going to hang out and do homework. Is that okay?" Remi called up to her mom.

# CHAPTER FORTY-SIX

"Of course, that's okay! Nicholas is a good boy; he is welcome anytime!"

"Thank you, Mrs. Lucas!" I yelled up the stairs.

"No problem at all, Nicholas. I'll be down in a few minutes to make cookies for you two hard-working students, all right?"

"Thanks, Mom!" Remi yelled, then motioned me over to the kitchen table.

"We can work here if you want," she said.

I pulled up a chair and sat down.

"I have to say, I have missed your mom's cookies," I said with a wink.

"She's missed having you around, I know," Remi replied. "We all have."

I reached across the table to give Remi's hand a squeeze.

"I've missed being here."

"You're here now, anyway," Remi said, brightening. "And maybe once we're done with homework and stuff we can go outside and talk for a while?"

"Or watch a Pixar movie?"

Remi laughed.

"Or that."

"Sounds good."

We got to work on our assignments for the day. At least, Remi got to work. I tried to focus on the math problems in front of me, but I just couldn't. I was so unbelievably happy that I was back at Remi's table, in Remi's house, with Remi. It was starting to feel real, but I still couldn't believe I was so lucky. I thought about all the plans I had to show Remi how much I cared about her. Our first date would be the start of them. But those daydreams aside, it was nice to know I could just be with Remi. It didn't always have to be special or a big exciting show when we were together. We could show love by just being together.

Remi chewed on the strings on her hoodie absentmindedly. I watched her eyes scan across the page. Her eyebrows crinkled as she was confused. Then her eyes brightened as she realized the answer and she did a tiny happy dance as she wrote it down.

Remi made me happy. It was a realization so sudden that I had to stop and think about it for a second. It was true. She made me happy. I was happy when I was with her. I was happy when she smiled or laughed. I wanted to keep her beautiful smile on her face always.

"I love you," I said randomly.

Remi looked up, blinking the math out of her eyes.

"I love you, too," she said, smiling at me.

Then she looked down and got back to work, leaving me entirely, completely, and utterly happy.

# Chapter Forty-Seven

Today was the day! I had gotten the go-ahead from my cheerleading teammates. That and a subtle go-ahead from Nicholas. I had hinted about my next big display of affection when he was walking me home, and he hadn't seemed opposed to the idea. So, I took that as a yes and went right ahead with my planning. The girls all agreed to help. They were always down for any sort of drama or attention.

It was second period. Just after the bell, when everyone was still scrambling to get to their classes on time. The hallways were just clearing out. It was our time to strike.

"What class is he in?" Mikayla asked, slinking behind me in the hallways.

"It doesn't matter, now shush!" Bethany hissed.

We strolled up to the office door and knocked twice on it. Sierra answered.

"Come in, hurry!" she said, "Mrs. Vella just stepped out to get a snack. If my calculations are correct, and they are, you have about a ten-minute window. Just enough time for Mrs. Vella to walk down to the vending machines in front of the cafeteria, spend two minutes standing and staring at the machine, decide on the same drink she gets every time, get her Dr. Pepper, and walk back up to the office. All that to say, hurry up already!"

We scrambled into the office. Bethany was having second thoughts.

"Can we get in trouble for this?" she asked.

"Shut up, Bethany! Aren't you willing to risk getting into trouble for love?" Sierra hushed her.

"I don't know, how much trouble are we talking about here?" Bethany snapped back.

"Would you quiet down, Bethany?" I asked as I walked behind the desk.

"Yeah, calm down, Bethany," Mikayla whispered, "The worst that could happen is that we all get detention."

"Detention!?"

"Shh!"

I fiddled around with the buttons on the desk until I finally found what I was looking for.

"Guys, here!" I said, "This is the button that turns on the loudspeakers for the whole school. And here is the microphone!"

I picked up the microphone and positioned my finger at the button.

"Is everyone ready?" I asked.

"I'll keep watch!" Mikayla said.

"I'll videotape it!" Sierra said.

"I'll stand awkwardly back here and hope to not get detention," Bethany said with a deep sigh.

"Okay, here we go! Sierra, give me a countdown!" I ordered.

"This is Love-Nicholas FM. We're live in three, two, one!"

The girls fell silent as I took center stage.

"Attention students! Before you begin your third-period class, I have a brief announcement. I would just like to announce that Remi Lucas thinks Nicholas Savage is her dream man and that she hopes he'll let her love him forever. That is all. Thank you and have a studious day."

I pulled my finger off the button, and we all exploded in a fit of giggles.

"That was awesome! Instant viral video. Thanks, Remi!" Sierra said, already uploading the video for all the internet to see.

"You guys, someone is coming! Oh, it's the principal! And he doesn't look happy!" Mikayla said urgently.

We all froze. We were caught. Surprisingly, it was Bethany who stepped up to save us.

"I know another way out, come on!" she said, grabbing the girl nearest to her, who happened to be me and pulling me toward the back of the office.

We all followed her blindly to the back of the office.

"Where are we going? Into the janitor's closet?" Mikayla demanded.

"It's not the janitor's closet. It's the door to the basement. Come on!"

Bethany pulled the three of us through the door and closed it just in time. The principal of our school burst into the room and angrily stormed around.

We listened through the door, barely daring to breathe, as the principal searched the room for signs of the student who had pirated the sound system. Soon, he came close to the basement door. We heard the doorknob start to turn.

"Come on!" Bethany hissed, pulling us down the stairs into the darkness of the basement.

Normally, we would have had second thoughts about descending unknown stairs into a pitch-black basement that was probably full of rats and spiders, but not today. Today we were all high on adrenaline and the angry huffs of the principal coming toward the door were enough to make us all dive into the abyss.

The principal did open the door. We clung to each other in the darkness and prayed that the light wouldn't reach as far as us. Thankfully, the darkness swallowed the tiny light coming from the doorway like a spider swallows a nat. The principal shut the door again and left us in the darkness.

"Are you guys there?" Bethany was the first one to speak.

"Yeah. Man, I thought for sure he was going to catch us. I had my eyes closed the whole time!" Sierra admitted. "I even forgot to film!"

"Me too," I said breathlessly, "About the eyes-closed thing, not the filming."

"Same," Mikayla chimed in. "I was too scared to open them. Not like I could have seen anything anyway."

"That's good," Bethany said, "Having our eyes closed is good. That's probably why he didn't see us. The light couldn't reflect off our eyes."

"How do you know all this?" I asked.

"Yeah, how did you know about this place? I've worked in the office for weeks and I had no idea this place was here," Sierra said.

"My dad helped design the building. I did a project on the history and architecture of the building a couple of years ago. I brought the real blueprints and everything. To be honest, I didn't know if this place was still here, or if they had boarded it up years ago. I guess it's still here!" Bethany finished with a deep breath.

"I guess so," Mikayla said. "Thanks for saving us, anyway."

"Yeah, thanks Bethany," Sierra repeated.

"Does anyone have a flashlight?" I asked then, growing uncomfortable in the dark.

"I have my phone; it has a flashlight on it."

"Same here," Mikayla said, "And I carry a flashlight keychain with me. I also have another small flashlight. It's on my back-pack... which I left in study hall."

"Then why would you bring it up?" Bethany snapped.

"Don't snap at me. I'm stressed, okay? I still have the keychain one."

"Guys, chill out. Here," I said, turning on my flashlight. "We're all okay, right?"

"Yeah."

"Okay, good. Bethany, did you happen to see any other exits

from the basement?" I asked. "We can't go up that way because we don't know if the principal is still there."

"Yeah, and even if he isn't, you can bet Mrs. Vella is," Sierra sighed.

"I did, actually," Bethany remembered. "There was one that opens into the library. I think I can remember the way."

"You *think*?" Mikayla asked.

"Don't be snarky. It's our only option right now," I said, "Lead on, Bethany."

So, Bethany led us deeper into the darkness.

# Chapter Forty-Eight

We had been stuck in the basement for hours. Now, we had all but given up.

"I thought you knew the way out," Mikayla moaned for the millionth time, "Or at least the way back to the Principal's door. I would have taken detention, or even expulsion, over sitting here in the damp dark."

"Can you shut up? I said I was sorry already! But it's dark down here, and I'm sorry that I didn't memorize the blueprints so completely that I could walk them blind!" Bethany defended herself.

"My battery is almost dead," Sierra said quietly.

"The phones are of no use anyway. We don't have service down here," I said, trying to comfort her.

"But they are our only form of light. Once they go out, what are we going to do?" Sierra asked.

"Die in the dark, obviously," Mikayla mumbled.

"Kayla, now is not the time," I scolded her.

She fell silent, reluctantly, as Sierra's phone died.

"My turn, I guess," I said and opened my phone.

I turned the brightness up just enough to see the other girl's faces, then turned off everything else that would use up power. We huddled around it like a campfire.

"Is anyone scared of the dark?" I asked quietly.

Everyone shook their heads.

"I'm not scared of the dark, but I am scared of dying lost in a dark basement," Mikayla said.

Bethany whimpered, beginning to cry.

"Mikayla, you seriously need to stop," I snapped.

"No, you need to stop kidding yourself. Remi, this is the last place anyone is going to look for us. And even if they did, it's huge! We've spent hours wandering around down here. Hours!" Mikayla argued.

"Yes, and that's hours our teachers haven't seen or heard from us! They'll be looking for us!" I replied.

"And where will they look, Remi? Bethany said so herself, this place hasn't been used in years. She wasn't even sure it existed anymore! The last place anyone will have seen us would be class. They wouldn't even know for sure that we were in the office! And even if someone recognized your voice, and even if they thought to search the office, and even if they found the door, and *even if* they sent someone down here, there's no guarantee that anyone will find us!"

"Mikayla's right," Bethany cried, bursting into tears, "The blueprints showed the basement is under the whole school. The whole school! They can't search every inch of it!"

"Bethany, it's okay," Sierra said, pulling Bethany closer to her. "Someone will find us, I'm sure."

"Should we keep walking?" I asked. "Maybe we will stumble across the principal's office door again."

"We tried that, remember? We even tried marking where we'd been with the chalk in Mikayla's backpack. But we kept going in circles," Bethany wailed. "There are walls everywhere, like a giant library! It's impossible to find the edge!"

"Shh, Bethany, try to calm down. Take some deep breaths," Sierra said to Bethany.

Then, turning to me, she said, "My dad said that if I was lost anywhere, I should just stay in one place. That would make it easier for people to find me. If I moved around, I could just get more lost."

"I'm siding with Remi," Mikayla said, "We need to move while we still have light. My phone and Sierra's are already dead. We only have Remi's and Bethany's left, and then we'll only have my little keychain light. Remi, what's your battery percentage?"

"Forty-one percent," I said gravely.

"Bethany, what about your phone?"

"Twenty-two," Bethany said, fresh tears rolling down her face.

"And I have no idea how much battery is left on this keychain. Remi, we need to move while we can still see our hands in front of our faces," Mikayla said.

"No, we need to stay here! If we wait here, someone will find us eventually," Sierra argued.

"Or they might not! Not before the phones die," Bethany interjected.

"Why is light so important? We can sit in the dark and wait for someone!" Sierra insisted.

"I'd rather get out of here myself," Mikayla snapped.

"Stop it, all of you! Let me think a minute!" I yelled. That gave me an idea.

"Hey. This might sound dumb but... what if we just yelled for help?" I asked.

We all stared at each other. In the panic of the past couple of hours and our desperate attempts to get out ourselves, we had forgotten.

"Should we yell all together, or one at a time to save our voices?" Sierra asked.

"One at a time," I said after thinking, "Then when your voice is too tired to yell anymore, I'll take over."

And so, Sierra started yelling. We all covered our ears and huddled closer together. Sierra yelled and screamed until all of us were nearly deaf. Finally, after what felt like hours, she tapped my shoulder, panting for air.

"Take over for me?" she gasped, her voice cracking like an antique plate on concrete.

I nodded, standing up. Everyone pulled their ears again, and I started yelling. It was kind of therapeutic, letting out all my anger, stress, and fear with my voice. But after a while, my lungs began to ache. I began to hate the sound of my own voice. Then it started to hurt. Every sound, every syllable, the nonsensical panic that came from my mouth rubbed my throat on the way out and grated as it echoed into my ears.

*Please, please.*

I kept thinking over and over.

*Someone find us. Please.*

# Chapter Forty-Nine

I had just sat down beside Timothy in class when I heard the announcement.

"Attention students!"

That was Remi's voice! I recognized it right away.

"Before you begin your third-period class, I have a brief announcement."

As the message went on, I blushed redder and redder. Remi had hinted that she would be doing another big stunt to show me how much she cared about me. But I had no idea it would be something this huge! It wasn't that I didn't like it, I absolutely did. It was such a sweet gesture and must have been rather difficult to accomplish. First, she would have to get permission to use the office speaker and... wait, would she? Knowing Remi, she wouldn't wait to ask permission. She'd probably just get a group of her friends together and break into the office.

"I would just like to announce that Remi Lucas thinks Nicholas Savage is her dream man and that she hopes he'll let her love him forever."

A gigantic smile spread across my face.

*I will love her forever.*

I thought to myself.

*Remi is my dream woman and there's no way I'm letting her go anywhere. I love her so much.*

"That is all. Thank you and have a studious day."

As the message ended, all my classmates turned to stare at me. I blushed even harder, smiling like an idiot.

"Dude," Timothy whispered from his chair.

I turned to smile at him. We fist-bumped as our teacher tried to begin the class. But we weren't listening.

"What was that all about?" Timothy said with a stifled chuckle.

"No idea," I replied, "I mean, Remi was talking about doing another stunt to show me she cared about me. But I wasn't expecting anything like this!"

"You're a lucky man, Nicholas," Timothy said with a shake of his head.

"I know," I replied, and on went the class.

After class, I hurried through the hallways, looking for Remi. I went to all her usual places, her locker, the hall in front of her class, and her friend's lockers. I even popped into the library for a second to see if she was there. Nothing.

I shrugged it off, guessing that I must have just missed her. I tried to go about my day without her, but her absence worried me.

Then came lunch. Timothy and I got our trays and sat down at our table to wait for the girls. Only they never came. I waited thirty minutes. Thirty minutes past the start of lunch. Thirty minutes past their usual time.

"They're usually here by this time. Where do you think they are?" I asked Timothy for the millionth time.

"No clue," he replied. "But you're right, they should have been here by now.

"Should I ask her friends?"

"No need. Look," Timothy said, nodding to where one of Remi's friends, Florence, was walking over.

"Hey, Nicholas, right?" Florence asked.

"Yeah," I replied, "You're one of Remi's friends, right?"

"Yes, I'm Florence," She introduced herself, not knowing that I already knew her name. "I'm on Remi's gymnastics team."

"Have you seen her today?" I asked.

"And Mikayla too, Florence, have you seen Mikayla?" Timothy added.

"No, that's just it. We were waiting for them in the hall, but they never showed up."

"What, go back. Who is 'they'?" I asked.

"And what were you waiting for them for, don't you have a class together?" Timothy inquired.

Florence looked lost so I motioned for her to sit down.

"You'd better start from the beginning," I said, and she nodded.

"Remi, Mikayla, Bethany, and Sierra were going to break into the office so that Remi could make the announcement," Florence started, and Timothy and I were already bewildered.

"Break in!?" Timothy exclaimed.

"Well, not technically. Sierra volunteers in the office so she'd just... let everyone in. Then Remi would make the announcement and they'd get out before anyone saw. The plan was to meet in the hall and all go hang out in the library. Then we could tell anyone who asked that Remi, Mikayla, Sierra, and Bethany were with us the whole time," Florence explained.

I nodded, understanding now.

"Go on," Timothy ordered.

"What happened?" I asked.

"That's just it, nothing happened. They did the announcement all right. You heard it, right? After all this, you'd better have heard it!"

I nodded, "It was very sweet. But we can talk about that later. Right now, I'm worried about Remi."

"And Mikayla," Timothy interjected.

"And the other girls," I added quickly. "Keep going. They did the announcement, but didn't meet you in the hall?"

"That's right. We all waited for them, the girls and I," Florence said, gesturing over her shoulder to a lunch table full of gossiping girls. "But they never showed up. We're starting to get worried about them," Florence finished.

"They don't look too worried to me," Timothy muttered. I elbowed him in the ribs.

"Have you asked a teacher?" I asked.

Florence nodded.

"Yes, all of Remi's usual teachers. No one has seen her since the announcement. It's like she... disappeared."

"No, she couldn't have just disappeared. Have you tried the other girls' teachers?"

Florence nodded silently.

"They didn't notice anything?"

Florence shook her head, looking defeated.

"You've certainly talked to a lot of teachers," Timothy said skeptically.

"They were all in the teacher's lounge," Florence explained, sounding rather offended at being questioned.

"Is there a chance she and the others were caught and put in detention?" I asked, trying to redirect back to the topic at hand.

"Why would detention keep them from their classes? Besides, any detentions I've heard of are after school," she said.

"Could they have been expelled?" I asked.

"For tampering with the speaker system? Sounds like a pretty hard punishment to me," Florence said hesitantly.

"We can't overrule any possibilities just yet. Come on, Timothy. We need to go talk to the principal," I said, standing.

"But I haven't finished my chocolate pudding yet," Timothy whined.

I ignored him and turned to reassure Florence.

"Don't worry. We'll get to the bottom of this. I have a study hall after this anyway."

Florence nodded and walked over to the table with her friends.

I hauled Timothy to his feet and marched him out of the cafeteria

"Come on, Watson. The game is afoot!"

# Chapter Fifty

"How long has it been?" Mikayla whispered, her voice raspy and weak from screaming.

I checked my phone again.

"Three hours," I replied, my voice also spent.

"Battery percentage?"

"Twelve."

There was a collective sigh. Sierra was laying on her back on the ground, her head on Mikayla's stomach. I was sitting on a crate we had found lying around. Bethany was standing behind me, braiding my hair for no apparent reason.

"You would think someone would have heard us by now," Bethany mumbled.

"I guess they're all too far away... or there's a lot more concrete between the school and the basement than I realized," I said quietly.

"So, what's our plan?" Sierra asked.

"I don't know," I replied. "Sit still and hope someone finds us?"

"How long can we wait?" Bethany asked.

"Realistically? Two, maybe three days at least. We all have our water bottles and some snacks, so we could probably wait a week or more for help to find us," Mikayla said.

"I don't want to be stuck here for a week," Bethany said with a sigh.

"None of us do," I said, "But don't worry. I'm sure someone will find us. They must have called our parents by now. They will be worried when they can't get in touch with us."

"Yeah," Mikayla said.

The rest of the girls said nothing, and we fell back into gloomy silence.

"Remi?" Bethany said.

"Yeah?"

"What is your battery at?"

I checked.

"Eleven percent," I admitted.

"Maybe you should just turn it off. I don't mind sitting in the dark if you guys don't. We might need the light later," Bethany whispered.

"Are you sure? It's so pitch black in here, without the light, I can't see my hand in front of my face," I replied.

"I'm sure. If you all are."

The others were silent for a long moment. No one wanted to sit in the suffocating darkness. The reality of our situation was starting to sink in, and with it fear and hopelessness. The darkness would fan the flames of panic and despair. But then again, who knew when we would need the light again? Or maybe we could find a place with cell service. We didn't know. And we needed to preserve our options. So, one by one, the other girls agreed.

"I'm all right with it. It's just darkness, right? It can't hurt anyone," Sierra said. Her voice started loud as she was trying to sound brave, but at the end of the sentence, her voice broke and faded away into a long sigh.

"Yeah, Remi. Go ahead and shut it off," Mikayla said.

"Okay," I said, reaching to turn off the phone.

"Wait, wait. We should all hold hands," Mikayla said, reaching out her hands for Bethany and me. "So, we don't lose each other."

I took Bethany's hand, and she sat down next to Mikayla. Sierra curled up closer to Mikayla and Mikayla put her free arm around her.

"Go ahead, Remi," Bethany said gravely.

And I shut off the light.

"I understand you two boys are concerned, but I really don't see how this is any of your business," the principal said, crossing his arms across his chest.

I took a deep, slow breath. We had been going back and forth with Principal Mitchel for fifteen minutes and were no closer to figuring out what happened to Remi and her friends.

"Have you even called their parents?" Timothy asked.

"There is no evidence the girls aren't in the school," the principal started.

"So, the answer is no," Timothy snapped.

"Four girls are missing, sir. Their friends haven't seen them, their teachers haven't seen them. I think-"

"I didn't ask what you think now, did I?" the principal snapped. "Students skip classes all the time. If I shut the whole school down every time they decided to skip out and go to the movies or something, nothing would ever get done!"

"I'm telling you, sir," Timothy said, a distinct sharpness in his voice, "That they didn't skip class. They aren't out at the movies, shopping, or anything else. They were last seen in this school. Now, they are gone. And we intend to find out what happened to them. By whatever means necessary."

"Are you threatening me, young man?" Principal Mitchel asked, a confidence in his voice. He was taunting Timothy, daring him to do something so that Principal Mitchel could dictate a punishment.

Timothy turned red and began to say something, but I stepped in the way.

"Come on, Timothy," I said, pulling Timothy away from Principal Mitchel's desk. "Let's go check the library. Maybe we missed them the first time around."

"Yes. Do that," Principal Mitchel said.

I could practically see the smoke coming out of Timothy's ears as I pulled him from the office.

"Oh, that man gets on my last nerve," Timothy said through gritted teeth. "We're trying to warn him that they've gone missing, and he won't listen! Did you see him? He was practically laughing at us!"

"I know, I know. Come on, we'll regroup in the library," I said.

"They have to be in the school somewhere, right, Nicholas? They wouldn't have skipped classes, surely?" Timothy asked as we hurried down the hallway.

"Without telling us, or their friends? Of course not! Especially after Remi's stunt with the speaker. She'd want to see me. She'd want to talk to me about it. I know it. Something must have gone wrong."

"How could something go wrong? They just sneaked into the Principal's office. Did they leave the school? Were they kidnapped?" Timothy asked, growing more and more panicked.

"Keep your voice down," I hissed as we walked into the library.

We smiled at the librarian and slunk to the back to sit at a table.

"Let's review the facts. Remi, Mikayla, Sierra, and Bethany snuck into the Principal's office, made the announcement, then... what? Florence said they didn't meet them in the hallway after- ward. So sometime between the office and the hallway, they... vanished," I said. I reached into my backpack, pulled out a note- book, and started writing all of it down.

"Florence said they were waiting in the front hallway. So, they must have seen them come out of the office, right? But they didn't see them at all. So, the principal must have kidnapped them!" Timothy exclaimed.

"Shh!" I hushed him quickly. "The principal couldn't have been in there, remember? Or he would have stopped them from using the intercoms."

"So, they got lost in the principal's office? That doesn't make any sense."

"None of this makes sense," I mumbled.

"What if something happened in the office and..."

I tried to zone Timothy out. He thought best when he said his thoughts out loud. I thought best when writing my thoughts down. I tried to ignore him while I mapped out what happened. But the more I wrote, the more confused I was. There was no way out of the office. They couldn't have just disappeared.

It frustrated me so much my head started to hurt. I was so worried for Remi; I could almost hear her voice. Wait... that was her voice!?

"Timothy shut up!" I snapped.

"Hey, I wasn't even being that loud, I-" Timothy started.

I reached across the table and covered his mouth.

"Shh, shh! Seriously, Timothy, shut your mouth for two seconds. There! Listen! Do you hear that?" I asked.

Timothy pulled away from my hand but didn't say anything. He listened intently.

"What am I listening to?" he asked.

Then the voice came again. It was faint and sounded far away, but it was definitely there.

"What is that?" I asked.

Timothy shrugged.

"Whatever it is, it sounds like it's coming from the other side of this door," he said, standing up.

"But that's just an old janitor's closet," I said.

Timothy tried the door, but it was locked.

"Locked, too. Ooh, maybe they're trapped in the closet?" Timothy suggested.

"The voice sounded too far away for that... there! There it is again, Timothy! Do you hear that?" I insisted, pressing my ear up against the door.

"Yes, you're right! We need to open this door."

"Right."

I looked around for a key. Then I mentally slapped myself in the face. Of course, there was no key anywhere around. So, what were my options? I could ask the librarian and risk her thinking I was crazy. Or, I could go to the principal, who already thought I was crazy. Or...

"The janitor! Old Sam!" I exclaimed.

"Shh, the librarian of death will hear you." This time it was Timothy's turn to shush me.

"All right, all right, I'll be quiet," I said. "But we need to go. The janitor, Old Sam, will have the keys to every door in the building. He has to! He has to be able to get into every room. We'll ask him!"

"Will he give them to us?" Timothy asked, skeptically.

"It's worth a shot, isn't it?"

With that logic, we left the quiet refuge of the library to find Old Sam.

# Chapter Fifty-One

"Y ou want me to give you the keys so you can do *what*?" Old Sam asked.

"We need you to open a door. We think some of our friends got lost behind it," Timothy said.

"A door. To rescue your friends," the janitor said skeptically. "That's a new one. What, do you want to use an empty classroom to vape or what?"

"No, sir! I've never vaped in my life!" Timothy exclaimed, offended by the mere idea of it.

"Sure, kid, sure. I have to say, as excuses go, that's one of the most creative ones I've heard. And that's a serious compliment, kid! I've worked here for twenty years."

The old man chuckled to himself and started to walk away.

"So, can you give us the keys please?" Timothy asked.

"No way, kid. Don't you have a class to get to?" Old Sam said.

I decided to take control of the situation.

"We think some girls are trapped behind the door in the library," I explained as quickly and rationally as possible.

Old Sam froze, his hand on the doorknob of the science classroom he had been cleaning.

"What door in the library?" he said slowly, his voice chilling me to my core.

"The... the one at the back. The very back. By the wall," I explained.

"Why do you think students are behind it?" he said. It wasn't phrased as a question, more of a demand. I answered regardless.

"They went missing in the principal's office, then we heard their voices in the library behind the door."

"The principal's office?" the janitor snapped, turning around quickly to face us. "You're sure that's where they last were?"

I felt Timothy jump behind me at the edge in the old man's voice.

"Yes, sir," I replied for the both of us.

"Come on," Old Sam said, grabbing the keys and hurrying out of the room.

Timothy and I exchanged glances and followed Old Sam down the hall. For an old man, he moved surprisingly quickly.

The three of us burst into the library, receiving a harsh glance from the librarian. Old Sam ignored it and stormed to the back of the library.

He unlocked the door as quickly as he could, but when he pulled on the handle, it didn't open. He tried again, with no result.

"Try it, boy," he said, pointing to Timothy.

Timothy froze, confused at the urgency in the man's voice. While he hesitated, I reacted. I pulled the door with my full weight, yanking on it as hard as I could. But the door didn't budge.

"It must have been shut off from the inside," the janitor said.

"What?" I asked, "What was shut off?"

Old Sam met my eyes.

"The old basement. It was closed off years ago for safety reasons. It's huge... enormous. The size of the whole school. But no lights were installed. To make things worse, wherever a wall is in the school, the same wall is in the basement. This creates hallways, rooms, twists, and turns. In total darkness, with so many walls, and only two exits... it's a death trap."

"And Remi is down there," I mumbled.

"I'm going to the principal's office. We need to call those girls' parents. What did you say their names were? And how many are down there?" Old Sam asked.

"I'll go with you," Timothy volunteered.

The old janitor nodded, and the two strode from the room. I think they thought I would follow behind them. But I didn't. I turned back to the door.

"Sealed off from the inside?" I said aloud, letting my thoughts carry me wherever they wanted in search of a solution.

"But with a maze underground and only one other exit, why would anyone do that? It doesn't make sense. No, it would be so much easier to seal off from the outside. But how?"

I felt along the edges of the door. It seemed to have been painted over a couple of times. My fingers found the hinges of the door. They were rusted, painted over, and wouldn't budge. Lucky enough for me, I had a screwdriver in my backpack. I pulled it out as quickly as I could, mentally thanking my dad for teaching me to always carry one. He told me, since I couldn't carry weapons to school, to carry a screwdriver in case I was attacked, because it could be used to stab an attacker. But in my case, I could use it to take the door off the hinges.

I looked around quickly. No one was in the library. Even the librarian had left with Old Sam to see what the commotion was about. I was all alone.

I heard the voice again. No, this one was different. It wasn't Remi. I didn't recognize it. It must have been one of Remi's friends.

"I'm coming!" I shouted, "Hold on!"

It was unlikely that anyone would hear me, but I did it anyway. Just in case they could hear and needed some reassurance.

It took a good fifteen minutes to get all the hinges off the door. I was afraid that someone would walk in at any moment and I would get in trouble for destroying school property. I also kept an eye out for the principal, or Old Sam, or Timothy, but they never came into the library. I wondered if Old Sam and Timothy were having a hard time convincing the principal of what was going on.

Finally, I got the door pried off the wall. I put it down carefully on the floor, struggling a bit because of its weight. Then I stood, staring at the place the door had been. It was a staircase descending into total darkness. It must have been the basement Old Sam was talking about.

I took a moment to collect my thoughts and formulate a plan. If the basement was as dangerous as Old Sam said it was, I would be foolish to go in alone. But at the same time, Remi was down there. There was nothing on earth that I wouldn't do for Remi.

I would go in, I decided. I would go in after Remi. But I would have to make sure I marked my route, so I wouldn't get lost in the maze. I rummaged through my backpack, searching for anything that could help. I found a flashlight that had a decent battery charge, which was useful. I put it aside. I found an extra shoelace, which I briefly considered using to make my way, but it was much too short. Then I found a box of thumbtacks. I could take them and some paper and pin up a white sheet of paper at every turn. The white would reflect the light from the flashlight very well, making it easy to see. And I could always write directions on the pieces of paper if I needed to.

I put the thumbtacks in my backpack and pulled my backpack over my shoulder. Before I left for the basement, however, I stopped to leave Timothy a note.

"You were taking too long," I wrote on a post-it-note, "So I'm going in after them. I'll leave a trail of white paper behind me. Wish me luck."

With that, I left the post-it note on the door I had removed from the wall. I turned on my flashlight and walked down the steep stairs into the basement.

The first thing I noticed was the temperature change. The

library was usually delightfully warm, but the basement was chilly. I hugged my jacket close to me, worried about Remi. Was she cold? Was she hurt?

I began walking down the hallway. I reached a fork in my path with three hallways spreading out in front of me.

"Remi?!" I yelled. "Mikayla! Is anyone here?"

The only answer I received was the echo of my voice bouncing back to me. So, I took the path in the middle. I stuck a piece of paper on the wall where the hallway ended, writing on it, "I'm taking the middle path." Then I walked onwards.

Old Sam was right. It was like a maze. I stumbled through the hallways, dead-ending into rooms with no exit, and ending up back where I had already been. The worst ones were the rooms with holes in their backs, leading to more paths. It was completely confusing. I tried to imagine the hallways above me for direction. I tried to picture the classrooms. But the walls down here were different. I had no idea what the architects were thinking when they built it. I could only imagine they were trying to make the rooms above more structurally sound by extending the walls into the basement. It wouldn't have been so bad if they left it at that. But whoever had built the basement had added walls, taken away walls, and cut holes in walls, creating a puzzling labyrinth.

Still, I continued onward, determined to find Remi and her friends. I left the pieces of paper at every turn and, every few minutes, I called for Remi. After about fifteen minutes of walking, I called again and this time I heard a reply.

"Remi!" I called into the darkness.

"Yes!" came the excited reply. "I'm here!"

"Remi!" I exclaimed, delighted. "Where are you? Keep talking!"

"Nicholas, is that you!?" Remi yelled back.

"Yes, it's me! Are the others with you?" I asked, trying to follow the sound of her voice.

"Yes, we're all here!" Remi replied.

There was a cluster of other voices, but I couldn't make out what they were saying.

"Hold on, guys, just hold on! Remi, keep talking, lead me to you!" I said, stumbling forward in my haste.

"How did you even get down here? We were beginning to worry that no one would find us!"

"I'm sorry it took so long, Remi. We didn't know where you were, or how you disappeared from the principal's office!" I replied.

"Oh, yeah, the office. I'd almost forgotten! Did you hear the announcement?"

"Yes, I did," I said with a laugh. "And I loved it. I love you."

"I love you, too!" Remi said.

"Hang on, now," I yelled, "I'm coming!"

~

"He's coming," I told my friends excitedly.

"We heard," Mikayla said, helping Sierra stand up.

"Remi, what if he gets lost down here, too?" Bethany fearfully asked.

"Nicholas!" I yelled, "Please tell me you marked your way in here so we can get out?!"

"I did!" I heard the faint reply. "I marked the way back with pieces of paper. Now keep talking, let me follow your voice!"

"Was everyone worried about us? Where did they think we went?" I asked.

"Your friends were worried. Florence was the one who told us about you being missing," Nicholas called back.

"Did the office call our parents?" I asked.

"I don't know. Timothy and Old Sam went to talk to the principal about it, but when just Timothy and I talked to him, he didn't believe us."

Nicholas sounded a lot closer now, so I kept asking questions so he could follow my voice.

"Old Sam? Who's that?"

"The janitor! He's the one who let me past the door in the library."

"The library? But we went through a door in the office," I replied.

"Yeah, there's two doors. How did you find the one in the office anyway?" Nicholas asked, his voice sounding even closer.

"Bethany found it. We needed an escape after using the intercom. But then the principal came in and we ran to hide in the darkness. The principal didn't see us, but by the time we stopped to catch our breath, we were totally lost. We were worried no one would even know where to look for us."

"You were right to be worried. I wouldn't have known you were here if I hadn't heard you yelling through the door in the library."

"You heard us yelling? We screamed until we were hoarse, but we didn't think anyone heard."

"Remi! Look, I see a light!" Bethany said, pointing excitedly.

"You can see a light?" I heard Nicholas's voice.

"Yes, I see it, Nicholas!" I yelled.

"Do you have a flashlight?"

"Yes, we have a phone light."

"Turn it up as bright as it can go and wave it around. I'll turn mine off and see if I can follow the light," Nicholas called.

I turned my phone's flashlight all the way up but noticed that my battery was dangerously low. I was about to tell Nicholas this, but he called out before I could.

"I see you! Wave the light around some more. Yes! There!"

"Nicholas! I see you!"

Nearly in tears, I ran through the darkness into Nicholas's arms. He held me tightly, rocking me back and forth, whispering into my neck.

"It's okay, you're okay. You're okay now. I'm right here."

"Ahem," Bethany coughed from behind me.

I pulled away reluctantly.

"We should go," Nicholas mumbled.

"Yeah, we should go."

"Come on," Nicholas said, turning his flashlight back on. "Follow me."

I took a firm hold of Nicholas's free hand as he led us through the maze of walls and rooms.

"You're shaking," Nicholas said quietly.

"Am not," I replied.

"Yes, you clearly are. I can see you! Are you cold?" he asked.

"A little."

Nicholas stopped for a second to take off his jacket, handing it to me.

"Aw, so sweet," the other girls chorused behind me.

But I tried to hand it back.

"No, then you'll be cold," I said.

"I haven't been down here for hours. Put it on, I'll be fine," Nicholas said. "Hurry up so we can get out of here."

I smiled and pulled the jacket over my shoulders.

"Better?" Nicholas asked.

"Much better."

"Good. Now let's get out of here."

# Chapter Fifty-Two

"Remi!"

"Mom?"

"Remi!"

"Dad?"

I smiled as I watched Remi run into the arms of her family outside of the school. They had been in the middle of arguing with the principal in the front parking lot. When we emerged, dusty and cold, from the basement, Old Sam told us they were outside, and we hurried through the halls to see Remi's parents, Mikayla's mom, Sierra's grandparents, and Bethany's dad. Timothy and I stood awkwardly to the side, our family unable to get away from work. Our phones, however, were blowing up.

"Dad?" I asked into my phone's receiver.

"Nicholas! Are you all right? The principal called me and said some girls were trapped in the basement. And you went after them?!" my dad exclaimed.

"Dad, one of the girls was Remi. I couldn't just leave it alone!"

"You could have told someone! A teacher, the principal!"

"We tried! They didn't listen to us!"

"All right, all right," my dad said, exasperated. "But don't think I'm going to forget about this. We'll be talking about this when I get home. Are you sure you're all right?"

"Yes, Dad, I'm perfectly fine," I said honestly.

"As long as you're sure. Do you want me to come and pick you up?"

"No, I'll see you at home."

"Okay, buddy. See you soon."

I hung up and resumed watching Remi talking with her family. Her mom would barely let her out of her arms.

"Nicholas?" Timothy asked, walking over.

"Yeah?"

Timothy surprised me by wrapping me in a hug.

"I was worried, my dude," he said.

"I'm all right. I found the girls," I said.

"Obviously," Timothy said.

I noticed that he wasn't looking at me at all. He was staring at Mikayla, who was hugging Remi.

"Go ahead," I said.

"Huh?"

"Go say hi to Mikayla," I answered, nudging him in Mikayla's direction.

"I... don't think she wants to..."

"Timothy, go," I said firmly.

I watched him walk slowly and awkwardly over, fidgeting and waiting while Mikayla talked with her mother. After Mikayla noticed him, she turned around and hugged him tightly.

"Nicholas!"

I turned quickly as I heard Remi's voice. She beckoned me over and I hurried to her.

"Nicholas, thank you so much for saving our precious Remi," Remi's mom said, giving me a hug.

"Yes, thank you," her father agreed.

"It was my pleasure," I said grandly.

"Come on, Remi. Let's get you home. You've had a long day," her mom mumbled, hugging Remi tighter.

"Nicholas, is your dad coming to pick you up?" Remi's dad asked.

I shook my head.

"He has to work and can't leave. Besides, I wasn't the one who was stuck in a cold basement for hours."

"I guess that's true," her dad admitted slowly.

"Come on, dear, come on," Remi's mom said, herding her family to the car.

Remi moved to go with them, then turned quickly and jumped into my arms. I held her tightly, thankful that she was safe and sound.

"Thank you, Nicholas," Remi whispered to me.

"Anytime, princess," I whispered back, kissing the top of her hair.

I watched them drive off before turning to go back inside. Timothy stopped me.

"My grandmother is coming to pick me up... do you want a ride home?" he asked.

"And miss robotics club? No thanks," I said, forcing a laugh.

He nodded, understanding, and walked further into the parking lot to wait for his ride. I walked back into the school building slowly. The principal was back in his office, probably stressing about the inevitable lawsuit that was coming. I felt a sense of justice. The basement was a safety violation. It was a miracle that a student hadn't gotten stuck down there before this!

A lot of my classmates had questions when I returned to my last class of the day. I answered as many as I could without getting in trouble for talking. In robotics, I worked on the computer program for Remi. It was nearly ready, but it wasn't quite perfect. And it had to be perfect for Remi.

It was only on the walk home that I really began to feel tired. It took so much effort just to put one foot in front of the other. My eyelids felt heavy, and whenever I closed them, even for half a second, I pictured myself back in the winding maze of the basement, desperately trying to reach Remi. It struck me how scared I had been then, in the darkness with only a flashlight and a paper trail to guide me. It hit me how terrified I was when I found out Remi was missing. I hadn't let myself feel scared at the moment, but now that it was long over and I was safe, I began to shake.

I dropped my bag on the floor when I got home, nearly forgetting to lock the door behind me. I let myself fall to the floor in the living room, my back against the couch.

It wasn't that bad. I kept telling myself the same thing over and over. It really wasn't that bad. It was just a basement. But it took a snack, a hot shower, and a solid few hours for the shaking to stop.

# Chapter Fifty-Three

I have to admit, I loved the fact that Nicholas had been the one to rescue us. Of course, I would have taken anyone. Any rescuer would have done nicely to save me from the dark and dismal dungeon. But it was especially perfect that it was Nicholas. And I had made sure to tell Mikayla that Timothy played a big role in saving her as well, which I'm sure she appreciated.

I honestly felt like I had grown from the experience. I had definitely gotten to know Mikayla, Sierra, and Bethany a lot better. We were much closer friends after our ordeal. I would go as far as to say that they were my closest friends, aside from Nicholas, of course. Nicholas and I had grown so much closer together that it felt like the last years of distance didn't even happen. We were those two best friends again, sharing every moment of our lives together.

We walked together to school hand-in-hand every morning since then, and we walked back from school arm-in-arm every evening. Nicholas made sure that I never walked alone. He'd been a bit more overprotective since the basement incident, which I did not mind at all. It was adorable the way he put his hand on my lower back to steady me in the hallway or stood between me and a boy if one approached me. But we still hadn't had our first official date, and I was beginning to get impatient.

"Why won't you tell me what you're planning?" I asked as we walked home from school one night.

"I want it to be a surprise!" Nicholas said.

I was immediately suspicious. I had asked him about our first date for about a week, and he always gave me the same answers. But today, he had a smug smile on his face. His answers had a tad more confidence in them.

"What are you hiding, Savage?" I asked, calling him by his last name.

"I don't know, Lucas. I guess you'll have to find out," he replied, giving me a wink that made me blush.

"Tell me!" I insisted, nudging his arm with my shoulder.

His backpack fell off his shoulder as a result, and he hoisted it back up before speaking to me again.

"I'm not saying anything," he answered with an annoyingly adorable smile.

"At least tell me when I'll find out. Please? When are you planning this!"

His face flickered and his smile grew. I seized those tiny nonverbal cues and used them as a trampoline to jump to conclusions.

"Is it soon? Nicholas, is it soon? You're smiling! That means yes! Right? Right! It is soon!"

"I'm not saying anything!" Nicholas repeated, miming locking his mouth with a key and throwing it away.

"No, no sir, I will figure this out. I will guess at least when it will be!" I promised him.

"No, you won't," he argued.

"Yes, I will!"

We stopped in front of my house.

"Goodnight," I said, turning to give Nicholas our usual goodnight hug.

Tonight, he held the hug a little longer than usual, which worried me.

"Are you okay?" I asked as I pulled away, only to notice that the smile on his face had grown bigger.

"Remi, would you like to join me for dinner tonight?" Nicholas asked, his voice deep and romantic.

I flushed with delight and excitement.

"You tease, you let me guess and ramble... all the time you were planning it for tonight?" I asked with a giggle.

He brushed a wisp of hair out of his eyes. I saw the sparkle in his eyes when he looked at me, and it gave me butterflies.

"I'm sorry I kept you waiting. I wanted the weather to be a bit warmer for what I had planned," Nicholas explained mysteriously, leaving me with more questions than answers.

"Warmer? Why would it need to be warmer to ask me to dinner?"

Nicholas closed my fence's front gate, separating us from each other with a white picket fence.

"I guess you'll find out. I'll pick you up in an hour? An hour and a half?"

"Bold of you to assume I'd say yes," I said coyly, leaning over the fence.

"Oh, so that's how you're going to play it, huh?" Nicholas replied.

He leaned over the fence as well, until our faces were inches apart. Then he kissed me. I leaned into the kiss, but he pulled away.

"Say yes?" he asked, sounding so sweet and innocent.

"You're horrible," I replied.

"Say yes," he whispered, the sentence sounding less and less like a question.

"Of course. I'll be ready in thirty minutes," I replied.

He pulled me back in for another kiss.

"What on earth are you two doing?" my mom asked from the doorway.

We both were gasping for laughter as we went our separate ways.

~

I could not wait to see Remi's reaction. I had planned this night for weeks, but I had to wait for the weather to get slightly warmer for my plan to work.

"Are you sure tonight is the night?" Timothy asked.

I had him come over to help me get ready for the special night, but he was skeptical when he showed up at the door.

"Completely sure. Thanks for coming over to help," I said.

"Anytime, buddy. Remind me what we're doing again?"

I whispered the plan to him as if Remi was somehow listening. He nodded and rolled up his sleeves to help.

"Dinner is almost ready, kiddo!" my dad said from the kitchen.

"Your dad is cooking?" Timothy asked.

"He makes a mean steak, actually," I replied as we walked to the backyard.

"Steak, on the first date? Man, you're really trying to make up for all those years you ignored her, huh?" Timothy teased me.

I laughed along with him.

"Yeah, I do have some making up to do. Anyway, Remi deserves only the very best."

"I can't argue with you there. She's a wonderful girl. Mikayla is always telling me about her," Timothy said.

"When are you going to ask Mikayla out?" I changed the subject.

"Tomorrow, actually. There's a movie coming out tomorrow night that Mikayla really wants to see. I got us tickets to the premiere," Timothy admitted, a pleased tone in his voice.

"Ah, bribing her with a movie she wants to see so she can't reject you. I see how it is," I teased him.

"Yeah, that's exactly how it is," Timothy said sarcastically.

We set to work then, preparing what I hoped would be the most magical night of my life.

When all the set-up work was done, it was perfectly ready for Remi to come over. Now, I just had to wait.

"All right, man. That looks to be it. Am I good to go?" Timothy asked.

I did a final look-over to make sure everything was perfect. Even I had to admit, it was flawless.

"Yup, you're good to go. Hey, stop by the kitchen, I had Dad make you a steak to take with you. But don't stick around too long, okay? Remi will be here any minute!" I ordered.

Timothy held up his hands and walked slowly to the door.

"All right, all right," he said, "I don't get underfoot. Wouldn't want to interrupt your *magical* night with your *beautiful* Remi."

He blew kisses at me as I glared back at him.

"Goodbye, Timothy!" I yelled when he finally disappeared inside.

"Farewell, Romeo! Parting is such sweet sorrow!"

I heard my dad laugh at Timothy's parting speech from inside, but I tried to ignore it. I looked around my backyard, making sure everything was completely perfect. Then I got an alert on my phone, and it immediately captured my attention.

The notification was a text from Remi that said, "I'm ready. Are you picking me up or...?"

I hurried from my backyard into my house.

"Dad, is everything ready?" I asked hurriedly.

"Yup, all good to go. Just let me know when you want me to bring it all out," my dad said, giving me a thumbs up.

"Thanks, Dad. So much. Really," I said, trying to get my nerves under control as I did so.

"Anytime, kiddo. I know Remi means a lot to you. Now, go! Scoot, you can't keep the girls waiting! They get fidgety, you know."

With these profound words of wisdom from my father, I ran

out my front door, only stopping to collect myself when my feet hit the sidewalk.

I took a long, slow breath, and straightened the collar of the most uncomfortable shirt I'd ever worn. I had bought it for a cousin's wedding that my dad and I attended, then had stuffed it in a drawer, hoping to never see it again. But I had to admit, I looked rather dashing in it, so I had brought it out of retirement just for tonight. I had paired it with a pair of equally as uncomfortable pants and tried to tame the bird's nest that was my hair. It was no small task, but I was ready for the night.

I strode up to Remi's front gate and opened it for myself. My confidence dwindled as I walked up the front steps. I didn't know why I was so nervous. I hadn't expected to be.

I took another breath to calm my quaking stomach before knocking on her door. Remi's father answered it, which rattled me even more.

"Hello, Nicholas. You look very nice tonight," Remi's dad said, standing in the doorway like a prison guard.

"Thank you," I choked out, "Is Remi here?"

Remi's dad pulled his head back into the house and yelled, "Remi! Nicholas is at the door!"

"Tell him I'll be down in a minute!" I heard Remi's voice from upstairs.

"Pretty sure he heard you," Remi's dad called back up to her.

"Tell him anyway!" Remi yelled back.

Remi's dad finally turned to me.

"She'll be ready in a minute," he said.

"So, I heard," I replied.

"See, he heard!" her dad screeched up at Remi.

"Oh, shoo, shoo," Remi's mom said, sweeping Remi's dad away from the door with her hands.

"Nicholas, dear, would you like to come in?" Remi's mom asked politely.

"Yes, please," I gratefully accepted.

I stepped into the hallway while Remi's mom tried in vain to shoo her husband out of the hallway.

"Honey, leave the poor boy alone," Remi's mom ordered. Remi's dad didn't listen.

"Nicholas, what are your intentions with my daughter?" Remi's dad asked harshly.

If I didn't know him better, I might have been unnerved by Mr. Lucas's stoic approach. But I had grown up with him. I knew that he was just fooling around. Still, I gave him an honest answer.

"Well, for tonight, I intend to give her a nice steak dinner," I replied.

"Ooh, steak. Any for me?" Mr. Lucas asked, causing Mrs. Lucas to swat him on the shoulder and drag him forcefully out of the room.

"No, none for you, you scoot. Remi, you'd better hurry up or your dad is going to end up on the date with Nicholas instead of you!" Mrs. Lucas warned.

"I'm coming, I'm coming." Remi's voice sounded closer and closer as she descended the stairs.

My breath caught in my throat. Remi was wearing a short red skirt with a navy-blue top, a silver necklace, earrings, and complementing makeup. She was more beautiful than I'd ever seen her, more beautiful than any other girl in the whole world.

"Too formal?" she asked me sheepishly, a hint of blush on her cheeks as she posed on the stairs.

"Not at all. You look gorgeous," I whispered, awestruck.

"Really? Because I was going for stunning," Remi teased me with a smile that made my knees weak.

"You are," I choked out, "stunning, that is. Perfectly flawlessly stunning. Breathtaking, even."

"All right, lover boy. Where are we going tonight?" Remi asked, flushing from my praise.

"And when will you be back?!" Mr. Lucas yelled from the kitchen.

"I'll have her back before ten, Mr. Lucas!" I replied.

"Sounds good. Have fun, kiddos!"

"Sorry about my dad," Remi apologized as she dismounted the stairs and stood beside me.

"No problem. I like him," I replied.

Remi smiled. "He likes you, too," she said. Then, as we walked out the door, she asked, "Where are you taking me to dinner tonight?"

"You'll find out," I said, pulling out a blindfold from my bag.

"A blindfold? Really?" she asked, giggling nervously.

"Yup. Only if you're comfortable with it, of course," I said.

She laughed and grabbed the piece of fabric from my hand.

"It sounds like fun," she said, putting it on. "Are we going in a car or are we going to walk?"

"Walk," I replied, taking her hand.

"Is it far? My shoes aren't exactly designed for a hike," Remi said.

I noticed she was wearing very nice sandals.

"At least they're not heels, right?" I teased her.

"Nicholas," she whined, "Tell me we're not walking far."

"We're not. I promise," I said.

I led Remi out on the sidewalk, and we walked up and down the sidewalk for about twenty minutes. I selfishly enjoyed holding her tightly against me, leading her in circles around the neighborhood. Soon enough, she caught on.

"Are we going in circles?" Remi asked after about five minutes.

"No, what? How would... why would we do that?" I asked, sounding very suspicious.

"Why do you sound like that?" Remi asked, laughing. "We are going in circles, aren't we? Nicholas where are you taking me?!"

"And we're here!" I said, quickly stopping Remi in front of my house.

"Can I take off the blindfold now?" Remi asked, reaching her hands up to her face.

"No, not yet!" I said, taking her hands in mine.

Slowly and carefully, I led her through my main hallway and into my house. My dad stepped out of the kitchen, looking amused, but I motioned for him to keep quiet. Finally, I led Remi out into the middle of my backyard.

"Okay... now you can take off the blindfold," I said quietly.

And I stepped back just in time to see her face light up.

# Chapter Fifty-Four

The whole backyard was aglow with the light of lightning bugs and fairy lights. There was a table set up in the very center with a candlelight dancing across two steak dinners. A glass pitcher of water in the center reflected the soft light of the candles and the pale flashes of the lightning bugs, making a tiny disco ball toward the back of the table. A tiny clay vase was on the side of the table closest to me. I recognized it from when I was in kindergarten with Nicholas. We had an assignment to make something out of clay. I made Nicholas a vase to keep flowers in, but I had made the neck of the vase much too small to hold more than one strangled flower. It held one flower now, a daisy. A single lightning bug sat on the daisy, lighting up the pedals every couple of seconds.

"Nicholas..." I mumbled, completely floored.

He wrapped his arms around my waist and kissed the top of my head.

"Do you love it?"

I could only nod dumbly.

"Tell me you love it."

"I love it," I whispered.

"I know," Nicholas mumbled, kissing my head again. Then he pulled one of my hands to his chest, kissed it, and bowed grandly.

"Your dinner, m'lady," he said with a wink.

I felt like I was in a fairytale as Nicholas led me to the table in the center of the backyard, which he had transformed into a magical fairy garden.

"How long did this all take you to set up?" I asked as he pulled out my chair for me.

"A couple of hours. But I had help."

As I sat down, I reached up and a lightning bug landed on my finger.

"How did you get this many lightning bugs in your backyard?" I asked, suddenly realizing just how many lightning bugs were currently in the garden. There had to have been at least five hundred of the bugs flying around.

"Some of them I collected, some of them I raised, and some of them I ordered online," Nicholas admitted as he sat down.

"Collected, how did you... wait, raised? Wait, wait, ordered?!" I exclaimed, even more confused.

Nicholas laughed. "Nothing less than perfection for the most beautiful princess in the world," he said, raising his glass of fizzy apple juice.

I laughed to myself. The apple juice looked like champagne and, in the glow of the fairy lights, lightning bugs, and candles, I really felt like a princess. I clinked my glass against his.

"What are we toasting?" I questioned before taking a sip.

"True love?" he suggested.

"Or soulmates," I added.

"True love and soulmates," he agreed and clinked his glass against mine again.

We both sipped our juice and ate our steak dinners in silence for a while, but it wasn't a hard, awkward silence. We were both so completely comfortable in each other's presence that we barely noticed the quiet. After a while, Nicholas reached his hand out across the table and held mine tightly.

"Remi?" Nicholas asked when we were nearly finished eating.

"Yes?" I said, looking up at him with shining eyes.

"Will you be my girlfriend?" Nicholas asked softly.

I was taken aback at his directness for a moment, then smiled to myself. We really were done playing games with each other.

"Yes, I will," I replied quickly.

"Wonderful." Nicholas took my hand and pressed his lips against it, making me feel terribly weak and powerfully strong at the same moment.

"Nicholas?" I mumbled.

"Yes?"

"Thank you." I looked up into his loving eyes. "I was beginning to think we would never be together."

Nicholas squeezed my hand tighter.

"I was beginning to think so, too," he admitted, his eyes growing sad. "I'm so glad you were patient with me."

Just then a lightning bug landed on my shoulder, and I let it crawl onto my finger.

"Do you remember when we used to catch lightning bugs as kids?" I asked softly, my eyes on the lightning bug on my finger.

"I do. I think about it all the time," Nicholas murmured. "I knew you were the one for me, even then."

"Did you?" I asked whimsically.

"Well, I didn't know I loved you like that. Not exactly. But I knew we were meant to be together."

The lightning bug crawled to the very top of my finger and flew away. I met Nicholas's eyes again.

"I love you," I whispered.

His face lit up and I smiled too.

"I love you so much, my princess," Nicholas replied.

Then, after a moment of staring at me, he asked, "Are you done with your dinner?"

"Yes," I said, pushing the plate away from the edge of the table slightly, "It was delicious. My compliments to the chef."

"The chef was my dad, actually," Nicholas said with a chuckle, "He wanted to do something to help me with our date."

"That was so sweet of him." I smiled. "Remind me to thank him later."

"I will."

Nicholas stood suddenly and walked over to a tiny table next to the only tree in their backyard. It had a CD player on it. He pressed the play button, and a slow jazz song began playing. Then he walked slowly over to me and held out his hand.

"May I have this dance?" he asked.

I blushed and stood up as he pulled my chair out for me.

"You may, my good sir," I replied, taking his hand.

"Thank you, milady."

Nicholas spun me around and I found his arms around me. I barely noticed the movements of the dance we were doing. I was lost in his eyes. I put my head on his chest as we danced together. The song ended and the next track began. We moved slowly together, losing track of time.

The lightning bugs circled around us, dancing with the music. The fairy lights reflected tiny sparkles in Nicholas's eyes.

But a gust of wind blew out the candles.

# Chapter Fifty-Five

Over the next few months, Nicholas and I grew closer together as a couple. It was strange at first, being officially together, but at the same time, nothing had ever felt more right or perfect. It was so much fun to tell all my friends that Nicholas and I were finally a couple. All the girls on my cheerleading team called us soulmates, and I had to agree with them. Nicholas and I were made for each other. He had been worth all the effort and all the waiting. Now, finally, we could be happy together.

Our second date was a double date with Timothy and Mikayla at an old-fashioned diner. It was surprisingly awkward at first. Since we were all such good friends outside of our relationships, seeing each other as a couple was strange. But it didn't take long for us to start joking around and goofing off. We soon got past the tension and have a fun time. After that, we went on a lot of double dates. It was fun to watch Mikayla and Timothy grow as a couple, as Nicholas and I did. I was overjoyed to be sharing my happiness with my best friend. Mikayla was happier with Timothy than I had ever seen her before in our friendship.

I tried to do little things every day to show Nicholas how much I cared about him. Ever since the basement incident, I decided against big shows of my affection. Nicholas seemed just as pleased with my tiny acts of love. Mikayla sometimes joined me, and we worked together to brainstorm ideas. Sometimes we would leave the boy's notes in their books. Other times we would leave treats in their lockers. Anything that made them feel wanted and special was planned and put into action. When Nicholas would do small things for me as well, I would immediately call Mikayla and she would do the same for me when Timothy did something special. In this way, we grew even closer as friends.

As for me, I was happier than I had ever been in my life, and Nicholas seemed to be happy as well. His happiness was very important to me, and I was delighted to see that he seemed more content and peaceful around me. We talked every day. Nicholas would walk me to and from school, and we'd discuss each other's days. Nicholas helped me with my homework after school. My mom made us snacks when we hung out in the afternoons. Our Saturdays were full of fun adventures, dates, and time shared together. Nicholas went to my cheerleading competitions and I loved going to robotics club with him. We celebrated each other's successes and comforted each other through our failures. Nicholas and I shared our lives with each other.

Now it was April. Prom was coming up soon. Mikayla and I obviously assumed that we would be asked to go by our boyfriends but, so far, neither of us had been asked. That's why, on that particular day in April, I was sitting on the bleachers behind the school after cheerleading practice, talking about the prom.

"Do you know if you're going to be free that night?" I asked, hinting at wanting to go in the most subtle way I could manage.

"I'm pretty sure I am," Nicholas replied, his tone not giving me any clues.

"Do you think you'll go?" I tried again.

"Maybe."

I internally sighed. This was going to be harder than I expected.

"Do you think you'll go with someone?" I asked encouragingly.

"Maybe. It wouldn't be fun to go alone," Nicholas responded dully.

"Do you think you'll ask someone?" I tried for the final time, my patience rapidly disappearing.

"Maybe."

"Nicholas Savage!" I exclaimed at last, "Are you asking me to the prom or not?"

Nicholas laughed and I swatted him lovingly on the arm. I blushed, embarrassed at my leading questions. I should have realized he was only teasing me.

"Shut up," I said, swatting him again.

"I didn't say anything." He laughed.

"Still," I replied.

He put his arm around me and held me tightly to him.

"If I'm going to the prom, and that's only an 'if', mind you, then I would be foolish not to ask out the most beautiful girl in the school," Nicholas mumbled.

"Who, Mikayla?" I asked innocently. "I'm afraid she's taken."

"No, silly. Guess again," he whispered, his mouth dangerously close to my ear.

I shivered a little and squeaked, "Sierra?"

"Nope," Nicholas replied. This time he kissed my cheek ever so softly.

"It's you, princess, you're the most beautiful girl in school."

"Just in school?" I huffed, pretending to be offended.

"I stand corrected," Nicholas said, lifting my chin with his finger, "You, princess, are the most beautiful girl in the whole world."

"You're too sweet," I mumbled.

"And you're blushing," Nicholas said with a stupid smile.

I put my hand behind his neck and kissed him.

"There, now we're both blushing," I said smugly.

Nicholas laughed aloud and I joined him. He hugged me tightly against his chest, and I relaxed under his touch.

"Seriously, though. Why don't you just come out and ask me to the prom? You know I would say yes," I said, "I just want to be asked."

"I know. You've just done so many wild stunts for me over the past year. I wanted to do something just as crazy to ask you to prom. I just need the right idea and some time to work out all the details. It has to be perfect to make you feel special," Nicholas said.

I could tell his mind was a million miles away, but I responded anyway.

"You don't have to do anything big to make me feel special. You already make me feel special every day. You make me feel special just by being my boyfriend," I said.

He wasn't listening to me, so I leaned in and kissed him again.

"Did you hear me?" I asked when I pulled away.

Nicholas pulled me back and kissed me again.

"You're too adorable," he murmured.

I sighed in blissful contentment.

"I have to go now, though. I have to talk to Mr. Humpheres about the robotics meet in a couple of days."

"The battle royale?" I asked, intrigued. "Did he get tickets for the robotics team?"

"Yup, he got the tickets. We're just doing final preps on the robots."

"Which one is competing?" I asked.

"You don't know? Oh, that's right, you skipped out on the last couple of robotics club meetings," Nicholas said, his tone scolding me.

"Hey, I had cheerleading practice! Don't judge me, Savage," I snapped playfully.

"I'm not judging! But I'm not telling you, either. You'll have to come to the battle and find out with the rest of the team."

"No fair!" I said, pouting.

Nicholas kissed my nose.

"You're cute when you're pouting. But I really have to go. I'll meet you out in front of the school in about fifteen minutes to walk home, does that sound good?" he asked.

"Yup, I'll see you there."

We gathered up our stuff. Nicholas ran inside as I took my time walking down the slippery bleachers. To my surprise I found Erica coming out the doors onto the field.

Erica stared at Nicholas walking past her. Nicholas ignored her and I felt a swell of pride and happiness as he did so. Then Erica turned her attention to me, walking over to me quickly.

"Huh, I guess you got your guy after all," Erica said sarcastically.

It wasn't the first time Erica had teased me about being with Nicholas. All through our relationship, she'd been trying to get between us. At first, I hadn't thought much about it. I had assumed she was jealous. But she had been getting more and more confrontational. Today, I had just about enough of her tone and her attitude. Looking back, it might have been an overreaction, but in the moment, I just snapped.

"Erica, what on earth is your problem? I've always been nice to you! I don't get why you go out of your way to be rude to me," I declared, my hands on my hips.

I could see Erica get irritated at being called out so directly. So, I braced myself, thinking she was going to yell at me.

But she just bristled and hissed, "You'll see. You just wait and see, Remi Lucas. Guys like that never stop messing with your head. I hope you feel really stupid for making a fool over him once you figure out what a self-centered jerk he is. You just wait and see."

I felt my face flush with anger. I didn't like anyone talking badly about the love of my life. But just as I was about to argue, Erica's voice softened.

"And when you do figure it out, I'll be here. Then maybe we can be friends."

I was surprised to see a flash of pity in Erica's eyes. My surprise was quickly replaced with anger. I didn't want her pity.

"Shut up! You don't know anything," I yelled, losing my temper completely. "Why don't you go away and stay out of my relationship!?"

With that, I stormed off, fuming. As I walked through the nearly empty school hallways, I was so angry that I was talking to myself.

"Erica is so jealous, it's almost sad," I muttered. "No, not sad. It's pathetic! Nicholas is such a sweet and wonderful guy. He loves me, cares about me, protects me, and makes me happy! I'd never let a snake like her turn me against him."

I burst out the front doors of the school to wait for Nicholas, still fuming. When Erica came out to walk to her car, I was so angry that I couldn't even look at her. But she looked at me. She took a long look in my direction and sighed before walking to her car.

A very tiny part of me wondered... did she know something I didn't?

# Chapter Fifty-Six

It was Saturday morning, and I was getting ready for the battle royale. The team and I had been prepping for this day for months. Our robots were our pride and joy, perfectly designed and lovingly crafted to be instruments of glorious war. We felt like a team of soldiers getting ready to march into battle.

Sadly, a lot of the girls weren't able to make it to the competition. They were scheduled to cheer at a home soccer game at the same time as the battle. We met up with them in the robotics classroom before we had to leave.

"Can't you just skip the game?" Nathan asked, scuffing his shoe on the floor.

"Nathan's right, it's just soccer. Not even football or anything," Timothy agreed, wrapping his arms around Mikayla's waist.

"No, we can't. It's our responsibility to show support to all of the school's teams," Sierra said sadly.

"Not the robotics team, though," Nathan said bitterly.

"I don't think the robotics club counts as a team. Besides, you wouldn't want the whole cheerleading squad doing flips and stuff while you're trying to battle, right?" Remi said with a chuckle.

"I would want you there," I said, kissing the back of Remi's neck.

"Aw, I wish I could be there," she said, giggling as I hugged her tightly.

"It's thanks to you that we're going anyway," David observed. "It was your idea to do the car wash and raise money to be able to go. It's not fair!"

"Life isn't fair, David," Bethany said with a dramatic sigh.

"And it wasn't all our doing, anyway," Remi argued. "You guys did all the hard work."

"It was Sierra's livestream that really got us the money. Her stream and her idea to let viewers buy us the supplies we needed," Timothy said.

"It was my pleasure, guys," Sierra said with a huge smile. "And it was Remi's idea to join the robotics club in the first place."

"It was a great idea, Remi," Mikayla agreed, "Joining the robotics club has been so much fun!"

The rest of the girls agreed, and David said, "We're glad to have had you."

"I'd never even been interested in robotics before," Sierra admitted, "But after hanging out with you guys for a while, I figured out I loved it!"

"Yeah, same!" Bethany agreed. "If I'd been exposed to robotics earlier, I might have even chosen to do that instead of cheerleading throughout high school. Don't get me wrong, I've loved being on the cheer team with all my closest friends, but it's impossible to do both. I'd never even considered robotics as an option."

"It is kind of expected that girls join cheerleading," Remi said, "I joined just because of gymnastics and it was extra stretching practice, but since I joined, I have noticed that people expect it of me."

"You're right," Sierra agreed, "Every cute girl is supposed to try out for cheerleading."

"Well, I, for one, would have liked robotics a lot more if pretty cheerleaders had been around the whole time," David interjected.

Everyone laughed. I saw Bethany nudge David playfully on the shoulder and was surprised to see him blush a deep crimson.

"Boys, we need to get going," Mr. Humpheres said, walking in from outside the school building, "The van is here."

"Good luck," Remi said, giving me a hug.

"Can I get a kiss?" I asked. "For good luck?"

Remi grinned and kissed me on the cheek.

"You don't need luck," she replied smugly.

"What about me, Mikayla, can I get one of those?" Timothy asked.

Mikayla giggled and kissed him on the cheek.

"Don't you dare ask us for a good-luck kiss!" Bethany exclaimed.

We all burst into laughter as the boys blushed. I noticed that David looked especially embarrassed. Could there be another romance budding between a cheerleader and a robotics guy?

"Seriously, guys, we're going to be late to pre-fight setup if we don't leave now!" Mr. Humpheres said urgently.

"Go on, you'll miss the all-important pre-fight setup," Remi teased, shoving me lovingly toward the door.

"Are you that anxious to be rid of me?" I asked, giving her a final hug.

"Never," she said with another kiss on the cheek.

"Now, get going!"

We all walked outside the school as a powerful, united team. It felt awesome, striding toward the car with my friends, off to battle, with our women waving us goodbye. Then Timothy tripped over his own shoelaces and fell on his face. He was fine, and we all had a good laugh before getting in the van and taking off to the competition.

# Chapter Fifty-Seven

My name is Erica Marrie Hudgents. I've been trying to get my own part of this story for some time now since I just know Remi and Nicholas will leave things out. Up until this point, I had a very minor role in the whole Remi and Nicholas romance story.

I knew something was off about Nicholas the first time I saw him. Yes, I will admit, I thought he was attractive at first. And yes, I did try to hit on him a few times. He shut me down quickly, however, which I must say, I am not used to. At my old school, I could have any boy I wanted. But Fort Hambrange High was not my old school. I learned that lesson over and over during my final high school years.

I'm getting ahead of myself. My addition to Remi and Nicholas's story really started when I was at the school on Saturday morning. I know what you're thinking. Erica, why on earth were you at a filthy school on your glorious Saturday when you could be doing something so much more fun? My question exactly. But apparently, my parents don't see it that way. They insist I go get extra tutoring in Chemistry. Chemistry of all subjects! When will I ever use chemistry in the real world? Especially since I want to go to school for graphic design. Honestly, I would have been fine squeaking by with my C+, but no, I had to bring up my GPA.

Enough of my ranting. The point is, I was at the school building on Saturday. It was the Saturday after Nicholas and his team of goody-goody computer nuts had gone off to compete in their Pacific Rim knockoff robot fight with a variety of Dungeons-and-Dragons-playing, six-library-card-owning, cat-loving nerds. The robotics classroom was empty of all of their ridiculous contraptions. At least, that's what I thought.

After my tutoring session, I decided to stop by the robotics classroom. My teacher always walked me to the door, so I pretended to tie my shoe so she would go ahead of me. I watched my chemistry teacher leave the building before doubling back through the empty hallways.

I ran my fingers along the green lockers. Ugly color, I always thought it was hideous. My old school had blue lockers, and I liked them so much better. Oh, how much damage I could do if only I could open all of these lockers. There were so many secrets locked behind those cheap combination locks. So many valuable secrets that I could use. But alas, they would remain secret. For now.

I stopped by a locker of one of the cheerleaders. Bethany. Such an idiot girl, out of all the idiots on the cheerleading team. I knew it was her locker because she had a magnetic heart on her locker. The rest of us weren't allowed to have any decorations on the front of our lockers, but of course, Bethany could. She was one of the oh-so-special cheerleaders.

I kicked the bottom of the locker. It left a tiny dent. I didn't care. She deserved it. All the cheerleaders deserved it. They were all stupid and only cared about themselves.

I know what you're thinking. Erica, didn't you try out for the cheerleading team? Yes, yes, I did. That was before I knew what miserable little two-faced liars were on the cheerleading team. I did a flawless performance at my try-out. Flawless! But they said I had 'no sense of balance' and 'couldn't even do a cartwheel right'. Really! It was really because they were jealous. They didn't like that I was better at cheerleading than them. I wasn't as pretty as them, too, or as popular. That's the real reason they didn't let me on the team. It had to be.

I stormed through the hallways, my anger making my face flush. I cursed myself for wanting to join their stupid team. And I cursed myself for ever wanting Nicholas!

I just... I thought Nicholas might have understood me. He was always quiet in class. He didn't like being called on, and he stayed mostly to himself. He was a loner. I was always a bit of a loner myself. Since I moved around my whole life, I never really had a chance to make close friends. Not to mention I never seemed to get along with other girls. I guess they were intimidated by me. I thought that if Nicholas and I could get together... maybe I would feel less lonely.

I sighed aloud and swore again in my mind. I was a fool for believing that Nicholas and I could be a good match. But it made sense at the time! I felt, and I still feel, that I really understood him. And now... but now...

I burst into the robotics classroom, the door shivering on its hinges at my force. Now he was dating a pathetic, mascara-running, lipstick-stealing, high-jumping cheerleader who threw herself at Nicholas in such a thirsty way. I didn't understand it! I had approached him very calmly; you could hardly even call it flirting! Remi's escapades put any of my attempts to shame. Yet, Remi is the one dating Nicholas. The guy was such a hypocrite! Going after me, saying he didn't approve of girls making the first move. He sure changed his tune quickly when a pretty and popular cheerleader made a move.

"AH!" I shrieked aloud. The noise echoed off the nearly empty walls of the robotics room and I sunk into a chair with a deep sigh.

It wasn't fair. It just wasn't fair. Nicholas was a complete jerk. He was superficial and dumb, just like every other guy. To top it off, when I tried to warn Remi about Nicholas's true self, she got mad at me!

"That's just what I get for being a nice person," I whispered to myself.

I stood up again and strode up and down in the room, trying to get over my anger.

"I just don't understand. What does she have that I don't? It's not fair!"

I stomped my foot, then was startled when I heard something fall.

"Hello?" I said stupidly before realizing no one was there.

"Oh, it was just a backpack. A backpack fell over."

I felt very stupid for getting scared over a backpack for a moment, but then I realized something.

"What's a backpack doing here? Did someone leave it?"

I hurried over to it.

"Wait, I recognize this bag," I muttered to myself.

I turned it over and over, trying to place it in my mind. Then I remembered! It was Nicholas's backpack!

"Jackpot!" I exclaimed, delighted.

"Let's see what secrets you have in here," I mumbled.

I unzipped his backpack and rummaged through its contents. It was a lot of usual stuff. Books for school, a pencil case filled with typical school supplies, some trash, and spare paper. There were a couple of hard drives which I didn't pay much attention to since he was in a computer programming class. Then I found something wonderful. Something that would change my destiny in Remi and Nicholas's story forever.

I found a very worn, dog-eared, written-in book called *True Love Needs Persuasion: Making Any Woman Fall in Love with You.*

"Now this is interesting," I whispered to myself, delighted at my discovery.

I curled up on the floor, my back against the concrete wall, and began to read. I flipped through the pages. I read all the notes

Nicholas had written in the margins. I peeled off some sticky notes filled with annotations and read those, too.

My eyes nearly popped out of my head. The grin on my face spread faster and wider than a flood. When I had seen enough, I snapped the book closed.

So many ideas were racing through my brain. I had so many options. There were so many different paths I could take. I could cause so many problems or perhaps none at all. The choice was in my hands. The power was making me sick and high at the same time. Suddenly, I was laughing hysterically, my hand over my mouth. I was going to have so much fun with this little book in my hands. So much fun, indeed.

"You know... maybe it's time I stopped being such a nice person..."

<h1 style="text-align:center">Chapter Fifty-Eight</h1>

The robot battle royale was much bigger than I was expecting. It was held in a neighboring high school's auditorium. We walked in, Timothy and David carrying our robot, and were immediately overwhelmed by the noise and the crowd.

"Why are so many people here for a robot fight!?" Nathan exclaimed.

I walked over to take Timothy's place carrying the robot. Timothy shot me a grateful glance and put on his headphones. Timothy had social anxiety and crowds overwhelmed him sometimes.

"This way, boys!" Mr. Humpheres called, waving his hands in an attempt to get our attention.

We could barely hear him, but we followed him anyway. What else could we do? Leave, I suppose. I could tell that we all wanted to leave. We had signed up for a small robot fight to showcase our mechanical creation, not to get all our nerves shot out by a gigantic crowd. It would take weeks to decompress after this.

Finally, we found our station. Setting up the robot was familiar and kind of therapeutic. Most of the guys put on headphones to try and drown out the noise.

"I'm sorry, guys. I didn't know it would be this busy!" Mr. Humpheres tried to apologize, but no one heard him.

"Team A12, please bring your robot to Arena 4. You will be fighting Team B12," an announcement said.

Thankfully, it was loud enough for us to hear. Timothy and I dragged our robot to the arena and hooked it up to the controls. It was decided that Nathan would run the controls. He had the most experience with a joystick and even had won a few videogame competitions for his skill with a controller.

We were all nervous about our first fight. The other team's robot looked pretty impressive. Lucky enough for us, it was poorly made. It started falling apart in the arena, and we had our first victory easily.

Our second fight was harder. I watched Nathan struggle a little as we all cheered him on. In the end, we won that one, too, and we were on our way again.

We fought our way through four more teams. Some were long fights, others were short, but the robots grew increasingly bigger and more powerful. All around us, other teams were fighting, and the winners moved on to fight the winners.

When there were only ten teams left, the battle royale was declared. Every robot would be put in the huge center arena in a fight to the death. We put in our robot, the Terminator. It looked small compared to the nine other bots, and we were all nervous. We had to go back to our station to get the rest of our supplies.

As we did, our anxiety peaked when the announcer gave us some new information about our fight.

"The winner will receive $20,000 in STEM funds for the school."

We were shocked. We stared at each other, wide-eyed, our mouths hanging open.

"Mr. Humpheres, did I hear that right?" Nathan asked.

Mr. Humpheres looked as amazed as we were.

"It's news to me, kiddo. But don't let it make you nervous, okay? Just fight your best!"

"Yeah, no. No way, guys, I'm out," Nathan said, putting the controller on our table and raising his hands.

We all panicked.

"What do you mean, out?"

"No, Nathan, we need you!"

"You're not quitting now, are you?"

Nathan got angry at our exclamations.

"Are you serious?! I've been piloting every fight up until this point. I can barely feel my fingers! Let someone else fight the battle that's literally worth $20,000!" Nathan protested.

"Come on, Nathan, you're the best, and you know that!" I tried to reason with him.

He was adamant.

"No way. If I lose, you guys will blame me. I couldn't live with myself. I've gotten us this far. I did my part! Someone else can take it from here."

"Backup plan, anyone?" David asked, twisting his fingers around his shirt anxiously.

"All contestants to the final ring. The battle royale will be beginning in two minutes," the lady said over the loudspeakers.

We panicked again.

"Someone needs to take the controls," Nathan said, "Timothy, you do it!"

"What, no way! I haven't used a controller in years! David?"

"Absolutely not, you're not putting that much pressure on me!"

"All contestants to the final ring. The battle royale will be starting in one minute."

"Oh, give me that!" I shouted finally, grabbing the controller and taking off toward the final ring.

My teammates followed closely behind me, but I didn't notice them. My mind was on the prize money. Our school could do so much with the money. Maybe it could expand the robotics club and hold more meetings. That way the girls could be involved with cheerleading and still fit robotics into their schedules.

I got to the ring and looked over at the other contestants' bots. One, in particular, caught my attention. It was from Mayflay High, our rival school. The school's bot was by far the biggest and most impressive-looking robot in the ring.

"I have an idea," I mumbled to Timothy, who was standing right beside me.

I didn't wait for his confused expression. I leaped over the boundary to make a final adjustment to the bot. Thankfully, I had a pocketknife on me with a few tools.

"What are you doing!?" my team exclaimed from behind the barrier.

"You have like ten seconds before the fight starts!"

"I only need ten seconds!" I replied, standing. It was done, and perfect.

"Contestants. The final battle will begin in three... two... one. Fight!"

I made it back to the controller just in time. The robots in the ring came to life, and they were out for blood. A couple of the rival schools' bots attacked each other immediately. A few more tried to get between them, taking out one or both while they were busy fighting each other. I hung our robot back, waiting by a wall until I had a clear shot.

Finally, I saw a chance. Two robots were fighting, and one was obviously top-heavy. I crept up slowly behind it and knocked it over. The robot it had been fighting finished it off for me. Unfortunately, it then turned on me. I backed up as far as I could while it came after me, then rammed into it at full speed, finishing it off with one of our robot's defensive attachments.

"Nice!" Timothy said with a delighted squeal.

I took my eyes off the robot for a split second to smile at him, only to realize I was being attacked by two different robots. I nearly panicked but managed to keep my cool. I drove as close to the wall as possible, with the robots following close behind. Then, quick as a wink, I drove between two fighting robots. All four robots collided in an epic battle, and I was free to pick my own fight.

It was time for me to pick a target. I picked a small robot that was hiding toward the back of the arena. Hiding was a good strategy at the beginning. It let the other robots pick each other off. But now was not the time for cowardice. I drove up to the robot, laying down my challenge. It came to life as it moved to fight me.

"You got this, Nicholas!" Nathan encouraged me.

I did have this. I had it in the bag. The smaller robot was no match for our robot's size and strength. I crushed it like a beetle. With no other robots near ours, I had time for a brief high-five from Timothy before turning back to the battle again.

That's when I saw the final robot finish its last victim. It was the Mayflay's robot. We were the only two bots left in the ring. The robot turned slowly, its attention fixed on our robot. I looked up across the room. The Mayflay's pilot looked at me with confidence.

An evil smile spread across my face. I had been waiting for this all day.

I put our robot on full speed and tore across the arena to meet my mortal foe. The bigger robot swerved at the last second to avoid a collision, giving me the advantage. I caught the bigger robot in the back before it could turn to face me, causing it to wobble. But then it recovered. It got in punch after punch on our poor robot, who barely held its own. The smile on my face didn't waver.

I waited for the enemy robot to come in for another punch, then I released our secret weapon. I had filled the cotton-ball-launcher Remi and I had made with a ball of sticky tar. It took forever to figure out a way to launch it successfully, but I had managed. Now, it worked perfectly. It stuck all over the robot's wheels, rendering it completely immobile.

I looked up again into the eyes of the enemy. The confidence had died, replaced by fear. I smiled again as I destroyed their robot.

The crowd went wild. My team screamed in my ear. Even Mr. Humpheres was jumping up and down. They cheered again when I was presented with the trophy and the check. The trophy I gave to Timothy, who raised it over his head without another cheer. The check I gave to Mr. Humpheres, who looked close to tears.

The whole team was elated. We cheered, sang songs, and toasted each other with flat sodas before Mr. Humpheres decided it was time to head home. Still cheering, we carried our robot on our shoulders like he was a returning hero.

After we loaded our robot in the car, I reached out to get my phone and text Remi the good news. That's when realized that I left it in my backpack... a backpack that was no longer on my back.

"Mr. Humpheres? Can I go back inside for a minute? I think I forgot my backpack," I said.

Mr. Humpheres looked confused.

"I checked the station, Nicholas. No one left anything. Are you sure you didn't leave it in the car, or at school?"

I checked the car but didn't see any sign of it. My joy immediately turned to panic.

"I... must have left it at the school," I said, partly to Mr. Humpheres, but mostly to reassure myself. "I'll get it when we get back."

"Sounds good. Hop in, everyone!"

The team loaded into the van, but my mind was racing.

I had to get my backpack.

# Chapter Fifty-Nine

I spent the whole soccer game wishing I was with Nicholas. As I walked home, I checked my phone every two seconds to see if he had texted me the results of the competition. All the girls were waiting to see how our beloved robot had done. But he didn't text me.

Finally, I got a notification from the school's social media account that said our robot won. I was delighted at first, throwing my fist in the air in happiness. But my smile fell when I saw that Nicholas still hadn't texted me.

"What is going on?" I asked myself, kicking at some pebbles on the sidewalk.

"Why hasn't he texted?" I asked the stone I was kicking. "Is he pulling away from me again?"

The rock didn't answer, so I kicked it again. I tried to convince myself that he was probably busy or tired from the long contest. I had been growing closer to Nicholas for months, I couldn't let my overthinking and insecurity get in the way now.

"I can't be silly," I told myself, "He's tired, or busy, or carsick or something. He'll text when he can."

I managed to put myself in a better mood for a while. That's when I turned the corner to my house. Erica was sitting on my front steps. I took a deep breath before walking up. She had a cat-like expression with a wide smirk. I steadied myself for another confrontation. Part of me couldn't believe that Erica would be here to bother me again after I had told her off only a couple of days ago. But the other part of me knew it was exactly something Erica would do. She was persistently annoying.

Still, I was not having it today. I had zero energy to fight with her, so I let her know that right off the bat.

"Get out of here, Erica. I'm serious. I'm done playing nice," I snapped.

"So am I," she replied.

She stood up, holding a backpack. I watched as she unzipped the backpack and dumped its contents all over my porch.

"I just came to give you your boyfriend's backpack. He left it at school."

My face flushed beet red.

"You need to go."

"Gladly."

Erica stormed past me, tossing her hair over her shoulder. I sighed, annoyed at her, Nicholas, my life, and just everything. I walked up to my porch, mentally cursing Erica out. I gathered up Nicholas's things, putting everything neatly back in his backpack. He had all the usual things, notebooks, schoolbooks, and...

*True Love Needs Persuasion: Making Any Woman Fall in Love with You.*

What?

I picked up the book slowly. It was very worn; the binding was nearly falling apart and had a couple of pieces of duct tape on the spine. Nicholas, or someone, had read the book a lot.

"Making any woman fall in love with you?" I read the title in disbelief.

For a moment, I thought about putting the book back in the bag without reading it and talking to Nicholas about it later.

"But he won't mind if I read it," I said to myself, "He trusts me."

So, I took the book inside, plopped down on the couch, and started to read. At first, I couldn't believe what I was reading. Then it started to sink in.

And with each page, another piece of my heart broke off.

# Chapter Sixty

The guys on my team kept singing 'We are the Champions' all the way home. I joined in once or twice when Timothy forced me, but I was too worried to sing. I stared out the window, trying to calm my nerves. I didn't understand why I was so nervous. I would find my backpack when I got to school. There was no reason to be so on edge.

Still, the minute we got to school, I hopped out of the van as quickly as I could. The other guys gave me high-fives and left to be picked up by their parents, but I stayed behind. I searched all around the outside of the school, in case I forgot to put it in the van. Nothing. Mr. Humpheres unlocked the school doors for me, and I ran in to check the lost and found. Still nothing.

"Did you leave it in the robotics classroom?" Mr. Humpheres asked.

The lightbulb went off in my mind. I had left it in the robotics room because I was helping to carry out supplies! I ran to the room, already feeling relieved.

My stomach dropped when I saw the backpack was gone. I searched the whole classroom and found nothing.

"Come on, Nicholas. Let me drop you off at home. You can

check with the office later, all right? I promised your dad I'd drop you off and I have to get home."

I reluctantly followed Mr. Humpheres back to the van. We drove home in silence and my voice was sad when I thanked him for the ride. Then I saw Remi's house, and my face brightened. I wanted to see Remi. I would go see her. She would make me feel better.

I skipped up and knocked on the door. Remi's dad answered.

"Hello, Mr. Lucas!" I greeted him with a smile. "Is Remi in?"

"Hey, Nicholas! How was the robotics meet today?" Mr. Lucas asked.

"We won!" I said proudly, trying to look around him for Remi.

"Congratulations! But I'm afraid Remi isn't feeling well. She's been in her room the past couple of hours."

I was immediately worried out of my mind.

"Is she okay? Could you tell her I'm here?!" I demanded, then after a moment's thought, added, "Please?"

Mr. Lucas disappeared into the house for a minute. I heard voices, one of them Remi's, but I couldn't make out words.

"She said she's too sick to come downstairs right now. Sorry, Nicholas," Mr. Lucas said apologetically.

My heart sank.

"Thank you, sir," I said politely, then turned and walked slowly back to my house.

As I was crossing my front lawn, I saw a movement in a window on the side of Remi's house. I looked up and saw the curtain move in Remi's window. She appeared at the window and met my eyes. I smile and started to wave at her, but she stared down at me with a heartbreaking frown. My gut clenched and my hand dropped back down to my sides. Remi stared at me a moment longer, and I swore I saw tears in her eyes. Then she dropped the curtain. I stood there another moment, but she didn't return to the window.

I felt like a tidal wave had destroyed my entire world. Something was terribly, awfully wrong and I didn't know what it was or how to fix it.

I tore through my house and up to my room. I flicked the lights on and off three times frantically. I threw myself to the window and stared at Remi's bedroom window. Her light remained on. I stared at the window for a long time. My whole world was falling out from underneath me. All I wanted to do was to run over and beg for forgiveness for whatever it was that I had done.

*You know what you did.*

I turned to meet the tiny voice in my head. It was sitting in the armchair in my mind, smoking all my raging emotions like a cigar.

*What?*

I asked it, desperate for answers.

*Your backpack is missing, and Remi isn't talking to you. Do you think that's a coincidence?*

I sunk down to the floor, my head in my hands. I didn't want the answer anymore. I didn't want it. I couldn't bear the thought.

*What was in the backpack, Nicholas?*

I couldn't answer. I couldn't think. My mind was on fire. Everything I loved was slipping away from me. I couldn't...

*Say it, Nicolas. What was in the backpack? What did you leave in the backpack?*

"The book," I mumbled miserably.

*That's right.*

"Oh, why didn't I get rid of that book?!" I screamed aloud, not caring if someone heard.

# Chapter Sixty-One

I didn't cry. That was the only decent part of that night. I didn't cry once the whole night. I didn't cry when I read through the book the first time. I didn't cry when I read all of Nicholas's notes, the notes about me. I didn't cry when I reread everything he had dog-eared or highlighted. I didn't even cry when I saw Nicholas outside. I was strong. I was brave. I didn't cry once.

No... that was a lie. I did cry once. I cried when I realized that I'd been kept at a distance for years for Nicholas's enjoyment. I cried when I thought about all the things I'd done for him that he'd watched for entertainment. I cried when I imagined myself as the desperate puppet in his sadistic game. I cried when I remembered all the years, I spent loving him, missing him, waiting for him... all those years wasted. I cried when I thought of all the times I just wanted to be with my best friend, only to have him push me away. I did cry, just once. I bundled all the emotions I was feeling into one good cry.

Then I realized that he wasn't worth my tears.

I'd never been so disgusted with anyone in my entire life. Disgusted wasn't even a strong enough word. He'd been manipulating me for years. All this time, since we were children. And for what? His own pleasure. His own entertainment. I was a doll to him, a toy. I wasn't human. I was an object. He used me. And I had loved him.

I wanted to burn the book. Or flush it down the toilet, page by page. I wanted to bite it, rip it, stab it, or bury it. But I didn't. I needed it as evidence. I needed it as a *reminder*.

I would never trust him again. And I couldn't be in love with someone I couldn't trust. It was over. The years of longing, of love, of waiting... it was all over. And the book was the final page of our story.

I closed the book and put it on my desk.

I wouldn't be angry, I decided. It would do no good. That's just what he wanted, a reaction. He wouldn't get any more public spectacles out of me. He wouldn't get any more begging, waiting, or loving. He would get nothing.

He would watch me go to prom with someone else. Mikayla, maybe. She would go with me. We would get all dressed up. We would look beautiful. We would have fun together. Then he would watch me graduate. He would sit and watch as I threw my cap in the air. He would watch me walk out of the high school.

Then he would never see me again.

I would fall in love, I decided. I would meet someone else, maybe at college. I would love him, and he would love me. He would be patient as I learned to trust again. He would prove himself again and again. He would let me cry about Nicholas. He would promise never to be like him. We would be happy together. I would be happy. I would be better off without him.

I would be happy again, I decided. Without Nicholas.

Because he would never make me happy again.

I woke up the next morning with a knot in my stomach. For a second, I didn't remember why. Then it hit me. I had lost Remi.

"No, no, don't panic. We don't know why she's upset. Maybe she just wasn't feeling well," I told myself.

I didn't believe myself. I got dressed and ate breakfast as quickly as I could. As I ran outside, I was hit with the realization that Remi might not be waiting outside for me. I might have lost her. I panicked for a moment. My heart was beating so rapidly I thought it would pound out of my chest and I gasped for breath.

I felt a sudden rush of relief when I saw her standing at the end of my driveway. But the relief vanished, replaced by despair when I saw the look on her face... and my backpack swinging limply in her hand.

She tossed the backpack softly, and it landed at my feet. I scooped it up, cradling it in my arms.

I called on the tiny speck of hope I had left and put on a fake smile.

"What's wrong?" I asked, my heart breaking as Remi stood staring blankly at me.

Remi pulled the pick-up book from behind her back. She flipped it open to a dog-eared page and read it aloud. I recognized the line. It wasn't from the book. It was one of the notes I had written in the margins. The notes I had written about her.

"Keep ignoring Remi until she's so hooked that you consume all her thoughts," Remi read. She snapped the book shut, and I winced.

"Remi, I know this looks bad-"

"No," she cut me off, "No. You don't get to explain."

"But it doesn't mean-"

"No!" she shouted, tears suddenly pouring from her eyes. My heart broke again. I had caused Remi to cry.

"You've been manipulating me. You kept us apart for years. I needed you! I needed you, Nicholas, I needed my best friend!"

I closed my eyes, trying to pretend this wasn't happening. It had to be a nightmare. Right? It had to be.

"Guess what, Nicholas. I don't need you anymore," Remi said.

The tone in her voice broke me completely, and I let a stray tear roll down my cheek. She didn't even sound hurt just... disappointed. I hated myself for what I had done. I hated myself for who I had become. I wasn't worthy of Remi's love. I was pathetic. A pick-me. Even now, I was so selfish that I was throwing myself a pity party instead of saying something.

"I'm sorry," I started, "I'll do anything to make it up to you!"

"There's nothing you can do, Nicholas!" Remi was screaming, completely losing her temper. "Do you hear me?! Nothing! You let me give you my whole heart and make a fool of myself while I did it, all while you liked me, for what?! You're own amusement? I hope my love was entertaining for you because you'll never see it again. I thought I had to win you over, but all the time you were just playing with me. Playtime is over, Nicholas. We're done."

"Remi, no!" I started, but Remi stormed off.

I tried to run after her. I wanted to walk with her to school, so we could talk. But Remi didn't walk up the sidewalk on our usual path to school. She got into her mom's car. I ran up to the driver's side, but she was already pulling out. She backed into the street and drove up the road to school... leaving me in the road watching.

I ran after her. I couldn't help myself. I chased Remi's car down the road, tears pouring out of my eyes, begging aloud for her to come back, to stay with me.

But she was gone. And so was my hope.

# Chapter Sixty-Two

I lived my life without Nicholas. For a couple of days, I felt really alone, but all of my friends came around to support me. Of course, I had gone to Mikayla's house to cry about the breakup for a while. She got me a gift basket of candy and bath bombs to make me feel better, which made me cry again. I started going over to Sierra's house on Saturdays, and I spent my afternoons practicing cheer routines with Bethany. We even had a girl's night out at a hotel when we went to cheer at an away game.

All the girls had dropped out of robotics to support me. I tried to protest. I didn't want them to give up something they enjoyed just for me, especially Mikayla, since robotics gave her an excuse to spend more time with Timothy. But they insisted. Instead, we practiced cheer, went out for ice cream, or went to see a movie together.

I threw myself into cheer and gymnastics. I practiced aerials more and more often now, slowly but surely getting over my fear of the flips. My gymnastics team was supportive as well, making sure to encourage me in my progress. I even got a part-time job helping teach a younger class of gymnasts.

I loved cheer, gymnastics, my work, and my friends. But I couldn't help but remember how much happier I had been with

Nicholas. I thought about forgiving him a few times, but I was always quick to push that thought away. He made such a fool of me and viewed me only as a toy for him to play with. He was scum, and I was much better off without him.

Still, I wasn't happy.

"Hey," Mikayla said softly, touching my shoulder. "Are you okay? You've got that faraway look you get when you're thinking about him."

"Yeah, I'm okay," I replied honestly, giving her a genuine smile. "I was just thinking."

"What about?" she asked.

"I was thinking that the next time I like a guy, I'm going to let him shower me with affection. I'll let him do the big stunts to prove his love. I'm done putting myself out there for a guy."

"Good for you, queen!" Mikayla said, giving me a high-five. "You are a goddess and deserve only the very best!"

I laughed. "Same to you," I said, "So if Timothy ever does anything wrong, you let me know, okay?"

"Sounds good," Mikayla said with a giggle.

It had been awkward at first, talking about Mikayla's relationship. I had even been a bit jealous at first. After a while, the sting of losing Nicholas had gone down, and I was able to be happy for Mikayla again. Timothy, unlike Nicholas, was a good guy and a real gentleman.

Suddenly Mikayla put her arm possessively around me.

"Heads up, shoulders back, walk like the queen you are," she whispered in my ear.

I nearly froze as I saw Nicholas. I was grateful for Mikayla's arm over my shoulders, helping me keep moving forward.

"Remi?" Nicholas said.

I forced myself to keep moving, though I wanted to shut down. Mikayla practically pulled me through the hallway. Nicholas didn't follow. When we turned a corner, Mikayla gave me a quick hug.

"Are you okay?" she mumbled. "Do you want to cry it out in the bathroom?"

"No, I'm okay," I replied, taking a breath.

"Are you sure? Ugly skank, he doesn't deserve to be on the same planet as you. What gives him the right to look at you? Or say your name? I should go back there and-"

"Mikayla, it's okay. Really! I just... I just can't stand the sight of him anymore," I admitted.

"Rightly so! Would you like me to put slime in his locker for you?"

"No," I laughed, "Better not stoop down to his level."

"You're right," Mikayla agreed, "The snake. Come on, let's not be late for class."

"Thanks for saving me from embarrassing myself," I thanked my friend.

"Of course, bestie! What are friends for? Speaking of friends, Timothy asked me out to dinner tonight. What do you think I should wear?"

As I talked with Mikayla about outfits and makeup, I felt very proud of myself. I had moved on from Nicholas very nicely. At least, I thought I had.

I wouldn't admit it to myself then, but I missed him. And that feeling wouldn't go away anytime soon.

# Chapter Sixty-Three

I wanted to pass out, cry, or just sleep until the pain went away. Every time I saw Remi at school, walking past her house, or with her friends, I felt as if my heart would simply give out from sadness.

My dad noticed my sudden change of mood. He started coming home early from work so I wouldn't be home alone on the days I didn't have robotics club. We would eat take-out and watch movies. It took some of the sting of losing Remi away, but whenever I went to bed at night and say her light on, the pain came right back. Eventually, I stopped looking out the window at night. But I still did our signal, if not for her, then for me.

Every day, the same thoughts played over and over in my mind. Every day from the moment I woke up to the moment I fell asleep.

*I could have had her the whole time. I caused all of these problems between us, all because of my own insecurity.*

*She deserves someone so much better than me.*

I tried to focus on my schoolwork and not think about Remi. Tiny memories of us would surface, no matter what subject I was working on. Even my fortress of math was penetrated by thoughts of her. I found myself scrolling through pictures of the two of us on my phone.

My friends tried to get me to snap out of it. They gave me tons of work to do in robotics club and kept reminding me of all the contests we were going to with our robots in the future. My eyes would keep drifting to Remi's empty chair.

I even tried to approach her once. I caught her eye and said her name. She walked by without a backward glance.

I slammed my gym locker closed, ready to be done with the horrible week. I was ready to mope and sleep at home all day Saturday, with no one to bother me. I wanted to be pathetic in the privacy of my own home.

"Did you hear? That hot chick, Remi, is single now."

I was alert immediately. I turned slightly to see who was talking. It was a guy I knew from American literature. A football player who always caused problems in the classes we shared. I hadn't met him officially, but I'd seen him around enough to know that he was bad news, and worse news if he was talking about my Remi.

*But she's not your Remi anymore, is she?*

The voice in my head said. I told the voice to shut up.

"No way," the football player's friend replied.

"Yeah way. Heard it from my sister Cassie who heard it from Remi's best friend. She dumped him."

"Don't blame her," the friend scoffed.

"Yeah. Anyway, I think I'll make a move. You know, now that she and the nerd aren't an item anymore."

"Dude, go for it. She's hot."

"I know, right? I love watching her in those tiny cheerleading uniforms. Though I have to say, I'd much prefer to see her without the uniform."

"Shut up!" I spoke.

It caught their attention. They hadn't noticed me in the locker room until that moment.

"What did you say, twerp?" the football player asked.

I bit my lip to keep from screaming. My fists were clenched so tightly that my fingernails bit into the flesh of my palms. I saw nothing but a red blur in my anger.

"I said, shut up."

He walked up to me, and I was suddenly aware of how much bigger he was than me. His friend was, too. I gulped but stood my ground.

"Say it again. Let's watch what happens if you say it again," the football player said.

"Yeah, tell him, Paul," Paul's friend backed him up.

"I said, shut up. You have no right to speak about Remi like that," I repeated calmly.

Paul threw back his head and laughed for a few minutes while I stood awkwardly, pinned against my locker.

"Yeah, you're going to regret that," Paul said.

Long story short, I ended up on the locker room floor with a bloody lip, a cut on my forehead, and badly bruised ribs. But as I lay on the cold floor in agony, I had a moment of realization.

The red cleared from my eyes and I pulled myself up to sit with my back against the lockers. I held my aching ribcage and wiped the blood off my face as I thought. The pain brought me clarity, and I had come to a decision.

I wasn't the sort of man to deserve Remi. Not at all. But I would become that man. I had to. There were so many despicable guys that would swoop in to make a move on her. She had always turned them down in the past, but that was because she spent the last few years in love with me. Now that I had let her down so badly, she might go out with one of those jerks that didn't love and respect her the way I did.

*But you don't love and respect her. If you did, you would never have manipulated her. You would never have led her on. You wouldn't have hurt her.*

No, no! I argued with myself. I had to do it. I had to. I thought I would lose her if I didn't.

*Yet you lost her anyways.*

I wanted to cry but any heavy breathing made the ache in my ribs become unbearable.

*I do love her. I would do anything for her. So, that's what I'll do. Anything. I'll do anything to win her back... before someone else gets to her first.*

Even if I had to make a public spectacle of myself, even if I had to make grand gestures, even if I had to embarrass myself in the process, I would win Remi back. I would show her that I could be a man who deserved her.

Even if I lost everything in the process, it would be worth it just to hold her again. I deserved to lose everything after what I had done to her.

*I am a selfish, manipulative jerk.*

"Nicholas, are you okay?" Timothy asked, hurrying into the locker room.

I turned to him with a glazed expression.

"I am a selfish, manipulative jerk."

Timothy sighed, used to my self-loathing by this point.

"Yes, I know. But can we get you to the school nurse right now and deal with your broken heart later?"

Timothy helped me, slowly and painfully, to my feet. He led me to the nurses' office, who called my dad to come and pick me up. All I could think about the whole ride home was how I was going to make it up to Remi.

I had to make it up to Remi. Remi was right when she said that she didn't need me anymore. I had only just realized how much I needed her. I would do anything and everything to regain her trust and win her back.

Because I loved her... and I had to.

# Chapter Sixty-Four

The moment I got home, I set to work on the computer program I was making for Remi. It would be one way I could show her my undying love. I'd been working on it since before the beginning of our relationship, but it still wasn't perfect. It had to be perfect for my perfect angel. It was close to being finished, but it still had a few bugs.

That night I threw everything I had into completing it. I coded and troubleshot until three in the morning when I finally passed out on my keyboard. The next morning, Saturday morning I woke with the letter C clearly imprinted on my cheek and a number of strange lines from the other keys. I crawled back into bed to get a couple of hours of good sleep before waking up again, eating a quick breakfast, and getting back to work on the program.

I was so close. But the program was only part of my plan. I had to get a tiny bit of Remi's attention, too.

That Monday, the program was ninety-seven percent done. It was time to try and get Remi to at least talk to me. It had been a while since our breakup, I thought. Maybe she had cooled down a tad? At least to the point where she would hear me out.

I saw her in the hallway between classes. It hurt so badly, seeing her. But I took a deep breath and walked up to her.

"Remi, I really need to talk to you..."

She didn't even turn to look at me. She stared straight ahead and marched past me like I didn't even exist to her anymore.

I was crushed. I didn't even try to hide the pain. I tossed my books in my locker and slammed it shut with a heavy sigh. In despair, I watched Remi walk away with a cluster of her cheerleading friends around her. That's when another idea hit me. If Remi wouldn't listen to me, maybe her friend would.

I hurried through the hallways, looking for Timothy.

"Timothy!"

He hurried over, recognizing the urgency in my voice.

"What's up?"

"Can you get Mikayla to talk to me?" I asked.

Timothy was confused.

"What? Why?"

"Please, I'll explain later. Hurry, before we have to get to class!"

Timothy ran off and I waited by my locker. A few moments later, he ran back up, half dragging Mikayla behind him.

"Here," he said proudly.

Mikayla scowled at me like I was gum on the bottom of her designer shoes.

"I don't want to talk to *him*," she spat, spinning around to walk away.

"Wait, Mikayla... can I talk with you, please?" I asked as politely as I could.

"What on earth do you want?" Mikayla snapped.

I held up my hands, trying not to seem argumentative.

"I just need your help. I have something for Remi, and-"

"Why should she accept anything from you?"

"Please, baby, just listen to what he has to say?" Timothy asked, rubbing Mikayla's shoulders.

I gave him an appreciative smile. It was always nice to have friends in high places or, in this case, places close to Remi.

"Fine. You have ten seconds," Mikayla said reluctantly.

"Thank you. I'm making something that I think will make it up to Remi, and-"

"Are you serious!? You can't just make up for something like this with a dumb gift, Nicholas!" Mikayla cut me off. "You broke her heart!"

"I know, I know!" I said hastily, "And I'm so sorry. I was so wrong to try and play games with Remi."

"Yes, you were," Mikayla agreed, "And you'd better not try anything like that again. Not with Remi, not with anyone."

"I won't, I won't, I promise. I've learned my lesson," I promised. "And I want Remi back. I'm willing to do anything for her. I want to pull off some grand gestures to win her back, the same way she did for me... to show her I've changed."

"You're copying her idea to show her you've changed?" Mikayla questioned with a skeptical frown.

"I'm showing her that I can humble myself and put myself out there," I explained, hoping what I was saying was making sense.

"Okay... I wouldn't expect Remi to take you back, though. She's pretty much blocked you out of her mind," Mikayla said.

"Yeah," I said with a sad sigh, "I'm sure she has. But I have to try anyway. Because I love her."

"Sure," Mikayla sarcastically said.

"So... can you help me?"

Mikayla considered for a long moment before answering.

"I won't put in a good word for you or anything. It's Remi's decision whether or not to take you back. Personally, I wouldn't, but as I said, it's her choice."

She fell silent again for a long time. Just when I was about to give up hope, Mikayla took a deep breath and met my eyes.

"Okay, I will help you. What plans did you have so far?"

# Chapter Sixty-Five

When Mikayla and Timothy asked me to join them for lunch at our usual diner, I didn't realize that David and Bethany would be there.

"Hey, guys!" I exclaimed, giving Bethany a hug. "I didn't know you guys would be here!"

"Yeah, David asked me out and Mikayla asked if we wanted to do a double date," Bethany said with a huge smile.

"No way!" I squealed with excitement.

"David, you'd better treat this beautiful princess right!" I ordered.

David blushed and nodded.

"Come on, sit down, let's eat!" Bethany said excitedly.

We all sat down, and I started to feel strange being the only one there without a partner. Apparently, Bethany felt my discomfort because she brought up the subject.

"How have you been doing with Nicholas, Remi?" she asked softly.

"Fine, actually. I've had a lot more time to spend at the gym. I'm teaching a beginner's gymnastics class now, you know," I said, sipping my water.

"That's awesome!"

"You should see her, Bethany, she's amazing with the little kids," Mikayla gushed.

"Have you thought about getting back with Nicholas?" Bethany asked bluntly.

"Beth!" Mikayla scolded her.

"What? I was just asking. I know he's been missing you," Bethany said innocently.

"That's true, Remi," Timothy ventured hesitantly, "He's been moping around for weeks, miserable without you."

"Well, he's just going to have to get over it. I have," I said confidently. But I didn't feel so confident. I didn't want Nicholas to be miserable. As mad as I was, I still cared about him.

"It's a shame. You two were so perfect together, too," Bethany said.

"Bethany, shut up!" Mikayla snapped. "This is hard enough on her."

"It's all right, Kayla," I said kindly. "Bethany is right, after all. We were great together. Too bad he turned out to be a manipulative snake."

That shut everyone up. There was an awkward silence for a while, so I tried to repair the damage I had done.

"Timothy, David, how is the robotics club coming? I heard you guys got a ton more funding from the prize money."

"That's right!" David said, brightening. "We've gotten a ton more club members and enough parts for the three robots we're building right now."

"That's awesome! Timothy, how's the building process coming?"

As we were chatting, a boy from the football team approached the table.

Bethany recognized him and cheerily said, "Hey, Paul!"

He ignored her and focused on me.

"Hey, Remi."

"Hey," I replied, confused.

I felt Mikayla tense next to me. I agreed with her. The guy looked like trouble.

"I was wondering if you wanted to come to a party I'm hosting at my place tonight? It'll be a lot of fun. I promise," he said with a wink.

I didn't like the way he said the word 'fun'. Actually, I didn't like the way he said anything.

"No, thanks," I said briskly, "I'm busy."

"Doing what?" he persisted.

"Your mom."

David snorted, choked on his drink, and started coughing.

"Come on, that's childish," Paul continued, crossing his arms over his chest.

"Not as childish as continuing to bother me after I said no," I argued.

"Just come already. It'll be fun!" Paul said. As he did so, he reached out and touched my hair.

My friends were immediately ready to fight. Mikayla reached over and slapped his hand as hard as she could.

"Back off!" I shouted, catching the attention of people at nearby tables.

"Is everything okay over here?" our server asked.

"This idiot is bothering me," I replied.

"Sir, I'm going to have to ask you to leave," our server said.

"Whatever! I was leaving anyway." Paul turned to walk away, yelling over his shoulder, "You're not even pretty anyway. Get over yourself!"

"Remi, are you okay?"

Timothy asked. Everyone at the table was looking at me with concern.

"Yeah," I said, but my voice cracked in the middle. I took a breath, trying not to cry, and tried again. "I think I'll go home now."

"I'll walk you out to your car," David offered, fury flashing in his eyes as if he dared Paul to try something in the parking lot.

"Me too," Mikayla said, standing up.

"No, no, it's okay. I'll just have my mom come pick me up," I said, already texting her. "See you guys later."

I excused myself from the table, not bothering to hear their replies. I camped out in the bathroom until my mom picked me up.

"Are you all right, honey?" my mom asked urgently.

"Yeah," I replied.

But I cried all the way home.

I didn't understand why all guys were so mean. Why couldn't they just leave me alone and stop messing with me?

# Chapter Sixty-Six

"Okay," Mikayla admitted, "I have to say, that is a pretty cool program."

Mikayla, Timothy, and I hovered over my laptop in the library as I showed them the program I had built for Remi.

"See, it is programmed to come up with routines based on the gymnastics moves Remi is strongest at. And I uploaded a ton of contest information into it, so it knows what moves Remi will score the best at. It also researches other athletes in the competition, so Remi can compare her moves with theirs. Oh, and look here! Remi can log how her progress is going, and the computer will suggest stretches and workout routines to help her progress."

"Dude, this is sick! How long did this take you?" Timothy asked.

"A while," I said modestly.

"I have to say, this is pretty useful," Mikayla said, sounding surprised and impressed. "I would use this program myself."

"I would hope it's useful," I mumbled, thinking back on all the late nights and long hours I had put into this project.

"So basically... you made a custom program just for Remi? That's kind of... cute. Romantic, even," Mikayla relented.

"I hope Remi thinks so."

Mikayla snorted.

"If you can get her to talk to you," she said.

"Can you help with that?" Timothy asked. "You could ask her to talk to Nicholas and maybe...?"

"No way, I'm not getting in the middle of this," Mikayla said, putting her hands in the air defensively.

Then, after a moment, she said, "Not directly, anyway. But I might have a couple of ideas about how to get her attention. I'm not saying for sure that they will work. But I'm sure they'd be better than anything *you* could come up with."

The last sentence stung a little, but I brushed it away.

"I will do anything," I said seriously.

"Good. So, here's my idea..."

~

"Remi Lucas, get over here!"

Mikayla waved me over frantically when I arrived in the cafeteria at lunch.

"What, what's up?" I asked, concerned and confused.

"Girl, we really need to talk," Mikayla said as I sat down at our usual table. "Where on earth were you this morning?"

"I had a dentist appointment. Why, what's wrong? Did something happen with you and Timothy?" I asked.

Mikayla waved the question away.

"No, we're fine. It's about Nicholas."

"What about Nicholas?" I said, immediately interested.

"He stopped me yesterday to talk about you," Mikayla said seriously, her voice low and urgent.

"What did he say?"

"He wanted to do some kind of stunt to win you back."

"What kind of stunt?! Come on, Mikayla, I'm not in the mood for guessing games!"

Before Mikayla had a chance to answer, a teacher was in front of the cafeteria, trying to silence everyone.

"Students, students, may I have your attention?"

Luckily it was only my grade's lunchtime, so it was relatively easy to silence the room.

"Thank you," the teacher said when we were mostly quiet. "Now, I have been speaking and working with a particular student who has something he would like to present. We thought that now would be a good time. So, please give a few moments of your undivided attention to Nicholas Savage."

The teacher clapped, trying to get the rest of the students to clap with her. They did not. Everyone was too confused, wondering what was going on. As for me, I was stunned. I turned to Mikayla.

"What on earth is going on?" I hissed.

"His big stunt," Mikayla groaned, "Do you want to slip out and go to the bathroom or something? I'll cover for you."

"No, thanks," I said decidedly. "I want to see this."

"Thank you, Mrs. Ramsey," Nicholas said as he walked to the front of the cafeteria.

He coughed twice, trying to avoid eye contact with me. I stared him down with my arms across my chest.

"I designed a computer program for gymnasts, and I wanted to demonstrate it for you."

Nicholas hooked his computer to a mini projector, and it projected his display on the lunchroom wall.

"It is programmed to come up with routines based on the gymnastics moves the gymnast is strongest at. I input specific moves and the computer rates them on a scale from excellent to proficient to beginner. The program then comes up with new routines based on the strengths of the performer. The bot also logs into nearby competitions to see what moves will score well with judges and adjusts the routine accordingly."

Nicholas's presentation went on and on. I could only sit in shocked silence. Mikayla reached out and took my hand at one point. I barely noticed her. The program was good. Excellent, even.

A few weeks ago, I would have been thrilled. It seemed like it would be extremely helpful in my gymnastics career. How long had he spent on the program? It looked complicated! All that, just for me?

For a minute, I thought about forgiving him. This gesture showed clearly how much he cared for me. He spent all that time making something that I would not only love but use on a daily basis.

Then the flashbacks came. I remembered that he had led me on for years. This was probably another trick. Another tip he got from a how-to book. Well, it wouldn't work. Not today. I wasn't his puppet anymore.

Nicholas turned to me at the end of his presentation. I looked away quickly to avoid his eyes.

"I made this for one great gymnast. She is probably the strongest, bravest, most resilient gymnast I've ever seen. She's stunning when she performs. Breathtaking, even. But she's beautiful in everything she does."

He paused and I looked up. That was a mistake. I stared deep into his tear-filled eyes and my heart broke all over again.

"I'm in love with her. I'm in love with you, Remi. This program is for you, this bot is for you. I love you and I'm so sorry I didn't say that from the very start."

I wanted to cry. No, more than that, I wanted to disappear. I wanted to sink into the floor until I was a puddle of non-existent nothingness. Was this how Nicholas felt during my stunt?

I felt all the eyes in the cafeteria on me, waiting for my response. I could feel Mikayla, worried for me. I took a deep breath and stood up.

"Keep your stupid computer program!" I shouted and marched out of the cafeteria.

I ran straight to the bathroom and locked myself in a stall. I tried to get my breathing under control, but I couldn't. I heard footsteps.

"Hey, Remi, are you in here?"

I unlocked the stall door and walked out slowly. Mikayla hugged me close to her.

"Are you okay?"

"I think so... no, not really," I said, starting to sniff.

"Girl, look at me," Mikayla said pushing me away to look into my eyes.

"If you don't want him back, don't take him back. You are a queen and a goddess, and you deserve a guy who will make you happy. Not going to lie, I thought the computer program was pretty cool, but that's beside the point."

I swatted her hands away, really starting to cry.

"I can't believe you're siding with him over me."

"I'm not!" Mikayla argued.

"You met with him!"

"Yeah, but that was only because Timothy asked me to."

"You could have warned me about that big stunt!"

"I tried to!" Mikayla persisted.

I was mad now.

"Well, I can't believe you helped him with that whole presentation. If he thinks he can win me back with a program he threw together in an hour, he's dreaming."

"An hour!? Come on, Remi, I know you're mad, but don't be an idiot. He worked on that for weeks and even pulled some all-nighters to get it done once you two broke up. Timothy told me! And you should have seen him... he was so excited to give it to you."

"How are you on his side?!" I yelled, bursting into tears again.

"Remi, I'm not..."

Just then we were interrupted by Mikayla's phone going off. She pulled it out and read the text.

"It's from Timothy," she said, "Nicholas wants you to know that he emailed the file to you. Timothy says that he said you can have it, even if you never forgive him."

"Good!" I shouted, "Because I'm not going to forgive him! And I'll delete the email. I'm not using any program he made.

Knowing him, he'll probably use it to stalk me or something. Anyway, I don't want anything from him. Except for him to leave me alone!"

Mikayla nodded, then said thoughtfully, "What if he doesn't? Leave you alone, that is. What if he keeps on trying to win you over, the same way you were trying to win him over?"

I had no answer to that question, but I spent the rest of the day thinking about it.

# Chapter Sixty-Seven

I wasn't going to give up. I couldn't! Remi was too important to me to give up after one try. I wouldn't give up. I would keep going until she noticed me again, or until we graduated.

I spent the next few days trying to come up with another grand gesture to win her over. I had to admit that all the ideas I came up with made me uncomfortable. I didn't like being so emotionally vulnerable in front of so many people. But after all, that's what Remi did for me. She deserved the emotional vulnerability.

With a sigh, I rolled over to grab my phone and call Timothy.

"Hey," he said when he picked up.

"I need help."

"Remi again?" he asked.

"Yeah. I just... don't have any ideas."

"Well, you could start by showing up to her gymnastics competition. It's in a couple of hours, right? I'm going to support Mikayla."

"That's right!" I exclaimed, slapping myself in the face. "That is tonight! But I have to do something, not just show up... what can I do?!"

"I don't know... what was her best competition?" Timothy asked.

"It was when she turned twelve. It was her first major competition or something. No, it was the first time she got a medal. She got second place if I'm remembering right. She came home and said something about she only won because a bunch of people wore yellow."

"Yellow?" Timothy asked.

I chuckled affectionately at the memory.

"Yeah. It's cute that she can be so superstitious."

Then a flash of brilliance hit me.

"Timothy, what time was the competition again?"

"Uh, it starts at eight, I think. Do you want me to text you the address?"

"Yes. Thanks!"

I hung up and jumped out of bed.

"Dad, I'm heading out."

"Okay, be safe!"

I ran out the door and got on the phone again, calling up all of my friends. I had a plan, but I would need some help.

"Girls, if you're not stretching right now, you're wasting your time!"

"If I stretch anymore, I'm going to tear a muscle or something," Mikayla moaned.

"Less complaining, more stretching!"

"Yes, Coach!" Mikayla and I replied.

"How are you feeling about today?" I asked.

"Pretty good," Mikayla replied. "You?"

"Pretty confident! We'll both nail it."

"Yeah, we will!"

Mikayla and I high-fived, then stood to walk out on the mat.

We were both competing at the same time on different mats, so we hugged each other before parting ways.

I took deep breaths as I stood on the side of the mat, waiting for my name to be called. As I did, I scanned the audience. My parents weren't there that day. They had a dinner party to go to. So, I wasn't expecting to see anyone I knew. Imagine my surprise when I noticed Nicholas in the audience.

I wiped my eyes and blinked rapidly to make sure I wasn't dreaming. Nope, he was there. Not just him but the entire robotics club! Nathan, David, other boys, and even some girls I didn't recognize. The new members of the team! Other friends of Nicholas were there, too, with Nicholas at the very center.

That's when I noticed something else. All of Nicholas's friends were wearing yellow! And Nicholas was dressed head-to-toe in yellow and was holding a huge bouquet of yellow flowers!

"Remi Lucas!"

I took a breath to calm myself down. I didn't know how to feel about Nicholas, but I didn't have time to figure it out now. I had a routine to perform.

As I strode out onto the mat, I glanced over at Nicholas again. I met his eyes without thinking. He smiled at me, although I noticed he looked pained.

I looked away quickly and moved to my starting pose. I was a bundle of nerves, fury, and hurt, but I was a professional gymnast. The show had to go on.

# Chapter Sixty-Eight

Remi's routine was flawless. She was in her element and it showed. The routine was difficult, but she performed every trick with grace. She was beautiful and elegant. I fell in love with her all over again, filled with longing. There were even a few flips in the routine. I was nervous when I saw her do them, but she landed them all perfectly. I was so proud of her. Gone was the hesitation and shakiness, replaced by confidence and skill.

At the end of her floor routine, I jumped to my feet and cheered along with my friends. We were, by far, the loudest group in the auditorium, but I didn't care. Remi deserved the cheers of a thousand fans.

Remi looked up at me before she walked off the mat. I half-hoped she would smile at me, but she didn't. She wrinkled her nose and frowned before marching off. I could barely wait to talk to her. But I had to wait until the competition was over.

When the winners were announced, Remi placed first in her category. My friends and I whooped and cheered as she walked forward to take her medal. The joyful smile on her face made my heart leap. I had to talk to her!

I ran up to the girl's van in the parking lot the moment I could.

"Remi! Remi, you did it! You landed all your flips! I'm so proud of you!"

For a brief second, Remi smiled and my heart leaped for joy, but she stiffened.

"Why are you here?" she snapped. "I didn't ask you to come here."

"I wanted to support you," I mumbled.

"You need to stop. And you need to stop trying to get my attention. I'll never forgive you. I'll never trust you again! This isn't going to go anywhere, so you might as well give up."

I took a breath to try and control the flood of emotions. I held out the yellow flowers, putting on my best smile, though I could barely look at Remi.

"Will you at least take the flowers?"

Remi shook her head, a little sadly.

"No. And don't bring me any again. This isn't something you can fix with flowers."

The girls got into the van and drove away, leaving me behind. I stared down at the flowers for a long time.

"I can't give up," I told myself, but the words had no determination behind them.

"But Remi's right. I need something much bigger than flowers. Something like she did for me with the robotics club."

A fresh idea struck me. I needed to show an interest in and learn about one of her hobbies! New motivation and inspiration consumed my mind as I hurried back to the building. My friends were there, waiting for me.

"How did it go?" Timothy asked.

"Awful," I replied with a brief sigh. Then, brightening, I said, "But that doesn't matter! I have a new idea. And I'll need your help..."

～

To be entirely honest, it was completely hilarious for everyone involved. Watching a bunch of nerdy, uncoordinated tech guys trying to learn a gymnastics routine was like watching giraffes doing the tango. There was a lot of bumbling around, stepping on each other's toes, falling in strange positions, and pulling muscles we didn't know we had.

"I will never call gymnastics easy again," Timothy panted, "I have no idea how Mikayla does this!"

"You're not kidding," I said, gasping for air.

"Why are we doing this again?" Nathan asked as he fell for the twentieth time that day.

"For Nicholas's girl, remember?" David replied, trying and failing at what should have been a simple somersault.

"You owe us big for this one, Nicholas," Nathan shouted.

"I know, I know! How about this, I'll take you guys to the new Star Wars movie on Saturday?" I asked.

"Your treat?" David asked, looking up sharply.

"Yeah, my treat. As a thank you."

"Yes!" David and Nathan high-fived then went back to failing the gymnastics routine.

"Are you sure this will work?" Timothy asked, sitting down stiffly, unable to feel anything at that point.

"No. But I'm hoping it will."

"I lost all function in my legs for hope?" Timothy moaned.

I laughed and slapped him on the back.

"I appreciate it, buddy."

"Nicholas, I hate to admit this, but I think we need help," David groaned. He had fallen on his face again

"I'd have to agree," Nathan yelled. "I literally can't even touch my toes."

"Time to call in the big guns," Timothy said, pulling out his phone.

"Who are you calling?" I asked.

"Not calling, texting. Mikayla gave me a couple of her cheerleading friend's numbers in case I couldn't get in touch with her at a practice or a competition. You have to admit, we need some experts."

I nodded. "Thanks, Timothy."

"No problem. Now shut up and let me text."

The guys and I took a quick break to rest and recuperate while we waited for the cavalry. And it didn't take long for reinforcements to arrive at the door.

I smiled to myself as my backyard grew crowded.

*This will work.*

I thought to myself.

*It has to.*

# Chapter Sixty-Nine

I was in an awful mood at cheerleading practice. Nearly half of the team was missing, and Coach was yelling at those of us who bothered to show up as if it was all our fault.

"Where is everyone?!" she demanded.

We all shrugged, texting our teammates, but getting no response. I was getting more and more annoyed. I didn't want to have to stay late and walk home in the dark. All I wanted to do was get through practice and go home.

"It's not like Sierra or Bethany not to answer," Mikayla said.

I turned on her.

"Do you know something about this? Is this one of you and Nicholas's plans?!" I demanded.

"No way! I mean... I can't say what Nicholas is planning, but I'm not involved. Now that I think about it, Timothy has been hanging out with him all weekend. Do you think they planned something for practice today?"

"Why would they? And how would they get nearly half the team to help them?" Mikayla asked defensively.

"I don't know!" I sighed. "I guess I'm just paranoid since the competition."

"I'm sorry about that, and the cafeteria."

"It's not your fault. I'm sorry I accused you of working with him," I apologized.

Suddenly, Bethany came running up. She was carrying a radio and looked excited. We quickly circled her wanting some answers.

"Bethany, I hope you brought the rest of the team with you!" Coach boomed.

Bethany gave Coach a winning smile and said cheerily, "Yes, I did! And I brought someone special, too."

She looked at me knowingly and winked. I groaned, dread consuming me.

"Is this another one of Nicholas's tricks?" I asked Bethany. By the way her smile grew, I knew I was right.

I stormed over to the stands and grabbed my stuff.

"That's it, I'm leaving. Everybody wants to see this guy make an idiot out of himself and I'm tired of it."

Bethany jumped up to plead with me.

"Please stay, Remi!" she begged, "It's not just him that worked really hard on this. A lot of people did!"

"Who else did he saddle into his shenanigans?!" I yelled.

Bethany ignored me. She ran over and pressed a button on the radio she had brought with her. The music began playing and I braced myself.

I spun around and saw Nicholas along with the guys from the robotics club and a bunch of my friends from the cheerleading team march out on the field.

Much to my dismay, I watched as they started an elaborate gymnastics routine. To be fair, it was a rather impressive routine. The girls on my team did a typical routine, but they had incorporated the guys and their various levels of skills. Nicholas was at the center, doing the most tricks. They were shaky and unpracticed, but he kept going diligently.

The routine ended with the robotics guys lifting Nicholas into the air. The others lay on the grass and spelled out the word "Prom?" with their bodies. The music shut off, and the world seemed to freeze.

I was shaking with anger. Not only had Nicholas embarrassed me again, but he had ruined cheerleading practice and used my friends for his schemes.

Nicholas got out of the pile of his friends and walked over to me, desperation in his eyes.

"Remi, please..."

"That was pathetic," I snapped, scowling at him. I didn't even try to mask my disgust and fury.

"In case you didn't hear me the first thousand times I said it or you're just too much of an idiot to understand, stop trying to win me over! I don't exist for you to play games with! Why can't you just leave me alone?!"

I didn't even look at the crushed expression on his face. I just grabbed my bag and stormed off the field. The only small satisfaction I got was Coach yelling at them to get off the field.

Mikayla walked me home. We didn't talk. She just held my hand. I was so grateful for her. I felt like apologizing again for accusing her of working with him, but I didn't want to ruin the moment. I would apologize again later. Now, it was just nice to be with her.

"You're not going to forgive him, are you?" Mikayla asked when we got to her house.

The question shook me.

"I don't think I can," I replied.

The next morning at school, I tried my best to ignore my friends and the guys from the robotics club. I hated Nicholas for making things awkward between my friends and me. I yanked open the door on my locker and a note fluttered to the floor. Curious, I picked it up. I sighed with frustration as I recognized Nicholas's handwriting.

*I'll be at the prom tomorrow night,* the note said, *I'll wait at the gazebo behind the gym. If you don't show up, I'll take that as your final answer, and I'll never bother you again.*

"I did try to warn you."

I turned around sharply to see Erica leaning on the locker beside me.

"He's a manipulative jerk."

I started to yell, but then I realized she was right. Erica had warned me. She'd been mean, cruel even, but she *had* warned me.

"Thank you," I said quietly.

Erica looked shocked. Her elbow even slipped off the locker.

"What?" she asked, staring at me with wide eyes.

"Thank you. For warning me, and for showing me the backpack with the book. I would have gone my whole life without knowing what Nicholas was doing to me. Without you, I would have been fooled. So, thank you," I replied.

Erica was quiet for a long moment, and I considered walking away. Then she met my eyes again.

"I'm sorry I was mean to you. I just saw how Nicholas looked at you."

"It's okay," I said and shut my locker.

"He does love you; you know. It's a weird kind of love, sure, and he is a jerk. But I think he was scared to lose you," Erica said honestly.

I stopped, considering her words. She turned and began to walk away

"Hey," I said.

Erica stopped and stared at me.

"Do you want to sit with me at lunch?"

Erica smiled.

"Yeah. I sure do."

# Chapter Seventy

"Do you even know what kind of tux we need?"

"There is more than one kind?!"

Timothy and I were completely lost. We were trying to find suits for the prom, and we were failing miserably.

"Mikayla said I need to get a silver one, so I'll match her dress," Timothy said nervously as we rifled through the racks.

"Are you nervous?" I asked, "About taking Mikayla?"

"A little, I guess. I just want to be sure she has fun. If she has fun, I'll have fun," Timothy replied.

He pulled out a silver suit and held it against him.

"What do you think of this one?" he asked.

I shrugged.

"It looks fine to me," I replied honestly.

"I better text Mikayla and see if she likes it."

"How are things going with you two?" I asked.

"Great," Timothy said with a huge smile, "I love every minute I spend with her."

"I'm happy for you," I answered.

Timothy looked apprehensive then as he asked, "How are things with Remi?"

"Nonexistent," I said with a sigh. "I left the note in her locker, so it's all up to her now."

"Are you really expecting her to forgive you?"

"Not really. But I'm hoping she'll at least hear me out. But I'll respect her decision and leave her alone if she doesn't meet me in the gazebo at prom."

"You'll give up?" Timothy asked, surprised.

"I'll have to," I admitted, "I'll have to move on. It won't be so bad... we've only got a few weeks of school left anyway. Then I'll never see... I'll never have to see..."

I broke off, trying to control my emotions. Timothy put his hand on my arm.

"Are you all right?"

I took another deep breath.

"I am," I answered. "I've made peace with the fact that I might have messed up so badly that I'll never win Remi back. I realize that my manipulative actions have consequences. I hope beyond hope that Remi will give me another chance. But I understand if she won't. If nothing else, I'll learn from my mistakes."

Timothy nodded.

"That's something, at least?" he said hesitantly.

"Yeah," I sighed. "That's something."

"You look amazing!" I squealed as Mikayla showed off her dress.

Her eyes got wide when she saw me.

"Are you kidding?! *You* look amazing! Look at you!"

We both giggled and hugged each other, although careful not to disturb our hair.

"We're going to be the queens of this party," Mikayla said, snapping her fingers in confidence.

"Naturally," I replied with a huge smile.

Mikayla grabbed her phone.

"Ooh, Timothy texted me! He's meeting me at the gym! Remi, we'd better get going..."

Mikayla trailed off as my face fell.

"What are you going to do about Nicholas?" she asked quietly.

I sighed.

"I've decided to go to the gazebo and at least hear him out."

"What?!" Mikayla exclaimed, "Are you sure?"

I nodded.

"If nothing else, I need the closure. He was a central part of my life for years, Mikayla. As much as I hate to admit it, I can't just move on. Not without a proper goodbye, that is."

"So, you're going to go with him to prom?" Mikayla questioned.

"I'll hear him out, at the very least. If I'm still disgusted with him, I'll walk away and never speak to him again. But I'll give him one more chance."

"Do you... want him back?" Mikayla asked hesitantly.

"I... I think a small part of me wants him to talk me into it. But a larger part of me is still mad. I don't think I can trust him, Kayla, I really don't," I admitted.

Mikayla gave me another tight hug.

"Well, whatever you decide, I'll support you. And don't forget, you look like a pop star, so you have that going for you."

I laughed.

"Yeah, even if I get my heart broken again, I'll look good while it happens."

"Totally girl, show him what he's missing."

I high-fived Mikayla and we finished getting ready.

"Girls, it's time to go!" my mom called from downstairs.

We giggled and flew down the stairs. After a photoshoot courtesy of my mom and a car ride courtesy of my dad, we were dropped off in front of the gym.

"Wow."

Mikayla and I both burst out laughing at the look on Timothy's face. He was speechless for a minute, so I encouraged him.

"Tell her she looks spectacular," I prodded.

"You do!" he gushed, "You look amazing, Mikayla, like... wow."

Mikayla laughed and took his arm.

"You look wonderful, too. Thanks for getting the suit to match. Now we really look like a couple."

Timothy could only nod dumbly, still awestruck by Mikayla's brilliance. Just as they were about to go into the building, Mikayla turned to me with a serious expression.

"Good luck. I'll be inside if you need me."

"Thanks," I replied with a smile that felt forced. "Have fun."

They did look wonderful together. It made me happy but at the same time, it hurt because it reminded me of Nicholas. With a deep sigh, I turned and began the nerve-wracking walk to the gazebo.

# Chapter Seventy-One

I had been at that gazebo for hours. In reality, it was probably about thirty minutes, but it felt like hours. I paced back and forth on the creaked wooden beams until I was sure I had worn a dent into them. I kept rehearsing what I was going to say over and over in my mind. I checked my watch every two seconds.

How long was I going to wait? How long until I had to accept the fact that she wasn't coming?

One by one, the agonizingly slow minutes went by as I waited for the love of my life. As I grew more and more impatient, I began to wonder what I would do without Remi. I would have to learn to live without her! I didn't think I could. She'd been the center of my entire existence for so long, losing her just might break me. Until this point, I had been trying to get Remi. That had been my only goal. What was I supposed to do now? I could never pursue another girl as I had Remi.

I could never love another girl as I had loved Remi.

I sighed and checked my watch again. I'd been waiting for forty-five minutes. I had my answer. Remi wasn't there.

"You do look handsome in that suit."

I whirled around, my heart beating out of my chest. I was breathless the moment I lay eyes on her. Remi was exquisite. Her blue dress complemented her blue-green eyes so they practically glowed, even in the dim light. Her hair lay gently on her shoulders and looked so very soft. Her face was as perfect and stunning as it always was, but it looked sad. It broke my heart to see Remi sad.

I exhaled, only then realizing that I had been holding my breath. It was time. It was time to lay it all out there and let the cards fall where they would.

"No more gestures," I said sincerely, "No more games. Just my honest feelings."

Remi nodded at me, so I clenched my fists and began.

"Remi, I'm sorry..."

At the beginning of Nicholas's speech, I wanted to hit him. I wanted to scream that he betrayed me. I wanted something more than an apology.

But then he went on. There were tears in his eyes and his voice was shaky, but he went on.

"My mother left my dad when I was little, you know that. He begged her to stay. He would have done anything. She still left. I grew up thinking that I would be left, too. By anyone who loved me. I saw what it did to my dad, losing Mom. At first, I swore that I'd never fall in love. We were friends, and you were everything to me, Remi. You made me happier than I've ever been. You were my shoulder to cry on, my playmate, my best friend in the whole world. When I realized I was in love with you, I was scared. So, I pulled away."

Nicholas took a breath and wiped his eyes before continuing.

"I pulled away because it was the only thing I knew to do. I'm so sorry for that. I was a kid, and I didn't know any better. I tried to stop loving you, I did. It was impossible. So, I figured I had to make the love... *safer*. I had to figure out a way that I wouldn't lose you, so I wouldn't feel the heartbreak my dad felt."

Nicholas paused again, looking up at me pleadingly.

"Go on," I said stiffly.

He took another breath and did so.

"I found the book in the attic. I think it was my granddad's or my dad's... I don't know. I never told anyone about it, and no one ever found out. Until... well, you know. I thought that if I did what the book said... you wouldn't leave. I realized too late that it was manipulating you. It was selfish, Remi. And love is never selfish."

Nicholas stepped off the gazebo and looked me in the eyes.

"I thought that if I did something wrong, I would lose you."

"You idiot!" I screamed, unable to control myself any longer.

"You did lose me! For years, we didn't spend any time together! I thought... I thought you couldn't stand me! And when I poured myself out to you, you kept me at a distance and played with me! You could have taken me then, Nicholas, that first day in the cafeteria."

"I know! I know, I screwed up. I screwed up so much. I should have just talked to you. I shouldn't have tried to manipulate you. I'll never do it again, to anyone. I swear," Nicholas protested desperately.

I bit my lip to hide my tears.

"Would you do it again if you knew for sure that manipulating would work and being straightforward wouldn't? If I never found out?" I asked quietly.

"No, no, I get it now. It's messed up. A lot of terrible manipulation tactics work, but just because they work, doesn't make them right. The right thing to do is be honest with people. I was so afraid of being rejected by you, I forgot that."

Nicholas took another step toward me.

"You're so much better than me, Remi," he said softly, "You're so pretty and sweet and good with people. I didn't think I could just be myself and have you like me."

"And what if you couldn't?" I snapped back, "What if you couldn't be yourself and have me like you?"

I saw the light go out of Nicholas's eyes. I felt his despair. I wanted to cry for him and me.

"I still wouldn't try to manipulate you again," he said slowly, "It's wrong, and it's not the kind of man I want to be."

"What kind of man *do* you want to be?" I asked faintly.

"The kind of man who is worthy of a woman like you."

He looked up again and met my eyes. I wasn't angry anymore. I didn't see him as the Nicholas who had betrayed me. I saw him as the boy he was when we were kids. Innocent, fun-loving, smart, loyal, caring... the Nicholas I loved and who loved me.

*He loved me. All that time, even as a boy. And he was scared to lose me.*

I was scared to lose him. I loved him, too. I had never stopped.

I took a step forward and threw my arms around him. He stiffened for a second, shocked. I pulled away and stared into his surprised eyes. I could tell he didn't believe what was happening. I pulled him in for a kiss, and he snapped out of it.

I felt his hands running up my back as he kissed me deeply. A tear rolled down his cheek and I wiped it away as he stepped back.

"I accept your apology. But you can't do anything like that ever again... and it might take me some time to trust you again."

"Thank you, Remi!" He laughed with pure joy. Then, serious, he said, "I promise I won't do anything like that ever again. And take all the time you need. I swear I'll work to rebuild the trust."

"Okay, then," I said with a smile. I felt the joy and peace fill me again and I was happy to welcome them back. I was happy to welcome Nicholas back.

"Now, can we go to prom?" I asked.

Nicholas bowed low. "Allow me to carry you, milady."

"What? Oh!"

I laughed as Nicholas scooped me into his arms. I rested my head on his shoulder and listened to his contented heartbeat. With the biggest smile on his face, Nicholas carried me off to the prom.

And the fireflies watched us leave.

# *Epilogue*

And that brings us to the end of our story. For now, at least. I'm sure Nicholas and I have more adventures ahead of us, don't we, babe?

I have no doubt, my darling Remi. Also, when was babe a thing?

I'm making it a thing, right now. Now shh, I'm trying to wrap the story up! We decided to both attend the same college, so we'll be together while Nicholas and I get our degrees.

And Remi is still planning on doing gymnastics in college! You got a very lovely scholarship, didn't you, love? I'm so proud of you.

Thanks! Yes, Mikayla and I both got a scholarship. Yes, that's right, Mikayla is going to college with me! Actually, and probably most surprising of all, so is Erica! She just happened to be attending too, so the three of us girls are getting a room together. Now *that* will be an adventure!

How long do you think it will take before you kill each other?

Nicky, shh! What else do I need to say?

Timothy is attending a school nearby, so he can visit me often. And Mikayla!

Yeah, I guess his girlfriend is important too.

Oh, David and Bethany are dating now! And they're adorable together.

The robotics team is still strong and growing.

I get to teach some young cheerleading teams over the summer!

I guess we've both got a lot of adventures ahead of us, don't we Remi?

I guess so. We'd better go out and start living them!

Together?

Together. Always.